Praise for Christina Freeburn's Mysteries

"A snappy, clever mystery that hooked me on page one and didn't let go until the perfectly crafted and very satisfying end. Faith Hunter is a delightful amateur sleuth and the quirky characters that inhabit the town of Eden are the perfect complement to her overly inquisitive ways. A terrific read!"

— Jenn McKinlay,
New York Times Bestselling Author of *Copy Cap Murder*

"An enjoyable read with a comfortable tone, plenty of non-stop action and pacing that was on par with how well this story was told...A delightfully entertaining debut and I can't wait for more tales with Merry and her friends."

— *Dru's Book Musings*

"Christina's characters shine, her knowledge of scrapbooking is spot on, and she weaves a mystery that simply cries out to be read in one delicious sitting!"

— Pam Hanson,
Author of *Faith, Fireworks, and Fir*

"A fast-paced crafting cozy that will keep you turning pages as you try to figure out which one of the attendees is an identity thief and which one is a murderer."

— Lois Winston,
Author of the Anastasia Pollack Crafting Mystery Series

"A little town, a little romance, a little intrigue and a little murder. Join heroine Faith and find out exactly who is doing the embellishing—the kind that doesn't involve scrapbooking."

— Leann Sweeney,
Author of the Bestselling Cats in Trouble Mysteries

"Battling scrapbook divas, secrets, jealousy, murder, and lots of glitter make *Designed to Death* a charming and heartfelt mystery."

–Ellen Byerrum,
Author of the Crime of Fashion Mysteries

"Freeburn's second installment in her scrapbooking mystery series is full of small-town intrigue, twists and turns, and plenty of heart."

– Mollie Cox Bryan,
Agatha Award Finalist, *Scrapbook of Secrets*

"Witty, entertaining and fun with a side of murder...When murder hits Eden, WV, Faith Hunter will stop at nothing to clear the name of her employee who has been accused of murder. Will she find the killer before it is too late? Read this sensational read to find out!"

– *Shelley's Book Case*

"Has mystery and intrigue aplenty, with poor Faith being stuck in the middle of it all...When we finally come to the end of the book (too soon), it knits together seamlessly and comes as quite a surprise, which is always a good thing. A true pleasure to read."

– *Open Book Society*

"A cozy mystery that exceeds expectations...Freeburn has crafted a mystery that does not feel clichéd...it's her sense of humor that shows up in the book, helping the story flow, making the characters real and keeping the reader interested."

– *Scrapbooking is Heart Work*

BETTER WATCH OUT

BETTER WATCH OUT

A **Merry & Bright**

HANDCRAFTED MYSTERY

FREEBURN

HENERY PRESS

For Tracy Hedrick,
my fellow scrapbooker/crafter, Disney and Marvel fan,
and one of my best friends.
We've shared many adventures,
seen each other at our best—and worst—
and our friendship has never wavered.
Thank you for always being there for me and having my back
especially those times when I just wanted to quit.
Your friendship and love make my world
brighter and more complete.
You are an amazing person. Never forget that.
I love you.

ACKNOWLEDGMENTS

A huge thank you to my editor Maria for helping make this book the gem that it is, putting up with all my angsting over the title, and for coming up with the perfect title.

Plus a thanks to all the other wonderful members at Henery Press for helping me make this book awesome.

I'd also like to thank my cropping buddies and friends, the encouragers who always pick up my spirits and help me through the learning curves of the new crafting mediums I jump into.

ONE

Right after Thanksgiving, Season's Greetings was full on Christmas. Everything was cheerful. Holidayish. Full of old-fashioned charm and visions of Christmas' past straight out of classic holiday movies. Large Christmas trees were erected at every intersection. The finest tree, a twenty-foot majestic Douglas fir, was at the end of Main Avenue. Multi-colored Christmas lights filled the branches from top to bottom, casting a kaleidoscope around the tree. At night, there wasn't a speck of evergreen noticeable because of the multitudes of colors twinkling all over the tree. It was my favorite sight of the holiday season.

Christmas coming alive in its full glory was what drew tourists to our town from the day after Thanksgiving to the first of the year. Season's Greetings knew how to do Christmas well. I was doing everything in my power to make sure it stayed that way. Even though a few people in town seemed determined to add a little Scrooge into the festivities. Like my neighbor Cornelius who always refused to decorate his costume shop or the outside of his home, and Jenna Wilcox who refused to share the theme of her float for the Christmas parade.

All I wanted was to have a perfect flow for the Christmas parade. I didn't want all the bands bunched up like last year, and the floats that threw out candy coming before the fire truck. Last year, it almost caused quite a few heart attacks as children ran out to snag the candy. Fortunately, Paul McCormick, the volunteer fireperson who drove the truck, had anticipated the issue and kept the truck far behind the floats and inched down the street. The parade lasted about an hour longer than usual but at least there weren't any injuries. My plan was to stop all potential problems before there was even an issue in anyone else's mind.

Jenna found my insistence at knowing highly controlling, and I found her unwillingness to comply with a simple request downright rude and Grinchy. She liked issuing orders but not following them. Jenna was a take charge, independent woman who took every opportunity to show it. She answered to no one though she expected everyone to kowtow to her. The woman was a force to reckon with and had no qualms of stirring up trouble in a person's life, even if it required making up a story, which was how I think she was voted onto the city council the last three elections even though no one particularly liked her. No one wanted to deal with the ramifications of not doing as Jenna wanted.

But Jenna was the least of my worries. There were eighteen days before Christmas, and I was nowhere near ready in my personal preparations for the holiday. Worse, I had twenty-six business hours left to mail out Christmas orders placed with Merry and Bright Handcrafted Christmas to beat the Christmas mail rush and finalize the lineup for Season's Greetings Christmas Parade.

Why oh why did I agree to organize the parade? This was the busiest time of the year for a woman who sold handcrafted Christmas items. Why had I done this to myself?

One word: guilt. Or rather, having a large soft spot for Christmas and my former stepdaughter Cassie. Nothing grabbed my attention quicker or had me volunteering my time than the thought of Christmas, anyone's Christmas, being ruined. My ex-husband Samuel had been in charge and his helpers dwindled away the closer it came to Christmas, and after Samuel was murdered, the rest—except his eighteen-year-old daughter Cassie—had bailed from the project and refused to take it over. If I didn't agree to organize the Christmas parade, then everyone in Season's Greetings would have their Christmas ruined. I couldn't let that happen.

I slowly drove down Main Avenue, taking in the sights. The light poles had a lighted, seasonal decoration attached to it: candy cane, wreath, silver bells, snowflakes, mistletoe. Red bows adorned the meters, sometimes making it a little hard to add money without moving the bow over. I wouldn't mention it as I'd rather move the large bow than have the city remove them. Everything needed a splash of Christmas during the holiday season.

Wreaths decorated the door of every store on Main Avenue, except for Cornelius's storefront. Not one decal on the window. Not one Christmas decoration to be seen through the window. His store was business as usual. Considering he ran a costume shop, I was surprised at how little care he gave to decorating. Though, I was happy he didn't put the Santa and elf suits near the front window. It wouldn't be good to spoil the Christmas magic for children. It might be easy to explain one Santa suit in the window, but not ten.

I pulled into a parking space in front of One More Page, a bookstore owned by my friend Rachel Abbott. This morning, I was dropping off a replacement naughty list sign. Her theme was Santa's workshop, but instead of the usual toy shop area, Rachel was depicting Santa's office, or more precisely his naughty and nice list. Someone had stolen the first sign and I had promised Rachel to drop off a new one this morning.

Not wanting to juggle the boards and the door, I phoned Rachel. "I have the new sign for you."

"I think I know who stole it. Jenna. She's copying it to make her own." The tenseness in her voice caused an iciness to run through my veins. Jenna's naughty list meant trouble in Season's Greetings. No one used that tone of voice for good.

"I'll be at your front door in a minute." I was surprised at the news. Not that my craft design was being copied, it happened every year to crafters. Come up with a cute project design and before you knew it everyone was selling one just like it. Though, I was surprised Jenna was doing it. She had never crafted anything in her life—that I knew of.

I removed the twelve-by-twenty-four-inch wooden sign from

the back seat of my SUV, being careful not to bang it against the side of the vehicle. I was more worried about nicking the sign than dinging up my car.

"We should have the conversation inside." Rachel herded me into the store, her brown hair with a few strands of gray was piled up on her head in a messy bun. Not a styled messy bun but one that was the result of waking up late and not having time to wash her hair. Her clothes were also in a disarray, buttons misaligned, one leg of her jean pulled up and the other tucked into a leather boot. Whatever was going on, it had Rachel in a tailspin. She usually had a more put together look and this said she scrambled out of bed and rushed to work.

"Is this going to ruin the holiday season?" I asked, carefully maneuvering through the door with the wooden signs, avoiding hitting the door frame and knocking my eyeglasses askew.

"Depends on how you feel about a twelve-foot-by-eight-foot naughty list sign displayed on a float with your and Samuel's name on it."

"Are you sure? Why?" Jenna and I weren't friends but not enemies either. I had no idea why she'd want to try and embarrass me, and Samuel was dead. She couldn't do anything to him. But it would hurt his mother and daughter, and they didn't deserve that.

"Because she's Jenna and..." Rachel cut her gaze away from me and pressed her lips together.

I knew what she was holding back and was glad my friend didn't feel the need to remind me that technically, Samuel Waters was still my husband since the louse, unbeknownst to me, hadn't actually signed the divorce decree when he and his lawyer said he had. I didn't want to be Samuel's widow. Samuel and my relationship had deteriorated quickly after our wedding, and I didn't want my name tied to his any longer. And, there was a woman in Season's Greetings who had believed with all her heart that Samuel had been free and clear to marry her and had been in love with him when he died. Bonnie had thought she was Mrs. Samuel Waters. She deserved the title of widow.

Hopefully, Brett, my first ex-husband, father of my two now adult children, and currently my lawyer, was able to clear up the marital status kerfuffle Samuel forced upon me and Bonnie.

"By now, I think everyone knows all of Samuel's faults," I said.

"You and Samuel aren't the only ones on the list. I have it on good authority that the mayor, the pastor, and a few other people are on the list. And, she's going to have the names lit up so everyone can see it."

What in the world was Jenna up to? The woman was on the city council, it made little sense for her to upset people. The group she was targeting, beside me and Samuel, had a rather large following of devoted fans and congregation members. The woman was going about getting reelected all wrong.

"I can't let her do that."

"That's why I wanted to tell you. She can't be allowed to ruin the parade."

The Christmas Parade was a huge tourist attraction. Visitors came from all over West Virginia and surrounding states to take part in our Christmas festivities. No matter Jenna's reason, I had to stop her. I couldn't allow her to suck away the joy and beauty. We needed the parade. It wasn't just a loved tradition but helped all the businesses in town have a profitable year. If the parade turned into an airing of grievances, no one would want to attend, and definitely not travel to see it next year.

Nor could I let her use the parade to start rumors about town residents. Everyone would wonder why certain people are on the list. Especially the mayor and the pastor. Me and Samuel...well, the residents would be able to figure that out pretty easily. Samuel was murdered because of a twelve-million-dollar lottery ticket, which the town now believed to be mine. I did have the ticket, as the true owner of the ticket gifted it to me, but I was still feeling a little reluctant to call it my own—and spend any of the money.

I stared at the naughty list still in my hands. On it were famous Christmas villains: Grinch, Scrooge, Mr. Potter, Scut Farkas—I should've added Jenna Wilcox to it.

TWO

The gravel road leading to Jenna Wilcox's home was a series of potholes and mud pits. I maneuvered to the left then immediately jerked the wheel to the right to avoid an even larger pothole. Blobs of dirt flew out from the tires. The six-bedroom farmhouse had belonged to Jenna's parents and was gifted to her once they decided to leave West Virginia and take up residence in North Carolina. They wanted to live in a place with less snow, more sun, and not have the overbearing humidity of Florida. It also helped they had another daughter and grandchildren living there.

It irritated Jenna that her parents packed up and moved, feeling they were choosing her sister and kids over her and Eric who didn't have any children. I didn't know Jenna or her parents that well, though it always seemed there was a tenseness to the relationship. I had actually been shocked when I learned they were related. The times I'd seen them at events, they acted like cordial acquaintances and not parents and child. I couldn't imagine treating or reacting to my child as if they were someone I was forced to see during the holidays.

My SUV slugged through the last half mile of mud to the Wilcox's home. Jenna and Eric lived in a large white farmhouse. It looked like it came straight out of a picture book along with the large red barn yards from the main house.

Jenna's brand-new yellow Renegade wasn't anywhere to be seen nor was her husband's faded red truck. I heaved out a sigh. Looked like I just wasted precious minutes I didn't have to squander. I should've called before making the twenty-minute drive.

The barn doors were open. Maybe someone was home. I parked in the driveway near the barn. Since I drove all the way out here, I'd peek at Jenna's float and check if the gossip Rachel heard was true. Maybe Jenna wasn't really using a naughty list as her theme's float, rather she just told someone that to rile up people. It was her favorite hobby. The float wasn't in the driveway, so my guess was in the barn or behind the house. The barn was the more likely choice as it kept it protected and hidden from anyone who might stop by. The best way to keep a secret was putting it behind closed doors...which just happened to be open right now.

I exited my car, shoes sinking into the mud. Fortunately, I was a sneaker or boots kind of girl and had opted for boots. Cats of all shapes and sizes rushed out of the barn toward me. There were about a dozen, weaving between my feet. Tails swished and trailed around my legs, it was like a multi-colored furry octopus was trying to drag me into the mud.

I was paying so much attention to the felines, I almost stepped into a deep rut near the barn. The open barn door called to me, begging me to step inside, kind of like a hidden, wrapped package wanting you to slit open the tape for a tiny peek.

I shooed the cats away, and slowly made my way inside the barn and tried not to think about the fact I was acting like I was on a clandestine mission. A flatbed trailer was covered by a tarp, giving the appearance of an area with hills and valleys. Excitement pinged through me. Jenna's float. I'd just get one little peek to discount the rumor Rachel heard then head home to work.

I lifted the end of the tarp. Lying flat on the bed was a large Santa naughty list. My mouth open. I stared. For the love of Christmas, what was the woman thinking? The list had two columns, one labeled "Name" and the other "Misdeeds." The twelve-foot list was filled with names of town citizens and a few of the misdeeds were written. My name was on it. Along with Rachel, the mayor, another city council member Norman, Pastor Benjamin

Heath, and her own husband. Fury rushed through me. Even her own family wasn't safe. Across from her husband's name was the misdeeds of drunkard and cheater. I took out my cell and tapped on the camera icon.

A hand wrapped around my wrist. The tarp slipped from my grasp and fell back over the trailer.

"What are you doing?" The question was a slurred mess of sounds and anger. Eric Wilcox swayed on his feet, his hair a tangled mess of unruly curls and lids drooping over his eyes. His ever-present red baseball cap was clutched in his hand. The man smelled like he'd taken a bath in rum and then ran a marathon. While the assessment of her husband wasn't incorrect, I couldn't believe Jenna would shame him before the whole town.

I leaned back, trying to break his grip and get away from the stench. While Eric had every right to be annoyed with my snooping, it didn't permit him to manhandle me.

"Looking for Jenna. Let me go." I used a firm, no-nonsense tone of voice.

He tightened his grip. "Under the tarp?"

"I wanted to confirm if the rumor about her float's theme was true."

"Not your business." His body tilted left and right, back and forth.

The movement was starting to make me nauseated. "It's my business since I'm organizing the parade."

"Don't mean you can trespass." His body swayed more, and he tightened his hold on my wrist. Pain vibrated up my arm.

I was starting to think he was holding on to me to keep himself upright, not for anything nefarious. But I still needed him to let go before he hurt me. A broken wrist was a broken wrist whether it was done intentionally or not. It would be hard to work one-handed. "You're hurting me, Eric. I need you to let go of my arm."

"Why? So, you can—"

"Let her go," Jenna's voice was a like a gun shot, loud, unexpected and terrifying, causing us both to startle and separate.

She tapped her foot on the wooden floor, her silver shoes sent sparkles of light around her feet. The woman was dressed like she was going to the Oscars. She wore a floral sheath dress, gold with hints of red throughout, that skimmed her modelesque body. Gold hoop earrings accented with crystals grazed her cheeks and her expertly curled hair tumbled about her shoulders. A Christmas-color hued scarf was tied onto a strap of her leather tote bag. Gold fringes from the scarf dangled down and skimmed her legs.

"She was nosing around." Eric jammed his hands into his front jean pockets and lowered his head. Miraculously, his swaying stopped, and he spoke every word in a careful tone.

"I stopped by to talk to you about your float," I said.

"It's not complete, but I can assure you it'll be done in time for the parade. Just a few finishing touches needed." She fought back a smile. Instead of being angry, she was happy I saw her handiwork before the parade.

"You can't use Christmas to shame people." I clenched my hands. "Santa is about magic and belief. Happiness and joy. Not to disgrace people. That's not what the holiday or the parade is about."

A Grinchy smile stretched her lips. "You do Christmas your way, I'll do it mine."

I drove straight to City Hall to chat with Mayor Vine. If Jenna refused to listen to me, she'd listen to the mayor. Or at least, I hoped so. What she was planning on doing would destroy the parade and ruin people's holidays. After pulling into a spot in front of the building, I dug around in my car for quarters, wishing the town had upgraded to new meters that accepted debit cards. I scrounged up two quarters, giving me an hour to talk some sense into the Mayor.

The moment I entered the building, I froze and gaped at the new setup of the entrance of city hall. There used to be a free-standing sign listing the various offices in the building. Now there was a tall, hunky man in a suit standing in front of a metal detector. Next to it was an eight-foot collapsible table with six plastic bins lined up. The metal detector was off to the side and didn't seem to be functional yet, judging by the fact the man's watch and metal tie tack wasn't setting it off.

The man had a dark beard shot through with gray. Dark hair flopped over his forehead, with a slight movement of his head, the hair moved from his eyes and a twinkling green gaze settled on me. He was almost like a toned and younger version of Santa. Santa's son who took very good care of himself and hadn't turned completely gray.

"I'm here to see Mayor Vine. Can I just go by? Doesn't look like all your security gadgets are hooked up."

"I need to inspect your purse." His voice was a deep rumble. He tapped a table in front of him and the suit jacket strained against his biceps. "Can you please place it here?"

"Absolutely." My voice sounded a little too gushy and flirty for a woman who recently lost her ex-husband, or husband, depending what the court ruled.

He opened it and his brows rose. On the table, he placed my cell phone, a weeding tool with a hook, a scraper, a pair of tweezers, sharp-tip scissors, a small, lighted magnifying glass, and a box of bandages. In my car was a plastic container filled with decals to weed. I always brought along a few projects in case I found myself with a long wait. It was a habit from when I drove my children to umpteen practices and I was instructed to wait in the car. I no longer drove anyone anywhere, and didn't have long waits, but still carried around craft projects.

"I'd have left my tote in the car if I'd known there was a new security procedure."

He placed the sharp objects into a bin. "You can pick them up on your way out."

Was he afraid I was going to poke the mayor with them? The guard's manner was a cross between polite and brusque, and he moved in a very efficient way. His eyes scanned the whole area the entire time. He took the job very seriously. I could guess what his prior profession was before becoming the security detail for city hall.

"Prior police officer?" I asked.

"No, military." The security guard handed me my purse. "Next, I need your name and business to conduct. After checking the appointment book, I can let you pass."

This was getting a little too big brother for me. Cute or not, I wasn't going to be forced into getting permission from some man to speak with the mayor. "I don't have an appointment. Mayor Vine has always had an open-door policy for his constituents." I hiked the strap of my purse back onto my shoulder. One he was likely to change after I threw a hissy-fit in his office.

"That changed last night."

"It's important that I speak with him. I'm in charge of the Christmas Parade and there's an issue regarding it. This is a big event for our town, and it can make or break the remainder of the holiday season. Which isn't that long to begin with."

He looked at me skeptically. "Christmas Parade emergency?"

"Yes. Call Mayor Vine and tell him Merry Winters is here to see him. He'll tell you to let me through." Or at least I hoped so.

The guard unclipped a cell phone from his belt, swiped his finger across the screen, and hit a button all while keeping his penetrating, yet twinkling gaze, on me. "There is a Merry Winters requesting to see the Mayor." He nodded a few times. "I'll make a note of that." He tapped the screen, twirled the phone around his fingers and holstered it in the clip attached to his belt.

"Can I see him?"

The guard moved the table out of the way. "Apparently, the seas are to part for you." The words were clipped.

Why did that irritate him? "The parade is important to this town and it's happening tomorrow. We have to work out all these details."

"I'm sure you do."

I had a feeling I was being judged by this man. Holding my

head high, I marched right by not caring why my ability to see the mayor annoyed him. Why should he care if my unscheduled appointment messed with other items on the mayor's agenda?

I stepped into the mayor's office and froze for a moment. The office was bare of all Christmas. Last week, there had been a Christmas tree in the corner and an array of porcelain Santa Clauses and reindeers on the shelves and lining the window sills. Now, there was nothing.

I walked over to the desk. It was littered with proposals. There wasn't a spot without a stack of papers. One was a large drawing of a park. The playground equipment was painted in traditional Christmas colors and statues were erected around the area of well-known Christmas characters: Rudolph, Frosty, Santa Claus. Hopefully, someone explained copyright infringement to the mayor.

I let nosiness get the best of me and nudged away a sheet of paper to get a better look at the next proposal. New street lights for Main Avenue. I liked the design, very old-fashioned, Charles Dickinson Christmas. The next one was for a new library. Our town desperately needed one, but I wasn't sure about the design. It was too futuristic in appearance, a lot of sharp lines with chrome detail and square windows with no shutters. Season's Greetings needed something more in line with our Christmas feel.

The door opened and the mayor's new secretary, Sarah Heath, stepped inside. The reason for the lack of décor was clear. The woman felt we focused too much on the secular celebration for the holiday and not the true reason. Sarah, also known as the pastor's wife, had wanted a more toned-down version of the Christmas parade, less kitschy parade floats, and more religious overtones with the school choir singing only Christmas-themed hymns rather than a mix of carols and popular Christmas tunes. Pastor Benjamin's wife had replaced Nancy O'Neil, the town's biggest gossip and his prior secretary of fourteen days. I was surprised Sarah took the job considering the Christmas holiday season was also the busiest time for a pastor.

"Afternoon, Merry, what brings you by?" She wore a plain gray dress that fell past her knees, a frock suitable for an Amish woman. Her light brown hair was slicked back in a severe bun. The woman appeared to be in her mid-sixties rather than her early forties. If her shoes were visible, I was certain they'd be practical chunky heels or mules rather than dainty heels. No makeup. No jewelry. Her only adornment and splash of color was a handmade silk scarf with a leaf pattern in muted tones of gold, red, and green colors suited for Christmas.

"The Christmas parade."

She flipped through the calendar on her desk. "You don't have an appointment scheduled."

"This issue just came to my attention." I walked to the door of the mayor's private office and rested a hand on the knob. "The mayor is expecting me."

"I should buzz him first. He doesn't like people barging in." Sarah gestured toward a couch. "He threw quite the fit when Jenna Wilcox walked in a few hours ago without knocking."

Had she already told him about her float and that was the reason for his fit? My confidence waned. If the mayor knew and hadn't been able to talk sense into her, I didn't know who else could. The parade was doomed. Was there a way I could salvage it? Where could I put her float that it would get as little attention as possible? I settled onto the edge of the couch, hoping it wasn't a long wait. There was a long to-do list waiting for me at home, half of it filled with crafting orders and the other parade prep. I pulled out my iPad and started designing some projects. At least some of my work was getting done.

The clacking of the keys was in tune to the Christmas carol playing from the radio. After a fourth song began playing, I heard a buzz and Sarah reminding the mayor I was waiting for him.

The mayor's static voice filled the room. "Send her in."

I walked into the mayor's private office and closed the door behind me. The mayor was standing in front of the large picture windows flanking the north side of his office and lining up a putt.

He glanced at me then returned his attention to the golf ball. The blinds were closed tight. He shifted his weight and tapped the ball. It rolled down the strip of green carpet and stopped halfway to the hole.

"Do you know what Jenna plans to have as her float's theme?" I asked.

"Unfortunately, yes." Mayor Vine sat down and placed the golf club onto the desk, gaze skittering to the door.

The security guard popped into my head. Was the mayor afraid he'd need it for another purpose other than golfing? For some reason, the mayor wanted the club nearby. Had someone threatened the mayor? "Are you stopping her?"

"No."

The mayor's one-word answered stunned me into momentary silence. No? That was it. No reason. No offer of help. Suggestions. Just no. "That's not acceptable."

"There is no rule about including residents names on a float."

"It's a naughty list. People will wonder why a person's name is on it. It'll hurt people's feelings."

"They'll have to get over it."

"Is that what you're going to do? Because your name is on it. I saw it."

The mayor refused to meet my gaze. "Jenna offered to do some editing."

Which meant the mayor's name was being taken off. "So as long as you're safe, you don't care about anyone else. What does she have on you?"

Using the golf club, he pointed at the door. "This conversation is over. You may leave."

"You can't sacrifice others in town to save your reputation."

"Don't be so sure my decision isn't to help others."

The look he centered on me caused a shiver to work up my spine. "Then stop her."

Mayor Vine tapped a folder on his desk. "I've read and reread the rules and guidelines about the parade. There's nothing forbidding a participant from using names or likeness of town members in their float."

There had to be something to stop her. "It doesn't seem like a good choice with reelections happening next year."

"I mentioned that to her. Jenna doesn't care. She's not planning on sticking around this town."

Which meant we had no leverage. She had nothing to lose by launching rumors and ill-feelings through the town. Merry Christmas to us.

THREE

Turning the corner to my house, I almost slammed on the brakes. It wasn't. It couldn't be. I blinked and blinked again. I wasn't having a nightmare. The monstrosity *was* parked at the curb in front of my house. The RV I had bought a few weeks ago to start a new life adventure but brought instead the worst moment of my life had returned. My son had taken it to Morgantown to sell it and had now brought it back. Was I stuck with it forever? At least it meant my baby boy was visiting me. I pulled into my driveway and waved.

My son and his friend Paul stood in the front yard, looking rather pleased. My heart tugged seeing my son in "street" clothes rather than his police officer's uniform. In his uniform, he was an adult. I couldn't even see a glimpse of the little boy I sometimes longed for. In jeans and a sweatshirt, and with his bright grin, I saw my little boy Scotland.

I rolled down the window and swallowed the lump in my throat. "What is that doing here?"

"We modified it. Come take a look."

I shook my head. "Bad memories."

Scotland draped an arm over Paul's shoulder. "They're all gone. Trust us, Mom."

Even believing I'd regret it, I slid out of my SUV and walked to the RV. There was no way I'd disappoint my son. With a flourish, Scotland opened the door.

"The renovations are a birthday gift from me, Raleigh, and Paul."

My birthday was a few days before Christmas, not really sure of the day as I was found in a stocking outside a church nearly forty-six years ago on Christmas Eve. I stood in the threshold of the RV. Tears filled my eyes. The RV was no longer the worst decision of my life. It was new. It gleamed. It was, without a doubt, a mobile crafting studio. "I love it. It's a crafting haven."

The dinette area, the area that had turned into my second ex-husband's place of death, no longer existed. In its place was a functional crafting area, suited perfectly for my needs. Instead of the dinner table for four with its two bench seats, there was a four-foot wooden table with two sturdy shelves attached to the wall. Everything that could be painted had a fresh coat, and all the old fabric was gone. In its place was upholstery and fabric in my favorite Christmas colors: gold, silver, and poinsettia red. There were even two poinsettia pillows on the couch.

The kitchen pantry unit had been converted into supply storage. Wine racks had been installed in the shelves to hold my rolls of vinyl, and the bottom shelf was left alone to stack cutting mats and other items I preferred to store flat. While my original plan had been selling and buying a new one, knowing how much thought and love my children put into making it perfect for me, this RV was growing on me.

"I looked at your setup in Raleigh's old room and used that as the blueprint for your studio area. I moved in some of your supplies."

"It's absolutely perfect." I hugged Scotland.

"What's wrong?" He pulled back, keeping his hands on my shoulders.

I wanted to say nothing, but after being a hostage of Samuel's murderer, I knew my son would think that was affecting me. It was better to tell the truth. "Jenna Wilcox is erecting a giant naughty list on her float and listed town members names and their naughty deeds on it."

"Are you serious?" Scotland was fighting back a smile.

"People are going to be hurt. She's using the parade to bully."

"She'll feel the consequences for her actions during the next election," Paul said.

"Mayor Vine brought that up to her. She's planning to move."

Scotland hugged me. "I know the parade is important to you, Mom. But you can't let Jenna get to you. I have the perfect thing to pick up your spirits. A present. It's in my car." Scotland ran out the door, leaving me and Paul alone.

I smiled. "Thanks, Paul. I appreciate you helping the kids fix it up for me."

He smiled back. "I know you plan to sell it, and the renovations will make it easier. Might be able to find someone at a craft event who'd be happy to take it off your hands. And please don't worry about Jenna."

"It's hard not to. I don't want her ruining the parade with ugliness."

"Then we'll just have to think of something to lessen it." Paul snapped his fingers. "We'll create a nice list and add the same names on it and beside them write forgiven. I'll tie it on the grill of the firetruck. We can come after Jenna's float. I'll get ahold of Norman, our town Santa Claus, and have him make an announcement that Santa decided to ditch the naughty list this year and there will be presents for all. It'll seem like it was planned."

"Like the names on the list were of people who agreed to be on it." I grinned. "I like it."

"I'm on it. Anytime you need help, I'm here for you." He pulled out his cell.

"I know." I walked out of the RV and watched my son wiggle out a huge box from the trunk of his car. "What did you guys buy me?"

"It's from Dad. He wouldn't tell me what it is, just that you might need help with it."

What did Brett get me that I might need help with? My first ex-husband, the father of my two amazing children, was a complicated man. Actually, our relationship right now was complicated as it was no longer at the easy friends-who-are-co-parenting stage. Our children were grown and living their own lives, and Brett let me know a few weeks ago he was interested in us rekindling our long flamed-out romance.

I wasn't sure why he thought all these years later we'd make a better couple. Parenting together had been our strong suit. It was other components of marriage where we clashed. Some people just didn't make good romantic partners. Friends, yes. Spouses, no.

Scotland placed a large box wrapped in birthday wrapping paper on the lawn. Brett and I gave each other token gifts for birthdays and holidays. Nothing extravagant and the size of the box said this was extravagant.

I walked around the box, eyeing it like one does a box left on the porch on April first. I didn't trust it.

"Is something wrong?" Paul studied me, a frown deepening on his face.

It was the hurt look on Scotland's face that galvanized me into action. I didn't want him to think I didn't trust his father. Heck, I did. I just wasn't comfortable with expensive gifts from Brett, knowing his feelings toward me.

I ripped off a strip of paper from the top of the box. The word inflatable was revealed. Even though Brett wasn't a big Christmas person, he gifted me something he knew spoke of my love for the season. I finished tearing off the papers. The bright red and green box contained an eight-foot inflatable hamster wearing a scarf and a Santa hat. A Christmas Ebenezer.

I hugged the box. "I love it."

"You have a good spot for it." Scotland pointed to the section of my yard that was without a Christmas decoration. The blank canvas of my yard was in the corner, almost tucked into the side yard. I hadn't wanted the good viewing spots in front of the house empty. There was no way I was putting Hammy in the corner.

"Hammy deserves a spot right in the front." I untied the ropes for the eight-foot snowman.

"You've named it Hammy."

"I've named them all." I patted the deflated snowman. "This is

Melty."

Without a word, Scotland and Paul helped me rearrange the inflatables. I couldn't wait to turn on the decorations tonight. It was going to be fabulous.

Scotland rested an arm around my shoulders and gave me a quick squeeze. "I feel bad that neither I nor Raleigh will be at the parade tomorrow. I didn't know the department was switching me to nights so soon."

"I understand." I smiled brightly, doing everything to hide my disappointment.

I knew the day was coming when traditions would change as my children's adult lives and schedules needed to take precedence over the ways of the past. The Season's Greetings Christmas Parade had been our big holiday event.

"I'll keep your mom company," Paul said.

"I hate to run off, Mom, but I have to head back to Mo-town. I have to work tonight. I wanted to see you before the parade and wish you luck. I know you've worked hard on it."

I squeezed him tight. "I'm happy to see you for any amount of time."

A few minutes later, I waved goodbye to my son and Paul. Paul had invited me out to dinner and I declined. I had a ton of work to do, besides, I wasn't in a place where I wanted to encourage more than a friendship with anyone.

I unlocked the front door. From his habitat, Ebenezer peered at me from under a pile of blankets, looking so sweet and friendly. The large habitat in the living room was created to give Ebenezer more roaming room in the house when I wasn't home. I didn't want him to have unsupervised free reign because there was a potential for him to get into something harmful. You'd never know he was an escape artist with an obsession for Christmas tree lights. It was because of him I had a baby gate around the Christmas tree. The critter just couldn't leave the lights on the bottom alone and having a pre-lit tree meant I couldn't move the row up.

"Don't you play innocent with me. I know you can get out of

there. What trouble did you get into today?" None! He was still in his guinea pig home. I scooped Ebenezer out of the cage setup and danced around the room. "You stayed in your house."

Ebenezer whistled and cuddled into my cheek. This morning I removed his jogging ramps out of his habitat. The little guy must've been using them to launch himself out of the caged area. Now, I knew why he loved them.

I put him on the ground. "I thought you'd be a breeze to take care of. You're almost as diabolical as a toddler."

Ebenezer beelined to the tree and tried to wiggle his plump body through one of the small holes. Yep, just like a toddler.

My phone pinged. I glanced at the screen. Bright. My business partner.

Deadlines going okay?

Yep, I fibbed. Bright had completed more than her fair share of the crafting projects over the last few weeks. There was no way I'd dump more onto her because of the Christmas parade. *I'll be caught up today. Mail out tomorrow.*

Don't keep yourself too busy. Remember to enjoy the holiday. Or try and avoid everything that has happened.

My finger froze over the virtual keyboard. Avoid everything that had happened. Bright knew me better than anyone else, even my children. Taking on the Christmas parade, and not putting our Etsy business "on vacation," kept me at an over-extended level, giving me no time to reflect or feel. The only emotion I was allowing myself to indulge in was anger. At Samuel. For what his schemes had cost me and left me to deal with. And most of all because his mistakes led to his death and leaving his daughter Cassie alone.

My simple life was now complicated. The biggest drama in my mundane world had been trying to recreate my life after my children had moved out and I was no longer primarily mom. Now, I felt like I was in a snow globe. Every time the world settled, it got shook up and all the pieces swirled around and all I could do was remain frozen until everything settled back down.

The only way to rid myself of the melancholy wrapping around me was to work. I knew the perfect project to complete orders and figure out the float line-up. One of my customers ordered three glass blocks with a Christmas scene. I'd cut out a vinyl decal to represent each of the floats like a sleigh for Santa's sleigh: Christmas trees for the florist, gingerbread man for the bakery, nativity scene for Harmony Baptist, and a giant bold "X" for Jenna. I'd take some photos (minus the X block) and let the customer pick the ones she wanted.

I lined the glass blocks in front of my fire place, placing Santa's sleigh at the end of the line and adjusted the fairy lights I had tucked inside. I plugged the nativity block into Santa then plugged Santa into an extension cord.

The blocks glowed, the soft orange-yellow light twinkled around the images. It was beautiful. I sat cross-legged on the floor and gazed at the décor. Everything was perfect. Except for the giant "X" representing Jenna. I should've pushed my irritation aside and made something more Christmassy for her. It would be easy to take off the vinyl and use the block but there was something so jarring and un-Christmas about the bold, giant "X." I had even made two marching bands, chorus of dancing women, and Boy and Girl Scout blocks. More thought should've gone into the representation of Jenna's float. I guess even I had my Scrooge moments.

Ebenezer crawled into my lap. I rubbed his furry head, shifting the strands of his multi-colored fur, still debating if Ebenezer had more white or brown fur. There were shots of red throughout. Guinea pig highlights. "What do you think?"

As if wanting to answer me, Ebenezer left my lap and waddle-walked over to the gingerbread block. He sniffed it carefully and in one quick movement, bit the cord.

I picked Ebenezer up and turned him to face me. "It's not for eating."

He wiggled his nose at me. I wasn't sure if that was guinea pig for "I won't do it again" or "I don't care."

The doorbell rang.

I deposited Ebenezer into his room and removed the ramps. I didn't trust Ebenezer not to launch himself out the moment I opened the door and go gnaw on the cords.

He squealed and whistled at me.

"You'll be fine for a couple of minutes. Stop all that fussing." I answered the door.

Rachel was standing on my porch, holding takeout from the family-owned Italian restaurant in town. They had the best breadsticks and chicken parmigiana. My mouth started to water even before the garlic and tomato aroma reached me.

"Saw you called the store. Since I was picking up dinner tonight, figured I'd swing by and share. I'm not much into leftovers and you know the entrees have enough food to feed a family of four. How did it go with Jenna?"

"Not good. She's going forward with the naughty list and has quite a few names on it."

"Who else?" Rachel carried the food to the dining room table.

"You're on it. Norman. Pastor Heath. The mayor had been on it, but he worked out a deal to get his name off and allow Jenna to trash others with her stupid sign."

"It's just names."

"She has a column that lists the naughty deeds."

Rachel spun toward me, one of the containers she was pulling from the bag slipping from her shaking hands. "She what?"

I grabbed the container before it hit the ground and we lost the chicken parmigiana. "Listing the reason someone's on the naughty list. She has her husband on it and by his name is drunkard. She hadn't finished listing the transgressions on the sign."

"Let's forget about all that. We haven't had a girl's night since..." Rachel trailed off, gaze drifting to the floor.

Since Samuel was murdered. It wasn't a conscious decision by either of us. The holiday season filled both of our schedules to the max, especially with us basically being one-woman operations.

"You're right." I sat down. "Let's eat before the food gets cold."

"I love your new decorations." She nodded toward the living room.

"I made the blocks to represent the floats. Trying to finalize the line-up. I decided to have everyone arrive at different times." As I retrieved plates from the kitchen, I explained my plan of having the floats arrive in pairs an hour before the parade in ten-minute increments.

"That sounds good. Last year it was a huge cluster with—" She stopped again.

I heaved out a sigh. "You can say his name, Rachel. I'm not going to collapse into a puddle of tears."

A smile twitched at her lips. "I'm more worried about you screaming and throwing stuff."

I waved my arm around. "I don't ruin Christmas." Almost everything in my house was something Christmas or family related. It was the basic theme of my decorating, during the holiday and not.

"That's true. There is no way you'd do anything to hurt Christmas." Rachel divided the salad into two bowls, both were overflowing with lettuce, cheese, tomatoes, and olives.

"What are your plans for the holidays?"

The holidays were a bittersweet time of the year for Rachel. She loved the Christmas season, the activities, the cold in the air, the spirit of togetherness and love that seemed to wrap everything. It was also a time that reminded her she was still alone. She got along with her family, but everyone lived far away from each other and were wrapped up in their lives. Her parents spent the holidays traveling from one brother's house to the other to visit their grandchildren. Rachel didn't feel comfortable leaving her business for a long time, especially around the holiday buying season.

A slight smile developed, and she picked up a napkin to hide it. "Nothing. This year I'm looking forward to a quiet Christmas at home. I plan to binge watch my favorite holiday movies and dinner will be frozen appetizers."

"Who is he?"

Her eyes widened. "He who?"

"The man that's making you smile."

"I don't have a man." She tore off a piece of bread and broke it into smaller pieces. The bread littered her plate.

"You can trust me." I grinned at her. "I won't tell anyone. Where did you meet him? How long have you guys been seeing each other? Is it the mayor's security guard? That guy is hot."

"There isn't a he." Anger and hurt sparked in her eyes.

I cut off a large chunk of chicken parmigiana and shoved it in my mouth, wanting something other than my foot in it. I had assumed Rachel was seeing someone, instead she had grown comfortable with her single status, a status she'd been trying to change for the last ten years, and I was ruining it for her.

We ate in a silence. Rachel occasionally fiddled with her cell phone. The quiet filling my house was not a pleasant one. Why had I teased Rachel about having a man? I knew it was a sore subject. She had wanted to be married. Instead, her last few relationships had been hook-ups that she thought were relationships with potential.

She had taken the initiative and brought dinner to me since neither of us were making time for our friendship, and I put a damper on the evening by telling her she couldn't be happy without a guy. I, of all people, should know a man didn't equal happiness. I had two failed marriages. I was living alone and happy.

The tension between me and my friend was my fault. "I'm sorry, Rachel. I shouldn't think a woman looks so happy because a man is in her life."

A phone binged. A text. I checked mine. No messages. Rachel tugged hers out and frowned. The lights coming from the lawn decorations highlighted her face.

I placed my hand on her arms. "Are you okay?" I tried to sneak a peek at her phone.

She shoved it back in her pocket. "Yes. I'm sorry, I have to leave. Might be an issue at the store." She hurried back into the house and grabbed her coat and purse.

"I'll come with you."

She shook her head. "No, it's not anything I need help with. I'll see you tomorrow for the final review before the parade." She hurried to her car.

Sadness welled up in me. I had this strong feeling Rachel had someone text her as an excuse to bail.

FOUR

The next morning with my spirits not so merry, I pulled into a parking space at the end of Main Avenue, the beginning of the Christmas parade, to start my final walk through. I owed Rachel an apology and hoped she'd accept it. I got out and fed the meter. Christmas music floated in the air. Where was it coming from?

Confused, I looked around and then glanced up. Attached to the light poles were speakers. This must've been one of the holiday improvements Mayor Vine was ecstatic over and the rest of the city council was a little peeved about. The mayor's choice of what constituted a necessary budget item was concerning to all of people in Season's Greetings. I usually leaned toward the side of what-was-he-thinking but I liked the addition of the Christmas music. Added to the atmosphere of our town being a Christmas destination. I'd find a way to tap a little bit into the lottery winnings and make an anonymous donation toward the speakers.

Everything was perfectly Christmas. The businesses had beautiful and tasteful decorations, ranging from contemporary to whimsical. The shops that were community stops had their small placards hung, designating them as either information, food, quiet, or if they had facilities available.

I trudged toward One More Page, spotting someone I hadn't expected to see standing in front of the bookstore.

Cassie's long blonde hair swung back and forth as she cleaned the front display window of One More Page. The front window gleamed. The naughty and nice sign were on opposite sides of the display unit, between them was a pair of glasses, a computer, and a picture of Mrs. Claus, all things Santa would likely have on his desk. Back and forth, Cassie's arm went. There wasn't a trace of dirt or dust on the window.

The high school senior should be in school, not on Main Avenue. At least she was helping Rachel rather than cruising the streets or causing mayhem. But, skipping school wouldn't help her graduate at the end of May.

Should I say something or not? She was eighteen and could opt not to go, but I hoped with all my might Cassie hadn't decided to drop out of school. I knew school was hard for her. Learning didn't come easy and she had to study for hours to get a passing grade. It was only a few months more. Her life would be so much easier if she graduated high school. Though, I was sure she didn't think her world could get much worse after her father was murdered and learning her grandmother's cancer had returned.

Sensing my attention on her, Cassie gave me a wavering smile. A woman walked inside the store. "Customers are going in. I need to help them."

I followed her inside, gently taking hold of her hand before she escaped behind the counter. "Rachel can assist the customers. We have to talk."

Cassie blew out a breath, puffing up her blonde bangs. "I know what this is about. I know what I'm doing. Besides, Rachel's not here yet. She had a slight emergency and is running late and asked me to open. Don't worry. I'm not skipping. The principal gave me permission to work at One More Page today rather than attend classes."

I crossed my arms and gave her my best stern-momma stare. "You expect me to believe that."

"You can call the principal. I'm not sure he can give you information. I'm an adult."

She was right. I had divorced Samuel before he died so the school didn't have to tell me anything. The girl was an adult in the eyes of the law and her life choices were up to her. And, I had stepped back from my relationship with Cassie. I had been so done with the man, I didn't want to have to look, think, or even acknowledge his existence. Which meant ignoring Cassie. A choice I regretted. It had hurt Cassie so much and left her feeling alone and abandoned after her father died.

Cassie blinked furiously, trying to starve off welling tears. "It's hard this week. All the plans for the parade. Kids griping about being forced," she air quoted the word, "to go with their parents and siblings. I just couldn't hear any more of their complaints. It hurts."

I hugged Cassie. I hadn't considered how difficult a time this was for her. I had been so wrapped up in my own angst and pain, I hadn't taken a good look at hers. "I'm so sorry."

Drawing back, Cassie ran her index fingers under her eyes. "Rachel got some new craft books in. You can browse while I make you a cup of cinnamon spice coffee and see what you think. We're planning on offering it tonight during the parade."

The bell jingled merrily. Nancy O'Neil, Jenna's best friend and the mayor's former secretary, walked into the store and scanned the area, a confused look blossoming on her face. The two women were so different it was hard to imagine they were friends. Jenna was put together. Fashionable. She dressed like an ad in a fashion magazine. Thirty-five. A private person who wanted to know all that was going on in Season's Greetings. Which I guess made it not so unusual she was friends with Nancy, a sixty-one-year-old who dressed in themes and knew everything that went on in Season's Greetings and loved to tell it.

"Can I help you?" Cassie placed the carafe on the counter, abandoning the coffee making to help the distraught looking customer.

"Jenna told me to meet her here this morning. Nine on the dot."

"No one is here but me and Merry. The store just opened at nine. Maybe, she meant a little later."

Nancy rummaged around in her purse. Tissues, slips of paper, and lip glosses tumbled out of her purse. She placed her phone on the counter and tapped it. "I have her text message right here. Said it was important. She sent the text fifteen minutes ago."

"You're welcome to wait for her." Cassie gestured toward a comfortable reading chair. "I was going to make some coffee and can bring you a cup."

Nancy moved her finger up and down on the cell's screen. "I have a list of errands to run this morning. Can you tell Jenna I was here on time?"

There was a fearful tremor in Nancy's voice. Maybe the two weren't such good friends.

"Sure," Cassie said.

"Thank you." Nancy rushed outside. A tall figure wearing a baseball cap, slammed into Nancy. Squealing, Nancy windmilled her arms to keep her balance. Her purse flew to the right, into the street, while she tumbled to the ground in the opposite direction. The man grabbed her purse and ran off.

I ran outside and helped Nancy to her feet. "Are you all right?"

"My medicine! My purse." She shook off my grasp and limped down the sidewalk after the thief.

"Thief!" I screamed and chased him.

"Merry, don't!" Nancy called out.

The purse snatcher ran, hunched over, digging in Nancy's purse. Where was everyone? I couldn't believe no one was else was coming to help. I huffed and puffed, glasses bouncing on the bridge of my nose. My pace was slowing down. The guy was going to outrun me.

He reached one of the small service roads. My spirits picked up. Half the time, there was a police car parked there, waiting for speeders who like to zoom down the road. The man started running across. A horn blared. A vehicle was shooting across the road. Another reason the police took up residence on the side street.

The man lost his grip on the purse as he planted a hand on the hood of the car and slid across. The driver slammed on the brakes.

The thief landed on his feet and kept running, leaving the purse behind.

The shaken driver jumped out and pointed at the guy. "He came out of nowhere. You saw that. Right?"

"He's not going to call the cops. He stole a purse and was trying to get away." I picked up Nancy's purse and walked back to One More Page.

"Oh my goodness." Nancy's hand was pressed against her heart. "That was scary."

Probably not the best idea to chase him, but the distress in Nancy's voice caused me to react. I had wanted to right a wrong. And that one seemed simple enough. "Are you sure you're okay?"

Nancy nodded. "You might want to check in with Cassie. She heard me yell for you."

I went back inside and saw a pile of items on the floor. The stuff Nancy dropped from her purse. I picked them up. Cassie was behind the counter, filling a to-go cup with coffee from a carafe.

Receipts. Four bank slips with Jenna's name on it. Wow, the woman sure did have Nancy hopping around for her. The slips were for four different banks. Cash deposits. Why so many different ones? Wasn't it easier to keep your money all in one place?

My eyes caught the sum. The travel business was booming this holiday season.

"You shouldn't have done that." Cassie held out a cup of coffee in a to-go mug.

The cinnamon wafted toward me. It smelled heavenly. Unfortunately, my hands were full. I crumbled the receipts and slips into a giant ball and shoved them into the garbage can behind the counter. I accepted the drink and took a small sip, nearly burning my tongue. "Delicious."

"Don't change the subject." Tears rushed into her eyes. "What you did was stupid. You could've gotten hurt. Killed."

"I wasn't in any danger," I said.

"You don't know that. That guy knocked into Nancy on purpose. What if had decided to turn around and hit you? Attack you. He might've been on drugs or something."

I opened my mouth to argue then stopped. As much as I didn't like getting a lecture from an eighteen-year-old, she was right. I made a dangerous choice. Whatever was in Nancy's purse wasn't worth my life. "You're right."

FIVE

Every ounce of sunlight had left, and the sky was a stretched canvas of black littered with twinkling stars. Flakes of snow drifted down. It was a perfect night for the parade. I just had to find a way to enjoy it. A melancholy had settled over me thinking of everyone's reaction to Jenna's float.

I adjusted my scarf. There was something about that twinge of cold that brought memories of Christmas past. The hope. The excitement. The childhood longing for Santa Claus and the wonders a young mind dreamed during this time of year. My children loved the Christmas parade. Even when they were teenagers, it was one of the events of the season that we always attended together. It was a nostalgic childhood tradition for them and I was thrilled they never felt too old to enjoy it. This was my first year without one of my children watching the parade with me.

Half the floats had arrived, ignoring the time-slots I had given them, and the drivers were in the process of getting into the proper que order. They were used to arriving an hour before the parade started. The biggest surprise was Jenna still hadn't arrived. I wasn't sure if that went on the naughty or nice side. Rachel was also tardy along with Paul McCormick and the fire truck.

The Harmony Baptist float was parked at the end of the parking lot. Pastor Benjamin was adjusting the cardboard star above Baby Jesus. The savior being represented by an American Girl Bitty baby doll. The pastor had wanted a real baby, but there wasn't a mother who was comfortable having their infant on a float during December. I couldn't blame them. The weather was unpredictable.

In the distance, I heard the siren of the fire truck blip. At least one more of my floats was almost here. Paul took up residence in my mind before I closed the door on those thoughts. He was my friend's son. A friend of mine. A man, thirteen years my junior, who wanted to be more than friends. At times the thought appealed to me and other times I wanted to hide from what seemed like a threat of romance. My track record of picking a mate was dismal. Two divorces.

A husband? Why not just a guy to hang out with? Have fun? That was something to consider. Who says I needed a commitment? Why not just have a friendship, with the possibility of a romantic entanglement every now and then? I was an adult. I didn't have children at home to worry about. Just have fun and not worry about the future of a relationship.

A loud ruckus drew my attention. A horde of boys in blue uniforms were running around. A frazzled looking man and woman tried to gather them up as the Boy Scouts darted off in different directions, trying to see if anyone needed help.

I tapped the book light I had attached to my clipboard and checked off the Boy Scouts. Now all my walkers had checked in: Boy Scouts, Girl Scouts, and the high school band. I was waiting for the high school dance troop, the competition cheerleaders, and dance team.

"Troop 113, checking in." The leader said, counting the boys in blue scattered around the parking lot.

"Got them." Fortunately, the church had installed massive security lights all around the church's parking lot, making it easier to track the troop who didn't seem able to stay in one place longer than fifteen seconds. Watching the darting bodies was exhausting. Where did the boys get so much energy this late in the evening?

"Shouldn't everyone be getting into place?" Pastor Benjamin Heath pushed up the beige sleeve of his Joseph costume and tapped his watch. "The parade begins in five minutes."

Where had the time gone? And where were the rest of the floats? "I'll get everyone in place soon. Waiting on a few more floats."

"We're ready." Pastor Benjamin waved his hand and a group of church members dressed as the figures in the nativity circled him. "I've had my float here ready for days."

It was easy for them to be on time as the stage area was the parking lot of Harmony Baptist Church, which was a block from the beginning of Main Avenue. Though I noticed he was short a wise man.

"I'm still missing a lot of the floats."

"How is Santa's sleigh?" Sarah adjusted the drape of her husband's robe then smoothed down the area of hers over her stomach. "Norman wanted authentic presents rather than fake ones like our previous Santa used. The church had already collected a lot and wrapped them ourselves, so we donated those gifts. It doesn't matter if the church gives the children presents or Santa."

I was glad to hear it though it was a change of attitude for Sarah. Usually she wanted Santa wiped right out of Christmas.

"I hope the sleigh isn't too full," the pastor said. "We don't want the gifts tumbling out as the sleigh makes its way down the street."

"I'll check on it," I said.

Santa's sleigh was in hiding behind the church underneath a tarp. No one wanted a child seeing it before Santa was suited up and in place. Frowning, I glanced around. Where was Norman? Norman Bail was seventy-two years old, the oldest city council member, and the most rule-abiding person I knew, besides my son Scotland. Norman loved Christmas almost as much as I did. He and his wife Angela built the most awesome Christmas display every year, it was like the North Pole was transported to their yard. Lighted sleigh. Eight lighted reindeer arranged around the yard, waiting for Christmas Eve when Norman moved them to the places in front of the sleigh. He usually was the second one who showed up, Pastor Benjamin always being first, including before the event's organizer.

Where were my missing floats? I pulled out my cell and called one of my stragglers.

A harried voice answered the call. "On the way. Traffic is stopped. A large plastic snowman is blocking the road."

That explained why so many of the floats were missing and the blipping of the siren.

"The fire department is helping the owner clear it. Good thing it was a bounceable plastic and the fire truck was behind it. It bounced off the road and hit the grill of the truck. Traffic is moving again. You'll have a slew of floats pulling in soon."

Panic welled up in me. How was I going to handle a bunch of floats arriving at the same time? There wasn't enough space in the parking lot to have them pull in and wait while I was lining up another float. I was a one-woman show.

"What's going on?" Norman said from behind me.

I spun around, never so happy to see someone in my life. Norman's flannel shirt was tight across his stomach. The man had taken his Santa role seriously and bulked up a few pounds.

"You can help me line everyone up. Half the floats are here, and the other ones will all be arriving shortly."

Norman's face scrunched up in confusion.

Taking in a few deep breaths, I centered myself and reexplained that I needed his help.

"The parade is starting?" Norman scratched his chin, fingers disappearing into his white beard.

I wasn't sure if he was asking me a question or stating the obvious. Either way, I was worried. "In five minutes. Starts the same time every year."

"Of course. I just—" Norman stopped talking and gazed around the area, seeming a little lost and confused.

A knot formed in my stomach. His mannerisms reminded me of my mom right before she was diagnosed with her illness. Confusion. Forgetfulness. And trying to cover it up by having someone repeat what was said or asking a question in a manner where it sounded like a statement.

Red lights flashed on and off. The fire truck, along with Paul McCormick and Chief Vandermore, had arrived. Hopefully, I could wrangle some help from them.

Paul parked the fire truck where it blocked anyone else from entering. Before I could tell him to move it, he jumped out and jogged over to me.

"Chief said to check in with you and find out if you want us to move the fire truck into position or pull it up a bit where only one float will be able to pull in at time from this entrance to the parking lot. He thought you might want some help controlling the flow of traffic."

There went the fantastic line-up I designed, though since everyone but Jenna had showed up, she'd be last. Once Santa arrived, no one would pay attention to her float. Her naughty sign wouldn't matter. "Sounds like a great plan. I'll get the ones in the staging area to pull up to the next one."

Norman wandered off toward the back of the church. Had he remembered he needed to get ready for the parade? Santa had to be suited up.

"Merry, are you okay?" Paul touched my elbow.

I blew out a breath. "I'm worried about Norman. He forgot about the parade. He asked me what was going on and I thought he meant about there not being a lot of floats here yet, but then I realized he meant why were there floats in the church's parking lot. It reminds me of my mom." My voice turned raspy as tears brewed. I handed Paul my clipboard. "Can you tell everyone the change of plans?"

"I'll go check on him and see if he wants assistance loading Santa's sleigh."

"I'll feel better if I talk with him." As I rounded the corner, I heard Norman cursing. He was sitting in the sleigh, leaning over so his head wasn't visible. Presents were tumbling from the sleigh to the ground. Santa's bag was overflowing. A few had toppled from the back and were almost underneath a new twelve-passenger van parked behind the sleigh. The white vehicle gleamed under the light. Harmony Baptist Church was expertly painted on the side.

"Everything all right?" I called out to him, not wanting to startle him.

"I had all these presents in Santa's bag last night. Someone was messing with my stuff. I had a tarp over the sleigh and it was off. A child could've seen it. Some of these presents are ruined. They were Secret Elves presents. Who would've done this?" He tugged on the hem of the Santa suit jacket.

I didn't have a clue. I was having trouble believing someone deliberately destroyed presents for children of low-income parents. "Let me help you pack up Santa's bag. I'll make sure the ruined presents are replaced before they're delivered."

Norman smiled at me. "You're a kind soul, Merry."

With his shaking hands and unsteady gait, I knew it would be easier for me to fill the bag. "You hand me the gifts, and I'll pack them." I climbed into the sleigh. The presents on top were piled up in a haphazard fashion, peeking inside I could see some empty spots. Norman wasn't a good packer.

"I had them all in here earlier." He handed me one. "It's like the presents got larger." He fumbled with the next packaged, nearly dropping it. His arms quivered with every move.

"Let me rearrange the presents in the bag first. There's not much room in here." I removed some from the bag. We'd have to start all over.

"Makes no sense," Norman grumbled.

I had a feeling Norman believed the presents were perfectly packed. From what I was watching, Norman wouldn't have been able to do so. He was moving in a jerky fashion. I was worried about him. I removed a present.

Jenna was staring up at me, scowling. I scowled back. Why was she hiding in Santa's bag? "I see our problem. Get out of there."

"Who's in there?" Norman hauled himself into the sleigh.

I grabbed Jenna's arm. It was cold. And rigid.

"She's dead." Norman said.

Norman and I exchanged a look of horror. Santa's sleigh wasn't going anywhere tonight. It was the scene of a murder.

SIX

Flashlight beams went back and forth over the asphalt area around the sleigh. Hunched over, Police Chief Hudson and Officer Orville Martin searched the area for clues of who put Jenna Wilcox into Santa's bag. Officer Brianna Myers was stationed near the entrance of the parking lot, directing the remaining floats to the end of the parade line-up. The sleigh was blocked by the church and no one could see the chief and Orville poking around in it.

Norman paced back and forth, muttering under his breath and tugging at the sleeves of his Santa jacket. His movements were frantic, gaze skittering from the police, to me, and the surrounding area. Paul was trying to talk to him, but Norman kept pushing him away, preferring to wander back and forth, a safe distance from the sleigh. It was a sight no one should ever see. Crime scene taped cordoning off Santa's sleigh from Santa. Presents littered the ground. An officer was carefully collecting them and placing them in evidence bags.

I shivered. Jenna was dead. Murdered. While I was worrying about missing parade floats, someone had snuck over to Santa's sleigh and placed her body inside. What if the killer had had time to place all the gifts back into the sleigh? Would Norman not have found her until he started handing out gifts to the children at the end of the parade? Was there blood on any of the presents?

My body trembled even more. Who would do such a horrible thing? Had I seen anyone going behind the building? I rummaged through my memory. No. The only person I saw going behind the church was Norman and that was a few minutes ago. Tears blurred my vision. I drew in small breaths to settle myself down.

"You okay?" Paul walked over and draped a heavy jacket around me.

The material weighed me down, making me feel claustrophobic rather than comforted. I shrugged it off. He caught it before it hit the ground.

"Who could've done it? I didn't hear anyone behind the church. Why didn't I notice anything? I could've helped her." My voice sounded broken. What was going on in our town? Samuel a few weeks ago and now Jenna. Why was hatred gaining such a stronghold?

"Don't put this on yourself. You don't know when it happened. And if you had seen something and went over, the chances are you'd be hurt or killed also."

I covered my eyes with my hands and drew in another deep breath. "What are we going to do? What am I going to do?"

"Nothing." Paul rubbed my back. "This is a police matter. There's nothing for you to do." There was a twinge of anger and fear in his voice.

I peeked at him through my fingers. "The parade. What am I going to do about it? It's supposed to start in a few minutes." What did he think I meant?

"That's a good question. I'll go ask the chief for you. Unless you prefer to ask?" he asked me, eyebrows slightly raised.

I shook my head. I preferred not to go anywhere near the sleigh and Jenna's body. Seeing it once was more than enough. "You can talk to him. What should I tell the parade watchers?"

"Hang tight, I'll be back." Paul jogged over to the chief.

Norman stopped pacing and came to stand beside me. "What's Paul doing?"

"He's asking about the parade. We have to tell the people waiting for it to start why it's not happening."

"It's not?" Norman flicked a gaze in my direction. "I hadn't heard the chief say it's cancelled."

"Jenna is dead in Santa's sleigh. I doubt the police are going to let you use it tonight."

He rubbed his chin. "What else could Santa arrive in tonight? The children expect it."

I gaped at him. There were some things that took precedence over Santa's arrival—like a woman being murdered. I highly doubted she climbed into Santa's present bag then died of natural causes. "Jenna was killed. You think we should just carry on as normal?"

"What else is there to do?" Norman asked. "Nothing we can do will bring her back and anything else, besides going on with the parade, will ruin the holidays for everyone else. Do you really want to announce to all those children that a woman was killed tonight? How will that affect them?"

He was right, but I hadn't planned on announcing Jenna's death. Her poor husband hadn't even heard about it. I sure wasn't going to allow him to find out through the parade grapevine. "I wasn't going to mention Jenna, just that something unexpected occurred with a float and the parade needed to be postponed."

"The business owners will love that. As will all the visitors who arrived tonight for the parade, arranged vacation plans around it. They won't mind coming back a different night. Heck, it won't bother them at all, and they'll decide to once again visit our town for Christmas rather than another Christmas-themed town."

The snarkiness shocked me. It was so unlike Norman. Before I let my temper out, I reminded myself he had just discovered a body. He was shook-up. Of course he wasn't acting like himself. It wasn't an easy situation to process. After I had found Samuel dead, it took days for me to feel like my world was stabilizing.

Paul and Chief Hudson walked over, neither looking happy. I steeled myself to accept whatever fate for the parade the chief determined best. Chief Hudson reminded me of an old-time gunslinger rather than an officer of the law. He had this rolling gait and I was always surprised to see him in a cruiser instead of on a horse, add in his long gray beard and hair and it was like he was the villain stepping out of a 1950's Western.

"The parade will go as scheduled," Hudson said. "Fire Chief Vandermore has agreed that Santa can ride in the fire truck this year."

"Are you sure?" I asked.

The chief nodded. "If the parade is cancelled, we'll have everyone returning to their cars and swarming this area. We'll lose whatever evidence is out there. We need to keep everyone where they are. The best way is for the parade to go as scheduled."

"Has anyone contacted Jenna's husband?" I felt sick. Eric was either waiting somewhere with the float, or among the parade goers waiting for his wife's float to go by.

"An officer has been dispatched to notify Eric Wilcox. If he's not at home, I have another officer searching the crowd for him. We'll make sure he's told before word gets out to the public. Did either of you see anything?" Chief Hudson switched his gaze from me to Norman.

"No," I said.

"What time did you arrive?"

"I got to the church parking lot at about four thirty," I said. "Pastor Heath and the actors for his float were just going inside the church."

He jotted down the information. "What time did you arrive, Norman?"

"I got here about three and was here about an hour. There was no one else around. I was done loading up the sleigh around four then went home for dinner. I don't like staying away from Angela for too long."

"Had the Pastor arrived or any of the church members who were on their float?"

"Nope. The lot was empty when I left," Norman said.

There was a thirty-minute time frame between Norman leaving and me arriving. Had I passed the person when I arrived, or had the church members and pastor showed up as the killer was about to leave? Was that why the presents had been left scattered on the ground?

"How did she die?" The question tumbled out of my mouth.

"I can't say."

It couldn't be too gruesome, or the police would be scouring the town for the spot she was killed. The area around the sleigh was pristine. Nothing was on the ground or marred the pockets of snow building up around the sleigh. I hadn't seen a mark on Jenna. Had there been any footprints when Norman walked over moments ago? I started to ask him then stopped. It wasn't my business.

Skimming the beam of the flashlight across the ground, Orville walked over. "Dispatch is getting calls about the parade. People are asking about the holdup."

"What will people say when they find out the parade went on after finding Jenna?" I asked.

"If we announce it now, I'll have to deal with the majority of the residents running over here along with tourists. This case is going to be hard enough as it is without potential evidence being destroyed or carted off," Chief Hudson said, his voice pained.

"If it even happened here," Paul said. "Who knows where she was killed."

"Then the killer has extra time to cover their tracks," I kept my voice low.

Chief Hudson pointed at me, Paul, and Norman. "I need the three of you to be my eyes. If anyone acts weird during the parade, anything unusual, tuck that information into your mind and let me know. Don't make a scene about it. Find a way to notify me as quickly as possible. Can you guys do that?"

Paul, Norman, and I nodded. It was a tall order. I had no idea what was out of the ordinary during the parade. We had a lot of weird things going on in previous years. Heck, one year Orville's parents drove down Main Avenue in their night clothes waving at the crowds with Orville chasing after them, threatening to arrest them for indecency. Orville's mom liked her nightgowns skimpy, barely covering her massive bosom.

"Get the parade started before people start wandering over here to see what's the holdup."

I headed for the floats. There were footsteps behind me. I glanced over my shoulder. Paul was following. "I thought you could use some help."

"This isn't going to be easy. People are going to know something is up," I said.

"They'll just think it's because this is your first year organizing the parade. There was bound to be some issues you overlooked."

I narrowed my eyes on him. "I didn't overlook anything."

He draped an arm over my shoulder and gave me a quick, one-armed hug. "I know that. But it wouldn't be unusual for something unexpected to happen or just to forget one thing. The town people know life has been rough for you lately, with Samuel's murder and being accused of it. They'll forgive you for a late start and any other bumps tonight. Use that to your advantage."

Paul was right. People wouldn't be surprised the parade didn't go off without a hitch. Why not use it in my favor? It was much better than the truth, especially since Chief Hudson wanted the truth concealed for the time being.

"What's happening?" Pastor Benjamin asked when I rounded the corner, adjusting the drape of his brown robe. Sarah, who was portraying Mary, was already on the float, settling baby Jesus into the cradle. "The officer won't let anyone behind the church. There's even an officer guarding the back door. Jenna isn't here. This is a ploy by her. She's done something to ruin the parade."

"Jenna's boycotting the parade," I blurted the first excuse to pop into my head and regretted it immediately. I had placed myself in a position of having to lie to everyone and creating a fictional fight between me and the recently murdered Jenna.

SEVEN

Pastor Benjamin drew back. "Boycotting? Why?"

Other float owners crowded around us. What now? I racked my mind for a good reason that wouldn't implicate me in her murder when the truth was out. The last thing I wanted to do was tie my name to another murder, or at least not as a suspect. I had found Jenna in Santa's toy bag.

I shrugged, hoping my non-answer would appease the masses.

Footsteps pounded behind me. I quickly turned, fearing someone was about to blurt out the truth. I wasn't sure who else would know by now, but there was a good chance me, Paul, Norman, and the police weren't the only ones who knew.

Like the murderer, the thought crept in.

Rachel was out of breath, her gaze skittered back and forth as panic crossed over her face. "What's going on? Why is the fire truck blocking the parking lot?"

"Paul and the fire chief parked it there to help with crowd control. Half the floats showed up at the same time and I'm having to change plans. Whatever order the floats were on the road getting here is the way they'll proceed down the parade route. What took you so long? You're just down the block." I rushed out the words, yammering on to bore and hopefully scatter the other float participants away. I didn't want to answer the Jenna question.

The pastor was listening to every word, an odd look on his face. I had a feeling he was suspicious about my earlier reason for Jenna's absence and was waiting to see what I'd say to my friend.

"My new part-time employee Garrett was late. I didn't want to leave Cassie alone in the store. A lot of shoppers and browsers. Cassie was so happy reading 'A Visit from Saint Nicolas' to the children that I hated asking her to stop and deal with customers. It was nice seeing joy on her face."

"Check in with Paul and he'll let you know when to merge your float into the line," I said.

"You're not going to say what's going on?"

"Don't have time to go into it. The parade was supposed to start ten minutes ago. There was an unfortunate delay because of a downed plastic snowman in the road. Since the police cleared that up, Officer Myers decided to give me a hand."

Rachel's eyes narrowed, and her head arched back a fraction. "Right. The police have nothing better to do than make sure floats are lined up. Shouldn't she be off duty?"

She knew I was lying to her. This was not going to help repair the rift I created in our friendship last night.

"I have to agree with Rachel," the pastor said. "Something huge is going on and you're keeping it from us."

This wasn't going well. I was never the best at keeping secrets. It was why my children learned a lot earlier than I wanted that Santa was the spirit inside of us rather than a real person. It had wounded me that I hadn't been able to stretch out that time of childhood with my children.

"No officer is off duty the night of the Christmas parade," I said. "You know how crazy traffic can get, not to mention there is always one child getting lost."

"That's all. Nothing else?" Rachel crossed her arms and tapped her foot. She wasn't going to budge until I revealed whatever I was holding back. "There's a police car blocking everyone off. Unless the officer moves his cruiser, there's no way I can get my float to the parade."

"I think the police are trying to stop cars from cutting through. Why don't you head back to your float? I'll see about getting the officer to move the cruiser until you pass." I shooed at her and the pastor. "I need you both at your floats. I'm starting the parade."

"Where's Jenna's float? Are you sure she's not the reason for the police presence?" Rachel settled a searching look, filled with concern, on me.

It was easy to brush off the pastor's question, not so much with Rachel. It was harder lying, or rather keeping information, from a friend. From the corner of my eye, I spotted the snowman float getting into position. A perfect excuse for me to leave this conversation.

"I need to check on that float. Wouldn't be good for the snowman to run away during the parade."

The local hardware store owner was checking the wire cord that attached the eight-foot-tall plastic snowman onto their float. The snowman had a few dinged places, black marks, and the carrot nose was slightly skewed but otherwise was in good shape. The owner was using some heavy-duty wire to attach the metal rings around the snowman's waist, pieces of rope were tossed in a pile to the side of the base of the float.

"Told you we should've used the trailer with higher sides," a young man said as he watched the owner scramble around the trailer to secure all the wire anchors.

"And I told you I wasn't asking for your opinion. Good thing I'm in love with your aunt, kid, or you'd be out of a job." The owner clenched his fists as he glared at his teenaged nephew.

The nephew grinned, a taunting smile that seemed to hope to push his uncle over the edge. There was no love lost between the two men.

"Hi guys." I approached the twosome, hoping to stall the brewing tension. "We have to get this parade moving. The residents and visitors are getting restless."

The owner dusted off his hands. "All stable. Sorry for delaying the parade. Tomorrow, I'll post an apology on social media and have the newspaper run a mea culpa."

"It's not necessary."

"I don't want people blaming you for the late start. We held up traffic."

The owner told his nephew to ride in the back then got into the cab of the truck. Grinning, the nephew eyed the snowman and the metal wires. I had a feeling I knew how the ropes failed. He was someone I needed to keep an eye on, but I had a more problematic person to be on the lookout for—a murderer. An annoyed nephew who wanted to toy with his uncle just didn't rank as high, but I couldn't let him fiddle with the safety wires of the snowman. Someone could get hurt.

I'd ride with the nephew to keep an eye on Frosty and get a good view of the parade crowd. It would be easier to spot Eric or anyone acting suspicious from the higher vantage point than walking. I tapped on the window of the truck.

The owner rolled it down. "I promise the snowman is secured. I added more ties to it and am using metal instead of ropes. I swore they were in perfect condition, but the slight movement of the snowman frayed them."

"In case the metal rings pop out, how about I help your nephew make sure Frosty stays put. If there's an incident, two people holding onto it is better than one."

Main Avenue was the definition of Christmas. Bright lights. Happiness. Decorations. Laughter. Trees, wreaths, and garlands were in the display windows along with gingerbread houses and other scenes that filled a Christmas heart. Except for Cornelius's costume shop but he had moved a couple of Christmas-themed costumes in front of the windows. I was thrilled at his effort.

Everything was perfect except for the secret lurking in the background—Jenna's murder. A foreboding tangled into my joy, robbing a bit of it. For the first time, I understood the mixed feelings others had about the holiday that most associated with goodness, love, and hope. It was hard to focus on the joy of the season when within the boundaries was wickedness. I didn't know how to deal with it, besides ignoring it for the time being and hoping it didn't consume me.

People filled every inch of the sidewalks on both sides of the street. Christmas lights hung in the trees, casting everyone in a golden hue. Children waved as we drove by. I waved back with one hand, keeping the other firmly on one of the wires holding the snowman in place. It was more from fear of me falling off the shaky trailer than from Frosty deciding it was a nice night for a second escape attempt. The nephew hid behind Frosty, trying to give him a voice and make the children on the left side of the street believe the plastic decoration was alive.

The other side of the street had a view of the young man's backside. A view some seemed to be extremely interested in. Since the chatty kid had told me he was twenty, I didn't feel the need to admonish anyone.

I was glad the young man decided to be the voice of Frosty as it gave me time to concentrate on my mission: scanning the crowd for Eric and someone acting suspicious. What did suspicious look like? Was it the man with his head tucked low like a turtle while two teenagers on either side of him held a conversation like he wasn't even there? Was it the woman decked out like she was attending a tea at the royal palace rather than a Christmas Parade in a small town in West Virginia?

There were too many variables to help the chief find a suspect. The only person I could lookout for was Eric. I knew what he looked like and that he always wore a red baseball cap and a denim coat with a flannel lining, which he never zipped. In the summer he didn't wear the coat, but he always had on the cap. Spring. Summer. Winter. Fall. It was like a grown-up version of a security blanket or stuffed lovie.

"I'm glad my aunt made me do this. It's kind of fun." The young guy grinned at me. "I'm Kyle, by the way."

"Merry Winters. The parade organizer. You didn't want to be in the parade?"

"Since I was here this weekend, my aunt said I needed to participate in their holiday tradition."

"Visiting?"

"I started attending the community college here this fall. Not sure my uncle likes the fact I took up residence in his empty nest. Sorry about making everyone late. I told my uncle we should've drove the float around the block a few times to make sure the snow guy stayed on the float. He said the ties were strong enough. He'd been doing it for five years and didn't need me to tell him how to build a float. I should've told him I got the idea from seeing the pastor testing out their float."

"Which church?"

"The one doing the nativity. Saw it driving down the back roads, even took a few sharp turns."

"You're sure it was Harmony Baptist?"

"It's hard to mistake the Harmony Baptist float with another. There aren't any other ones with a manger and a star."

She's done something to ruin the parade. The pastor's earlier comment popped into my head. How did he know that Jenna was up to something? The only people who knew about Jenna's naughty list was me, Rachel, and the mayor. I doubted Jenna had let word get out as she seemed to want to surprise the town with her design. "What time?"

The young man shrugged. "I wasn't paying attention too much. It was on my way home from work and it was dark. Thought it was a little strange to be out that late on the backroads, but it made sense since the parade is at night."

"Frosty. Frosty." Children chanted and begged the well-known snowman to sing them his song.

Kyle slid behind Frosty and started belting out the first verse of the song. Over and over again. It was the only part he knew.

"Watch it!" The angry words reached me over the cheers of the children and the parents who sung along. It seemed like our town only knew the first verse.

Another belligerent shout rose above the singing. Someone was causing some ire. Was it a possible suspect? I searched the area. A man was glaring at a figure rapidly moving through the crowd. A person wearing a red cap with the ends of the coat flapping at his sides. Eric. "Can you get your uncle to slow down?"

Kyle stared at me, an almost shocked expression in his eyes. "We're barely going five miles an hour."

"I need to get off the float."

His eyes widened. "Now? We'll reach the end of the block in a few minutes."

I didn't have time to explain the situation to him; I had to get to Eric Wilcox. I also couldn't just jump off the float. We were only going about five miles an hour, but if I fell, I could get seriously hurt. I didn't want to be incapacitated during the Christmas season.

"Someone is pushing through the crowd. I'm responsible for keeping everything under control." I pointed at myself. "Organizer."

"There's no way to get my uncle to stop. He won't answer his phone while driving and I can't knock on the truck's back window from the trailer." Kyle stretched out his arm, showing me what I should've been able to figure out myself. "I could try climbing into the bed of his truck. That should get his attention."

And get the young man hurt. The figure wearing the red hat was moving away. Soon, I wouldn't be able to see him in the crowd. I had to get off the float. It was a shorter distance down from the trailer bed than the truck cab. I was going to have to bail. I hitched a leg over the side.

"Hold up," Kyle said. "Gingerbread lady is handing out treats. The floats are slowing down because kids are trying to run out into the road."

That was one tradition the town might want to revamp, but fortunately it was still in place tonight. The truck inched along.

"I'll help you down." Kyle jumped from the trailer and held out his arms.

I hated being treated like a child. Though, it would be hard for me to get over the rail myself, especially with the vehicle moving. One of the drawbacks of being short. I grabbed Kyle's outstretched hands, stood on the thin railing and jumped. His grip kept my feet from sliding on the candy that had been thrown by other floats.

Another tradition to reconsider.

"Thanks!" I called out over my shoulder, pushing my jostled glasses back up the bridge of my nose as I ran toward the sidewalk, avoiding all the wrapped sugary treats littering the road.

The moment my feet touched the sidewalk, I realized my huge mistake. The streets were crowded and being shorter than half the parade watchers meant I couldn't see Eric over the heads of people in the crowd. Now what?

Tucking my arms to my side, I wiggled through the crowd, heading for the buildings. Cornelius's store had a two-foot-tall brick planter out front, perfect to stand on and get a bird's eye view of the street. I reached the planter. Placing my hand on a sign Cornelius erected saying "No Standing" in the dirt now planted with poinsettias, I boosted myself onto the bricks, staying clear of the plants.

From my new vantage point, I saw over people's heads but the blinking lights from the display window across the street was creating a strobe effect. I had to turn my head away and blink. Spots were in front of my eyes. How was I going to find Eric?

"But Mommy she is," a child whined.

"You can't be up there," an exasperated voice said. "If you ask one more time, I'll take you home."

"I can't see." Feet thumped up and down on the sidewalk. A young boy, about five, was near the planter. "Pick me up too."

The mom was holding a toddler on her hip. She glanced at the planter then at me, quickly looking away when our gazes connected. I saw the tears brewing in her eyes.

"What are you doing up there?" Cornelius snapped at me.

"Told you so," the mom told her son.

The little boy shot me a cheeky grin. "You're in trouble."

"I'm trying to find someone in the crowd," I said. "It's important."

"You're going to fall off and break your leg."

Red lights swirled. Santa was coming.

"Santa's on the fire truck." People announced.

"No, I won't." I shielded my eyes with my hand and scoped out the area. A man wearing a red baseball cap entered One More Page. Eric. I hopped down.

"Mommy, I can't see. I want to see Santa on the truck." The little boy jumped up and down, tugging on his mom.

"Santa will see you."

"Pick me up. It's not fair he can see, and I can't." He poked his baby brother in the leg.

"Climb up here." Cornelius removed the sign. "You'll be able to see him real good."

The little kid looked at Cornelius with wide eyes. "But the sign said not to."

"It's my sign and my planter so I can change the rules for it. I'll even hang onto you, so your mama don't worry about you slipping off."

I scurried away before Cornelius saw my grin. There *was* a Christmas spirit inside of him.

There was a crowd in front of One More Page, laughing and snapping pictures of her window display. People were standing with their back against the window and pointing while a friend snapped their picture. I peeked between the shoulders of a couple. Coldness swept over me.

On the bottom of the naughty list, in white letter stickers, was Jenna Wilcox's name. A stark contrast to the gold glitter vinyl I had used. The white seemed to shine out, demanding everyone's attention.

Why had someone added Jenna's name to the list? When? Why? My stomach rolled. Someone pulled the sign from the window and held it near their check, laughing hysterically at Jenna's name on it.

Get the sign. The loud order in my head galvanized me into action. I pushed my way into the store, snagging the sign as another person reached for it. Without explaining myself, I headed for Rachel's office. I had to get the sign in a protected place. I had to get the police here. Someone had put Jenna's name on the list.

Was it her killer? A chill swept over me. I yanked my cell from my pocket and called Paul. No answer. Of course not, he was driving the fire truck. I hoped 911 agreed this was an emergency.

"What's your emergency?"

I pressed myself into a dark corner between the main store area and the hallway. I scanned the bookstore. Hundreds of people, or it appeared that way, were in the store. Was the culprit still here? Had they already fled? "Jenna Wilcox's name was added to Santa's naughty list sign at One More Page."

Rachel's emergency phone call. Had someone broken into One More Page last night and added the name? No, I had seen the sign this morning. No one had tampered with it.

"What's your emergency?" The dispatcher asked again.

"I'm at One More Page and the naughty sign had Jenna Wilcox's name on it. I know it wasn't made that way. It was added." I lowered my voice. "With what happened to Jenna, I thought Chief Hudson would like to know."

"An officer is on their way."

Cassie was reading a book to a group of children and her co-worker, a tall, blond young man with a friendly smile, was ringing up a large purchase.

I thanked the dispatcher and hung up, ignoring her instructions to stay on the line. I slipped out of the corner before Cassie spotted me and hurried to Rachel's office. I needed to safeguard the sign. After I secured it for the police, I'd look for Eric. I hadn't seen him leave, but my attention had been on the sign.

The door to Rachel's office was ajar. With my shoulder, I nudged it open. A soft glow emitted from the monitor. The computer was on. The screen was angled away from the door, only a smidge of the image was visible. It was the front of the store. The security camera. I could check it to see if Eric was still in the store.

I stepped into the dark office and ran my hand along the wall for the light switch.

There was a shuffling sound behind me. I started to turn, and something hit the back of my head. Hard. The world turned dark.

EIGHT

Muffled laughter, cheers, and crying worked its way into my conscience. Groaning, I tried pushing myself up. Hands gripped my shoulders and helped me sit up.

"Merry talk to me," Cassie's tearful voice worked its way through the fuzz in my brain.

Her image tilted and twirled. I closed my eyes and drew in deep breaths. I touched a spot on my head that throbbed. It was a little sticky and tender to the touch. Someone hit me in the back of the head. Where was I? What had happened? Everything was a blur in my mind but soon focused into place. I was in Rachel's office. The naughty sign.

"The sign," I said.

Cassie glanced around. "On my goodness. I'm so sorry. I was supposed to remind Garrett to fix the plaque. The nail was coming out of the wall."

On the floor beside me was a decorative plaque with one of Rachel's favorite quotes from Harry Potter. There was a large hole in the drywall. The naughty sign was gone.

I rose to my feet, resettled my glasses properly on my nose and looked to see if the naughty sign fell further away from me. No. It was gone. My knees almost buckled.

Cassie wrapped her arm around my waist, keeping me upright. "Maybe you should stay seated until Paul gets here."

"You called Paul?" Maybe sitting was a good idea. The leather office chair creaked as I lowered myself into it. The screen was blank. Had Cassie turned it off, or had the person who had struck me with the plaque turned it off?

I wanted to ask Cassie but was afraid of her answer. If she said no, then she'd know that someone hit me. Possibly the murderer. It was best for her not to know anything about that.

Cassie nodded. "I left him a message. You were unconscious on the floor. I didn't know what was wrong with you until you mentioned the sign."

There was small ruckus coming from the main area of the bookstore. The after-parade party was in full swing.

"I need to go help Garrett. Will you be okay by yourself?" She glanced toward the open door.

"I'll be fine. I just want to sit for a couple of minutes."

"You should stay back here until Paul comes."

"If the parade is still going on, he won't be done for at least thirty minutes. Santa is on his truck and he'll go slow."

"Santa's arriving on the fire truck? Why not his sleigh?"

Oops. It was amazing how a simple, unassuming detail led to almost giving away a big truth that needed to remain a secret. "There was an issue with it. Norman couldn't use it tonight. The fire truck seemed like the best alternative to the sleigh."

Garrett stuck his head into the office. "I'm getting slammed up here."

"I'll be back to check on you." Cassie followed Garret back into the main store.

I leaned forward to get a better view of the monitor. It was off along with the CPU unit. Someone had turned off the computer and the screen. I doubted Cassie would've done that before checking if I was all right. Someone had hit me. The sign didn't come down on its own, not to mention the fact that the naughty sign couldn't have carried itself out of the room.

But who? Eric? Had he noticed I was following him and decided to follow me? Why? Carefully, I stood and tested out my legs. No dizziness. No double vision. I think I was going to be okay.

And to think this morning my biggest fear about the parade was that Jenna planned on starting rumors about townsfolk with her list.

My breath stuck in my throat for a moment, almost choking me. Was that why Jenna was killed? Had someone harbored a secret they feared would destroy them and decided to silence Jenna forever? My whole body quivered. I yanked back the office chair and dropped into it. Whose names were on it? I remembered mine, the mayor, Pastor Heath, the others flowed in and out of my mind without me being able to grasp them.

Wait! Eric. Eric's name had been on the list. Where was he? Why wasn't he looking for me? The parade was either over or ending soon and Jenna wasn't in it. The man should be looking for me to find out why his wife's float wasn't in the parade. Especially if word was getting around that Jenna was boycotting the parade. Eric would want to know why—unless he already knew she wasn't participating in it. If a wife turned up dead, it usually ended up that the husband was responsible.

Stop it. It was that kind of thinking that made me the prime suspect for my ex-husband Samuel's murder. I shouldn't jump to the obvious conclusion. Of course, Eric would know if his wife decided to bail on the parade. It was likely he was the driver of her float and would've known of any changes to the plan. Jenna was more the stand-on-the-float-and-wave-to-the-crowd type than stay inside in the cab and be invisible. But Jenna hadn't made any decision to boycott the parade. The choice to participate in it was taken from her. The most likely scenario was Eric was drunk and had no idea he should be concerned about anything.

"Santa is coming!" A little girl screamed, her voice filled with joy and wonder. "Santa."

The easiest way to figure out what Eric knew was to make myself visible. If Jenna hadn't decided not to show up tonight, Eric would look for me to find out why his wife's float wasn't in the parade.

I walked out into the store. Cassie and Garrett were helping customers. I waved goodbye and weaved through the crowd gathering near the window to watch Santa come to town. Children jumped up and down in excitement. Some adults were in the moment and others had a far-off look in their eyes, either remembering Christmas pasts when they eagerly awaited Santa's arrival or devising a route to get to their car first and beat the after-parade traffic.

A customer opened the door and I slipped outside. The cold wrapped itself around me, pepping me up a bit. This was my favorite part of the parade. Santa's arrival. I remembered the anticipation on my children's face and how they'd wiggle and jump, barely able to contain their excitement. Longing filled my heart. How I wished my children were here tonight. Like all our past Christmases. On second thought, I was glad my children weren't here tonight. This was going to be a parade to remember, but not in a good way.

The red lights of the fire truck swirling behind them caused me to blink and turn away as the motion started a headache at the back of my head. The pain in my head spread to the sides, tiny throbs that seemed to beat in tune to the rotating lights. I was feeling a little out of sorts and wobbly. Since most of the children were on their feet, I snagged a vacant spot on the curb.

"That's my child's spot." A mom glared at me.

"Parade organizer," I said. "Need to watch the floats and if I sit, children behind me can see."

"My child needs to sit also." She snagged the belt loop of her squiggling and dancing school-age child and dragged him back toward his seat.

"I see better by my friend." He tried to break from his mom's grip.

"Sit," she said between clenched teeth.

I totally forgot how territorial people were over their parade spots. It had been a long time since I worried about my children not being able to see or having to worry about carrying a tired child back to the car.

"That lady is there. I don't mind standing."

"Sit."

Sighing, I placed my hands on the curb, readying to push myself into standing. I didn't want to get the little boy in trouble.

"I'll scoot over." The little girl beside me plopped herself onto her mom's lap. "Plenty of room for you and him."

"That's okay," I said. "I'll stand."

"My mom's lap is comfier." She grinned at me. "Can you get me a private meeting with Santa."

I laughed. "I think I can arrange that."

The little boy on my other side pouted. "I could've met Santa if you let me stand."

"I'm sure she'll let you."

I wanted to snap at the woman but the fatigue on her face stopped me. My days as a single mom weren't so far past me that I couldn't remember when my exhaustion had my patience stretched to the breaking point. For some reason, taking her child's spot was the thing that broke her fragile Christmas spirit. It was Christmastime. Time of love and charity. And sometimes charity wasn't about money, it was about giving your kindness.

"You can both meet him."

The truck towing the trailer bed of the Harmony Baptist Float drove by. Something fell from the underside near the tire well. I leaned forward, straining my eyes. It was a dark lump. The base of the trailer bed was large, the tires missing the lump on the ground. As the truck and trailer pulled past the fallen item, I walked out onto the road to get a better look.

It was a large clump of mud with strips of a glittery gold material mixed in. The Wilcox's driveway had been a muddy mess yesterday morning, and likely still had been that night. Gold strips of fabric. Fringes. Jenna's scarf. Theories flowed fast and furious in my head, and one made itself right at home. The pastor had "guessed" Jenna was up to no good. He knew about her float because he had been to the Wilcox home and saw her naughty sign with his name on it. Had Jenna added his naughty deed to the list and the pastor silenced her? I hoped the road my mind was veering on was wrong, but in case it wasn't, I had to do something.

The siren from the fire truck blipped on and off. I motioned for Paul to stop and ran to the driver's side door.

Paul rolled down the window. "Are you okay?"

I held up my phone. It was loud. The only way for him to hear me was to yell, and it wasn't something everyone needed to know.

Mud fell from underneath the truck pulling the Harmony float. The pastor said the float had been parked by the church for days. Wilcox's place had tons of mud. I hit send and looked up at Paul.

He checked his phone. His eyes widened, and he glanced down at me, concern etched on his face. Cassie's message. I pointed at my phone then myself. He looked down.

"Need you to move away from the truck, Merry."

That was all? Move?

The fire truck inched forward. Children were yelling and screaming for Santa.

What now? What was I going to do until I could get an officer's attention?

The truck stopped, right over the mud that had fallen from the nativity float. Paul was protecting the potential evidence.

NINE

"You saw Jenna's body?" Cassie asked as I unlocked the front door.

Her tone was making it hard to decipher if she was interested or creeped out by the thought. The girl had asked millions of questions on the drive to my house. Part of me wondered if her interest stemmed from her father's murder. It was easier for her to ask questions she had wanted to know about Jenna's death when it was someone she really didn't know that well or had liked.

I didn't want to talk about it, especially with an eighteen-year-old girl. The parade turned into a disaster and my head was spinning not only from the knocking it took but also from all the thoughts and suspicions swirling around in it. Did the pastor, his wife, or both have something to do with Jenna's death? If not, who? Why?

The woman wasn't the nicest person in the world and enjoyed riling people up, but it wasn't a reason to kill her. And why Santa's bag? Was it the only place available?

Ebenezer tried to bolt out the door. The critter loved snow and had once again found a way out of his habitat. Fortunately, Ebenezer was enthralled with my guest and stopped mid-run.

Cassie scooped him up and carried him inside. "I'll make us some hot chocolate. Want me to make some popcorn?"

"I still have some Christmas sugar cookies left from my last baking session."

"We'll get them." Cassie and Ebenezer headed into the kitchen.

"Watch him. He'll try and eat them all." I settled on the couch, gently resting my head on the plush cushion.

To help move the crowd away from the fire truck, Norman had climbed down from the fire truck and announced Santa was going to read a story at One More Page. He invited all the children and parents to followed him. Santa saved the night. The children were excited about a bedtime story read by Santa. It was hard for parents to say no even though I could tell a couple of them wanted to stay and see what was really up with the stalled fire truck.

Orville told me to go home since the parade was over. My official duties were done. I wanted to tell him about the naughty list, but Cassie had stepped outside to check on me and the officer was preoccupied with evidence he was able to get his hands on. Telling him about the sign later wouldn't hurt anything.

Paul had examined the back of my head and while he agreed I was fine to go home, advised me to have someone stay with me. Cassie volunteered. I was about to argue until I heard my name scattered about conversations. Most of it related to my and Jenna's "fight" and not about the awesome job I had done with the parade. A fight I had made up in a moment of panic by telling the pastor I had banned her. If Cassie was with me, she wouldn't be hearing rumors about me that I'd have to explain away.

"Here we go." Cassie placed a tray with hot chocolate in two of my Twelve Days of Christmas mugs, and a mix of decorated sugar cookies. She picked up a reindeer and bit off his head.

I cradled a mug of hot chocolate, the warmth from the beverage spreading to my limbs. A tension I hadn't known I was carrying slipped off me like I shrugged off a sweater. I hadn't realized how drained the day made me. Tears welled in my eyes. I blinked them away. Where were they coming from?

"You okay, Merry? This hasn't been an easy day for you."

I swallowed down grief bubbling up in me. I knew Jenna, but we weren't close. Finding a body was a horrid experience, though not as traumatizing as finding my murdered ex-husband. "I'm fine."

"I'll turn on the indoor Christmas lights. That should cheer you up." Cassie rushed around the room, switching on the multitude of lighted Christmas decorations in the living room and kitchen.

The Christmas blocks glowed from near the fireplace. The giant "X," eliminating Jenna, brought tears to my eyes. It was ugly. A sharp contrast not only in design but in spirit to the other images on the blocks.

Cassie sat on the arm of the couch. "Can you teach me how to make a vinyl decal?"

I drew back, the request a little confusing. Was Cassie trying to take my mind off what happened tonight? "Sure."

"Great. I'll get Ebenezer settled and I'll meet you upstairs in the craft room."

I went upstairs and booted up my program and clicked on the icon for the Design Space software, which was the easier of the programs to explain to a beginner. I pulled over my rolling cart with the die cutting machines and inserted the USB port from the Cricut into the laptop. By the time Cassie arrived with a plate of sugar cookies and hot chocolate, the machine was ready to go.

"What did you want to decal?"

"A glass block. We should add something to the one with an 'X.'"

My face felt hot.

Cassie hugged me. "I noticed it upset you. That was Jenna's float wasn't it?"

I nodded.

"She wouldn't tell you what it was and now you feel bad that she was x'ed out."

"Actually, I found out the theme of her float and x'ed it out because I was angry with her." The tears trailed down my face and Cassie's image wavered before me. I took off my glasses to swipe away the spots on them.

Cassie brushed away the tears on my cheeks. "Let's change the design to something more festive. How about a dancing Santa? Nothing is holly jollier than Santa dancing. What do you have?"

"Click on new project, then images, and type Santa into the search box." I pushed the rolling chair away from the computer, giving Cassie space to bring another chair forward. "There's a few in the library. If you don't like any of them, we can look through the Santa folder on the flash drive."

"I'm surprised you don't have a flash drive just for Santa Clauses." Cassie scrolled through the Santa images.

"You can look in my projects area. There are some Santas I designed."

Cassie clicked over. "Are these all from this year?" There were about fifty different Santas. "You're one busy woman."

"Santa is one of the biggest requests I get this time of year."

"That's it," Cassie squealed. She hovered the cursor over a silhouette of Santa dabbing. "He'll be perfect. We can cut him out in a glitter green and put it over the black 'X.' Add the North Pole onto the 'X' and it'll look like Santa is dancing after returning to the North Pole."

I hugged her. "You're brilliant."

"Can I borrow the block to use as my art project for class?" She grinned at me.

The child had an ulterior motive. At this point I didn't care. She made me feel better and changed something I regretted creating to a teaching moment. "Absolutely."

"Now I won't be lying to Bonnie that I came over here for help on homework."

"You told Bonnie that you were staying here?"

Cassie nodded and resized Santa by pulling down the arrow in the lower left-hand corner. "Since we're living together, I thought it was the nice thing to do."

"How's that working out?"

Cassie shrugged. "It's weird. She's trying and I'm trying. I don't think we'll ever be friends but it's a little better since I know she didn't kill my dad." Her voice hitched on the last three words. "I can't throw her out. My dad loved her. And she is paying for all the expenses right now while we're waiting to see what the court says about who owns the house."

Another complication that arose with the question about our divorce. Would I be legally responsible for the mortgage? I couldn't remember if it was paid off. "I won't claim ownership. I want you to have the house."

"I just don't know if I can afford it." Cassie drew in a deep breath.

"You can live here." I made the offer again. The first time was right after her father's murderer was arrested—and Helen confessed she was dying. Helen couldn't take care of her granddaughter and didn't want the girl to watch her die.

"I want to live in my house, Merry. Mine and my dad's house." Her voice shook. She drew in a couple of breaths and squared her shoulders. "I want to be happy tonight. Let's think and do happy things. Here's the design I want, what do I do now?"

"Pick out the color of vinyl you want and put it on the cutting mat."

Cassie followed my instructions, first choosing the colors for her project, white for the words and glitter green for Santa.

"Click on make it and the software will show you which color to put on first. Load the mat with the vinyl and press send."

"This isn't too hard," Cassie said. "Kind of fun. You know, I could always help you out at your shop during the holidays."

"I might take you up on that."

The doorbell rang. Cassie was the first one down the stairs and opened the door. "Hi Officer Martin."

Orville was standing with his hands resting on his belt, looking very serious and police professional. Ebenezer's feet scratched on the floor. The critter was racing for the door.

"Hurry, he's trying to make a break for it." I knelt to intercept Ebenezer as Orville stepped inside and shut the door.

"I need to speak with you, Ms. Winters."

Ms. Winters. This wasn't a neighborly visit. He wanted to talk to me about Jenna's death. "Why don't you get Officer Martin a cup of cocoa and some cookies?"

"Okay." Cassie volleyed a concerned gaze from me to Orville and back to me.

"Orville's been working non-stop today. He could probably use some refreshments."

"I saw some sub rolls on the counter. I'll make us some sandwiches. I'm starving," Cassie said.

Orville sat in the recliner, leaning forward and resting his forearms on his knees. "I'm curious why you thought the mud might be evidence in Jenna's murder. McCormick showed me a text you sent him."

"Pastor Heath had said that he hadn't moved his truck from the church's lot. There's no mud there."

"Doesn't mean he went to the Wilcox's."

"When he saw the police cars, he assumed it had something to do with Jenna trying to ruin the parade. How would he know it was about her unless he saw her float?"

Orville frowned. "What float?"

"Her theme was Santa's naughty list and the huge sign had a lot of resident's names on it. And a spot to put the reason for being on that list."

"Which residents?"

I told him the names I could remember. "There were a few others, but I can't recall them."

Orville wrote everything down. "Did you speak to Jenna today?"

"No. I hadn't spoken to her since I stopped at her house to check on her float."

"What time was it?"

"Yesterday morning. Right before I went to speak to the mayor. I was hoping he could talk sense into Jenna. I didn't think airing grievances was the proper theme for a float."

"You also called about a sign."

"I made a sign for Rachel to use in her display window. It was Santa's naughty list and had the names of Christmas villains. Someone added Jenna's name to it today. I had checked the stores this morning and the sign hadn't been vandalized."

"Whose names were also on it?" Orville snuck a glance up at me. He was trying to hold back disappointment.

I straightened my spine. "I did not add Jenna's name to the naughty list or any other resident of Season's Greetings. I used the theme of famous Christmas villains. Grinch. Scrooge."

It dawned on me that Jenna had a main theme also. City council members. There were a few names, like her husband, that didn't fit. I wasn't sure why Jenna would add the extra names, it wasn't like the sign was subtle. Everyone would figure out she had a problem with everyone else on the council.

"What are you thinking?" The disappointment was gone, worry was in its place.

"Just that those names are council members. Why would Jenna single them out?"

"Where's the sign you saw in the bookstore's window?" He ignored my question.

"I don't know," I whispered. "People were picking it up. I took it to put it in Rachel's office. Someone knocked me out and took the sign."

"What?" Orville's head jerked up. "Someone hit you and took the sign."

I nodded. "They snuck up behind me."

"This happened at One More Page?"

"Yes."

"Was Cassie working there today?"

I knew where this was going. "I'd rather she didn't know about this."

"Merry, this is serious."

"I don't want her to worry about me. She's been through a lot."

"But she might have seen this person."

In every corner of One More Page was a security camera. Rachel had installed them a few years ago when she had a rash of "editors/censors" marking up sections of books they didn't approve of or wanted to fix. There were a few instances where entire paragraphs of a racy novel were crossed out with a black pen.

"There are security cameras at the bookstore. Let me call, Rachel. She'll let you see the tapes." Before he argued with me, I punched in my passcode and called Rachel.

She answered on the third ring, sounding breathless. "Is everything all right?"

"The naughty list was stolen," I said. "Can you give the police the tapes from your security camera?"

"I'm sure the police have more pressing problems. Tell Cassie not to worry about the missing sign. We can just have a nice list."

"Someone had put Jenna's name on the list."

Rachel gasped.

"I went to put it back in your office and someone stole the sign. Can you meet Orville at the store? He needs to review your footage."

"The cameras don't work," Rachel whispered, tears in her voice. "Money has been tight. I had to cut some expenses, and the monitoring service was one of them. The cameras are for show."

It was hard to keep a business afloat year-round in a small town. Our best months were October through January. After that visitor numbers trickled down and as the lack of visitors affected everyone's bottom line, it was hard for locals to spend a lot to support stores, especially one considered "luxury" items: crafts, reading, accessories. If your businesses didn't focus on necessities, your income took a hit during the rest of the year. One More Page had a few extra months—August to September when school started—of selling than the rest of us "luxury" businesses, but not enough that it would keep the business out of the red during the slower months without having to make some sacrifices.

I hung up. "The cameras are for show."

Heaving out a sigh, Orville pushed up on his knees. His joints cracking as he stood. "I don't appreciate you doing that, Merry. I would've talked to Rachel myself. You have to let me do my job."

He was right. That was a huge overstep. My heart went out to him. It couldn't be easy investigating the people you knew and considered friends. Somebody in Season's Greetings, somebody he knew, had murdered Jenna Wilcox and Orville had to dig for the truth.

"I'm sorry. I feel like I have to do something."

"From here on out, I got it."

TEN

"It's Beginning to Look a lot Like Christmas" played from my bedside table. I snagged my phone and swiped my finger across the screen. The alarm stopped. Briefly, I thought of closing my eyes and getting another hour of sleep, but I had a long list of tasks to complete today, including packing for a class that I was teaching at Season's Living, the assisted living facility where my mom resided. I didn't want her or residents to be disappointed by being ill-prepared.

First, I needed to complete the orders I had to mail Monday morning. Any later and there was a chance they wouldn't arrive on time for Christmas. I fumbled for my eyeglasses, slipped them on, then snuck downstairs and brewed a cup of coffee. I moved around my house like I was Santa sneaking gifts under the tree. There was no reason Cassie should have to be up at six in the morning.

Carrying my coffee back upstairs, I put together a game plan in my head. Shower. Dress. Complete two orders. Email Bright an update on the orders. Finish preparing for the class. As long as I stayed focus, I'd have it all done by ten before I had to leave for class.

After making myself presentable, I settled into my office chair and got to work. The first order came together easily. The next one was testing my patience. Too big. Too small. Finally, just right. Exhaustion washed over me. It had taken me fifteen minutes to adjust the size of the font for the personalized Santa nice list I was creating for an order where the customer wanted to add "just one more name." That one more name required me to adjust the font setting. At this rate, I wouldn't be done until after Christmas. I had tried to get a good night's sleep. Between Cassie checking on me every other hour and my mind conjuring up suspects, I had gotten less sleep last night than when my children were infants.

A message notification popped up on my computer. Bright. I switched over to the window with Facebook opened on it. Usually, I didn't have any tabs for social media open when I was working, and turned off notifications on my phone, but today I wanted to keep updated on what was being said on the town's Facebook page. It wasn't good to be unaware of the gossip when you stood a high chance of being part of it.

Who was murdered?

I blinked at it a few times, the question startling me. How did Bright know? I wouldn't have thought a murder in a small town would reach where Bright lived. Unfortunately, murders weren't that uncommon in the world—though before a Christmas parade in a Christmasy-named town was liable to turn a story viral.

I moaned and plopped my head against the leather rest of my office chair. My kids would find out. While it might mean I'd get another visit, I didn't want my children worried about me. Or thinking they had to become involved because they believed I was involved.

If the police didn't release it, I probably shouldn't, I responded.

I was hoping you'd say you didn't know. Bright ended the message with a sad face emoji.

Hard not to when I was in charge of the parade.

So, it did happen during the parade. How horrible? How many people saw?

I hovered the mouse cursor over the Google icon. Don't look, I scolded myself. I didn't need to fill my head with all the rumors that were going around the internet, just the ones in my home town. *Before. No one saw anything.* That we knew of.

Had someone? I envisioned the parking lot of the church where the sleigh had been parked. No one had been there when I arrived. Had Norman possibly seen someone before he left? He had told the police no, but his memory wasn't the best right now.

Are you there? Are you okay? Merry? Concerned messages filled my screen.

I'm fine. I just remembered something. I should call the police.

Is someone with you? You should call your son.

I'm fine. There's no reason to call my son or have a babysitter. I didn't see anyone but there was someone there who might have. And this person might not realize they know something.

I wanted to keep my explanation as vague as possible while also reassuring Bright I was okay. I didn't think she'd be able to contact either of my children, but I didn't know for sure. There was a chance one of my children—Scotland—friended her on Facebook to monitor our friendship. My son wasn't keen on the fact that I was best friends and in business with someone I only knew through social media. In the almost eight years we've known each other, we only talked on the phone once and have never met in person.

The situation sounds dangerous to me.

It's not. If I think something is wrong, I promise I'll ask for help. I signed off, trying to block from my mind that I hadn't come away unscathed. Someone had hit me in the back of the head for a sign. Who?

I didn't have time to ponder it. There was a phone call to make and a long list of orders to complete before I left for my class. I called the station, hoping to catch Orville before he was off-duty. The administrative assistant put me through to him.

"What can I do for you, Merry?"

"Last night, Norman said he hadn't seen anyone in the parking lot or around the church. I'm worried that he might have and could be in danger. He's been having trouble remembering things." I relayed what happened last night.

"He didn't remember about the parade?"

"No. He was confused on why all the floats were there."

"That is concerning. I'll stop by Norman's on my way home and chat with him. See if a good night's sleep has him remembering anything. I appreciate you letting me know."

"You're welcome. What should I—"

Orville cut me off. "Do what you're doing now. Any concerns bring them to me or another officer. Don't be surprised if you get a call from a reporter. The best thing to do is tell them no comment or to contact the town's public relations department."

"Jenna was the town's PR person."

Orville drew in a deep breath. "That's right. Tell them to call the police chief." He hung up the phone.

The tone of Orville's voice changed when I reminded him of Jenna's job. With her travel agency, it made sense for her to act as the town's spokesperson. It was a part-time job that blended in perfectly with her business. Did it relate in some way to her murder?

I popped onto the town's website and hopped around the site. There wasn't anything there that would make someone want to kill. The time of the parade, the businesses participating, emergency contact numbers, phone numbers of churches that could help with electric bills or financial help for the holidays. All the best about Season's Greetings, not one thing about any shortcomings the town or its residents might possess. And if I didn't want any customers taking to the internet to talk about mine, I needed to get back to work.

I closed the window and returned to my design software. Adjusting my noise-cancelling headphones, I hit the blinking button on the Cricut. Since I had a slight headache, I was blocking out the machine noise. The mat fed through and the first project of the day was being cut. A few days ago, I had uploaded a picture of the naughty and nice lists to my Etsy page and received some orders for them. Even though the lists were the last things I wanted to create, I didn't want to cancel them since customer service made or broke a crafting business.

If you got a reputation of being flaky, or even worse, a scammer, you were done. Merry and Bright Handcrafted Christmas wasn't just me. I didn't want to disappoint Bright or push off too many orders onto her shoulders. The last few weeks she'd been picking up the slack. It was time for me to do my part.

Pulling the vinyl from the mat, I held it up to the window, inspecting it. Perfect cuts. A shadow loomed over me. I startled, dropping the vinyl onto the floor. Ebenezer raced into the room and dragged the project under the desk.

Cassie stood behind me, wearing my Buddy the Elf shirt and looking a little sheepish. I slipped off my headphones.

"I hope you don't mind I borrowed your shirt," Cassie said. "I wanted something holiday themed to wear to work today and I don't have anything. I knew you had a ton."

I heard paper—vinyl—crinkling. I hoped it was his paws and not his teeth causing the sound. Imitating a guinea pig, I lowered myself onto my hands and knees and shimmied under the desk. "That's fine. If you need to borrow anymore, just let me know."

"I will. That's why I started your wash for you. Some of your best shirts were in the hamper."

"That's not for you." I scooped up Ebenezer and carried him back to the door. I placed him in the hallway and he plopped over, looking at me with pathetic eyes. "You're not allowed in here. That won't work on me."

"I didn't mean to scare you," Cassie said, picking up the list of names for my customer's naughty list and putting it on my desk. "I wanted to let you know I was leaving, and Ebenezer seemed really upset that he wasn't with you."

"He just doesn't like the fact he's not allowed in the craft room. I try to keep this room as allergy free as possible. No fragrances. No pet dander."

"I'm sorry. He just looked so sad pawing at the door."

Ebenezer wasn't happy that there was a part of the house closed off to him. With his short stubby legs, I had thought it would be hard for him to get upstairs. Nope, he had found a hop-jump gait that worked. The guinea pig was relentless.

"I'll be taking a coffee break soon." I was going to need more than one cup to get through the day. Of course, once I went downstairs, Ebenezer would decide to play in the tunnels Paul and I made for him. If I was available and wanted some snuggles, Ebenezer had something better to do. The critter wanted my undivided attention when I was working or on the phone.

"Do you need a ride?" I asked. Cassie had driven me home in my car. Her vehicle was still at One More Page.

Cassie waved goodbye and bounded down the stairs. "No, my co-worker Garrett is stopping by to pick me up."

"Wow, Rachel must be expecting a lot of business this morning."

Cassie paused at the door and turned slightly to face me, her cheeks blushing a bright pink. "He's off until this afternoon but offered to take me in this morning. He was there last night and knew I drove you home."

"Should I plan dinner for two?" I hoped the answer was no but made sure my voice didn't hint at my preference. When my children first moved out, I was lonely and hated the quietness and not having anyone that needed me. After some time being alone, I was starting to like my freedom and having no one else's schedule to consider.

"Nope. I'm going over to Grandma's to cook dinner." Cassie's expression softened. "I've never made dinner for us before and Grandma agreed as long as I came over to her place. She's not up to leaving her house."

"That's wonderful." I maintained a light and airy voice even though I wondered if Helen was going to tell her granddaughter the truth about her health. It wasn't my place to hint at anything.

Cassie eye's widened and she dipped her head. "You can join us if you'd like. I'm so sorry for not inviting you earlier. You've had me and grandma over tons of time."

"I have a back log of orders. The parade put me behind

schedule, and I've been looking forward to a quiet evening at home. I have some chili in the freezer I'll thaw out and put some Christmas music on in the background."

"If you're sure..." Cassie trailed off. There was a beep.

"Your ride is here. You should get going." I turned back around, giving my attention to the computer screen. If Cassie pressed enough, I'd relent, and if Helen was planning on telling her granddaughter the truth about her health, I didn't want my presence to alter any plans. I fussed with the image on screen even though I had already cut out the design. Which was on the floor and might be torn thanks to Ebenezer. Quickly, I undid the changes.

Cassie clomped down the stairs, smoothing down her hair. There was a bounce to her step.

Someone should be checking up on the guy Cassie was interested in. I needed to ask Rachel some questions about him. All I knew was that he was a little flaky. He had showed up for work late yesterday, making Rachel late getting to the parade. Once again, I was focusing so much on my issues, I was ignoring Cassie. I jumped from my chair and ran down the stairs.

"Cassie..." The front door closed. Too late. I opened the door and stepped onto the porch. The car, a gray well-kept sedan, was almost at the corner. Drat. I couldn't see the driver. I stopped myself from racing outside and waving down the car. That was a little too dramatic. Besides what would be my excuse for flagging them down? Changed my mind about dinner? Wanted to appraise the guy she liked?

Someone had to look out for Cassie. The only one Cassie had was me. It was my duty to find out about this guy and make sure his intentions toward her were pure. *You don't even know if he likes her. He might just be being neighborly.*

That was true. Was it safe to err on the side of caution? I had wanted to know about the guys my daughter Raleigh had been interested in, and the girls Scotland dated, wasn't it normal to wonder about the boy that caught Cassie's eye? Or had my belief in seeing the good in everyone taken a hit? The world had shown me a little of its dark side when Samuel was murdered and now it lurked in my mind.

I didn't want to dwell on it but could no longer pretend it didn't exist. I'd talk to Rachel and if she didn't know much about Garrett, I'd see if Scotland could dig anything up on him, unless that would get my son into trouble at the police department. The last thing I'd ever want was to create a problem for my children.

The doorbell rang two times. One after the other.

"I'm coming." I hoped the unexpected visitor didn't mind a Christmas tree sweater that lit up. Not that I planned on pushing the button to get the lights twinkling. The flashing lights bothered me after a bit. I only turned them on when I either wanted to entertain a child or annoy an adult.

I opened the door. A furious Sarah Heath marched into my house. Her pale beige, almost colorless, trench coat flapped open around her calves, revealing her calf-length brown skirt. Her dark hair was twisted into a knot and dangled in a blob near her neck. The heels of her beige pumps click-clacked on the hardwood floors as she stomped into my living room. She glanced around, a distasteful look crossing her face as her gaze landed on Ebenezer.

He whistled at her, angry and drawn out. He didn't like the woman.

"Come on in," I said, hoping I didn't regret those words.

"How dare you accuse my husband." She dropped onto the recliner and crossed her arms over her chest. "We are going to have this out right now."

Yep, already regretting my hospitality. I should've thrown the woman out. Technically, I didn't accuse the pastor of anything. I just told Orville that pastor fibbed about the float having been in the lot and that the man's name was on Jenna's naughty list—along with the other city council members. Jenna and Mayor Vine had a tense conversation earlier in the day. It was likely she overheard and told her husband about it. Sarah was of the mindset that whatever she knew had to be shared with her husband. Nothing was kept from him.

"I didn't accuse your husband of anything."

She shook with rage, digging her short nails into the cushions of the armrest. "I know you're the one who planted the idea in the police's head that my husband had something to do with Jenna's death."

"All I did was answer questions."

She leaned forward, almost nose to nose with me. The trembling stopped, and a calm took over. An eerie calm. "In a way that steered the police toward my husband—and away from yourself. I know what you're up to, Merry, and it won't work. You're trying to save your reputation by besmirching my husband's good name."

From his habitat, Ebenezer shrieked. My guinea pig was a good judge of character. "My reputation isn't on the line."

"I know you were one of the last people to see Jenna alive."

A feeling like I had eaten a dozen Christmas cookies in one sitting settled into my stomach. Was that true? Had I—and Eric—been the last people to see Jenna alive? "It's time for you to leave."

Her face turned as red as a velvet bow. "I'm not done talking to you."

"I am. I have a class to teach." I stood and walked to the door. "Goodbye, Sarah."

Sarah dug her fingers into my arm. "I will not stand by and allow you to accuse my husband of an atrocious crime."

I held her wrist tightly until she let go of my arm. "Leave. Now."

"Don't try and ruin my husband. You will regret it." She stomped out the door, angrier than when she arrived.

Gaping, I stared at her retreating form. Had the pastor's wife just threatened me?

ELEVEN

Around Christmas time, the landscape at Season's Living always filled me with joy. The staff at the assisted living facility did everything they could to make the environment festive. It was cheerful and filled with the holiday spirit. The trees had white lights that twinkled at night and large white bows made from plastic kitchen garbage bags. It was a project the residents worked on every year. I loved how the director incorporated items the residents created into the seasonal décor. She wanted them to feel it was their home and not just a place where they lived.

It was why I knew it was the perfect spot for my mom, and why I believed my parents had decided to settle in Season's Greetings in their golden years. They were planning for a future in which one of them could no longer reside at home.

I pulled into a front spot near the doors. Fifteen minutes to spare, not a lot of time to set up, but I had it down to a science and the class kits were prepared with everyone's choice of paint and saying placed in a small box. I texted the director that I was unloading and popped open the trunk then wrestled out my collapsible storage wagon. It was a beast to get in and out of my SUV but worth the effort. With the boxes stacked properly, I only had to make one trip.

There wasn't much I could set up until after the class attendees took their seat. The students had ordered their signs ahead of time and I had to match the correct decal to the proper sign, or they wouldn't fit. The nurses and director wanted the residents to be in control of as many choices as possible. You never knew if there was a falling out between anyone or if a memory loss patient was having a bad day. It was easier for the patient to have some control over their situation on those days.

I understood that. My mother's memory slipped in and out every day. Some days she remembered me, other days not. Because the attendees might not have remembered what they ordered, I had brought along a few extra decals and signs. I wanted everyone to be happy with their project and planned on leaving the originally ordered decal and sign behind.

Carefully, I stacked the boxes and extra supplies into the cart, rearranging a few pieces when the pile started to tip. I should consider two trips. I had created more extra pieces than I realized. I could leave some of the extra in the trunk and return if I needed them. It was either that or make two trips. Something was going to fall if I stacked any higher. My craft supplies already looked like a Jenga one tug away from falling over.

"Merry, I must discuss something with you," the stern voice of Pastor Heath reached my ears.

Nope. I wasn't in the mood to deal with a Heath again. I pretended not to have heard him and grabbed the handle, beelining for the door. Hitting the key fob, the back hatch lowered. How I loved automatic closing doors and not having to look back. The wheels of my wagon bumped over the curb. The boxes shifted. *Please don't fall.* I didn't want to deal with the pastor right now. A few more feet and I'd make it to the door.

"Let me get that for you." Pastor Benjamin grasped the door handle but didn't open it. "I really need to speak with you."

"Your wife already talked to me. I have nothing further to say."

He drew back, hand slipping off the door handle. "Sarah talked to you?"

"Yes, this morning she showed up at my house as angry as Scrooge being asked to donate to a charity."

"What did Sarah say?" A nerve along his jaw twitched.

"She was mad because, according to her, I accused you of an atrocious crime. I tried to explain to her that I was only answering questions the police asked me. It's not like I could ignore them." I refrained from mentioning her threat.

"No, it's important to answer the police truthfully." A slight smile curved his lips.

There was something about the expression that shook me. "I'm running late. Class starts in a few minutes."

"Then I'll get right to the point. Thursday morning, I had spoken with Jenna. But it wasn't what you think it was about. I had no knowledge of a sign she was making. As the Vice Mayor, I went to talk to her about a troubling discovery with the budget. There was no money for the Christmas parade. It, shall we say, had disappeared. Along with funds for a few other budget items."

"What?" How did the Pastor know about it but not Mayor Vine? He hadn't seemed concerned about the town's budget considering all the proposals he had laying around. "The Mayor hadn't mentioned anything to me."

"I doubt he would since he suspected Samuel, your husband, had something to do with it."

The sick feeling in my stomach intensified. "That's not true. And, he's not my husband." I couldn't stop myself from adding the disclaimer.

Samuel was the cheating kind, but I doubted he was the thieving kind. He loved the Christmas parade. And more importantly, Cassie loved the parade. There was no way Samuel would do anything to ruin it or shame his daughter. It was one thing to run around on your wife, and quite another to steal money from the town. One was a moral crime while the other was a felony resulting in prison time.

"Time will tell," the pastor said.

I wasn't sure if he was referring to the accusation he made against Samuel, or my claim of not being married to the man. Either way, he was wrong on both accounts. My mind slipped to the bank receipts—with large deposit amounts at different banks—

Nancy had dropped. "Jenna was the treasurer. She had access to the funds. As only the parade organizer, Samuel didn't have the authority to withdraw funds from the city's account."

"People's bank accounts are hacked all the time. Samuel didn't need permission to get into an account and steal from it."

I was done with the conversation. He was wrong. I yanked open the door. With one violent tug, my wagon was over the kickplate and into the main area of Season's Living. It was freezing inside, either the heat was out, or the director wanted the temperature to match the winter wonderland theme created in the reception and visiting area. I was thankful the pastor didn't follow me inside, though his words had come with me, shoving out the Christmas joy from my heart.

Nope. I wasn't going to let it happen. No one would put a damper on my happiness of spending the morning teaching my mom and her friends a new craft.

The recreation room of Season's Living was filled with Christmas cheer. A six-foot tree was filled with ornaments crafted by the residents. A large Santa and Mrs. Claus vinyl decal was on the back wall. I had delivered the decals a week ago and the residents had been excited at all the decorations going up. I loved how happy it made the residents. Especially my mom.

Warmth filled my heart as I remembered her bragging to everyone that her daughter crafted the decorations. She was always so proud of me. She had been my biggest cheerleader when I mentioned turning my Christmas crafting hobby into a business. Every year, I made new décor for my home and was running out of room. I had wistfully said I wished I could share my love and talent with others.

"What's stopping you?" my mom had asked.

And it was that question, and my mom refuting every excuse I came up with, that brought to life the idea of having a crafting business.

Residents walked in and took seats. There were six eight-foot-long tables set up for two residents to be seated at. I wanted each resident to have enough space to work on their piece. I was waiting until they all chose a spot before passing out the wooden signs. My mom and her nurse, Bonnie, were the last two to enter the room.

"Good morning!" I beamed at my mom.

Bonnie sent a sad smile in my direction and shook her head. My heart grew heavy. I knew what that meant.

"Morning." My mom sat in the front, linking her hands together and placing them on the table. She smiled at me, vague and polite. Today was a day she didn't remember I was her daughter.

For a moment, I turned my back to the class attendees and blinked away the brewing tears. Pasting a smile on my face, I faced the room and placed the sample signs on the table, arranging and rearranging them while I got my emotions under control. Should believe come before joy or after it?

Bonnie gently rubbed my arm. "Want me to pass out the class materials for you?"

I wanted to say no, but I was having trouble uttering a sound. I nodded instead, grateful for Bonnie's compassion even though I didn't deserve it from her. Bonnie and I had a difficult relationship. She had been married to Samuel when he died. Making him, and her, a bigamist when he was killed.

Samuel had meet Bonnie when he came with me to visit my mom. Bonnie had been her nurse, and after we were divorced, I requested a new nurse for my mom. Switching nurses had been extremely hard on my mom so I relented, putting my feelings secondary to my mother's well-being. It wasn't like I had been pining for Samuel. It was just that I didn't trust him, so it made me not trust Bonnie.

Swallowing the lump in my throat and drawing in short breaths to stave off the tears, I started the class. "Welcome to Christmas crafting with Merry. Today, we will be working on signs. There is a decal to place on the board, I'll be showing you how to adhere it to the board, then we'll paint over the entire board with the color in the cup. After a couple of minutes, we'll peel off the vinyl and the original color will show through. I do have some extra colors and phrase options if you'd like to swap out."

I chose my words carefully, not mentioning preorders, so the memory care patients weren't left confused if they forgot what they requested or even the fact they had signed up for the class. From the corner of my eyes, Angela Bail, Norman's wife, snuck into the class, heading to a seat in the back row. Angela wasn't a resident at Season's Living. I glanced over at Bonnie who shrugged.

Another nurse walked behind me and whispered, "Day guest. It's okay."

Angela had a heart condition. It must be getting worse and Norman didn't feel comfortable leaving his wife at home. I was sure Norman was spending a lot of time at city hall trying to figure out where—and what to do—about the missing money.

If it was true.

My mom, Gloria, picked up the board in front of her and carefully considered the color. It was snow white. She had wanted a "Believe" decal and wanted to paint the sign Santa suit red, so the word "believe" showed in white. Everyone said I got my Christmas love from my mother. I loved being told that as a child because sometimes I felt out of place. It made me feel even more that I was their Merry.

She picked up the small lidded cup of red paint beside her and shook it. "I'd like the board in green and use white for the word. I'm not fond of red."

I tried to hide my surprise. My mother loved red. It reminded her of Christmas. Santa Claus. Velvet ribbon. Rudolph's nose. The color of the stocking I had been found in. Red was an "official" color of Christmas. This was something new—my mother forgetting an ingrained part of her spirit.

I pushed down the troubling thoughts swirling in my head and ignored the slight frown tugging down of Bonnie's brows. "It's better to paint the board with the brighter color, have it on top, as some of the color can bleed through if you have the darker color as the base."

My mother pursed her lips and twisted them back and forth a few times. "Can I have green instead to cover the white board?"

"Of course." I hurried over to my supply tote and grabbed a cup of Christmas-tree green. For my example, I'd make the same sign as my mom, using her original color choices and give it to Bonnie. She could swap it out later if my mother wondered why her sign was green instead of red.

The class went smoothly, besides my mother not knowing who I was. Angela had the process down and helped the gentleman sitting beside her. He was having trouble peeling up the tape. I should've thought of that. Many of the residents had trouble with fine motor skills. I needed to find a way to alter the process so residents with arthritis or other joint issues could still enjoy the craft classes. Crafting was great stress relief and helped the mind.

The class attendees beamed. Joy filled my heart. Nothing picked up my spirits more than people loving the crafts they created, well besides Christmas. It was time to turn the media room in my house into the classroom I dreamed about. I hadn't done it because I hated the thought of turning my house from where my children grew up into just a place I lived and used for my business. But it was time. My children had their own lives, were following their own dreams, in Morgantown. Ninety minutes wasn't too far away. It was time to get my new life fully started.

"Our class time is over for today. I hope everyone had an enjoyable hour. I'm planning on having a class every month."

"Sign me up," Gloria said. "I never considered myself a crafty person, but I really enjoyed myself."

I kept the smile on my face even as another arrow pierced my heart. My mother and I crafted all the time together. It was how we spent our summers. Every special activity, every passion, we shared seemed to have vanished from her head. Hopefully, they were still somewhere in her heart.

I packed up my supplies, distracting myself from watching my mom walk out of the classroom. Other craft students gathered up their creation and wandered out, talking of their lunch plans.

Carefully, I placed everything into my wagon, jostling it to make sure nothing fell off. Everything was secured.

Angela sat at the table, looking down at her lap, she lifted one hand and swiped at her cheek. She was crying.

I went over to her. Before I asked if anything was wrong, I plopped into the seat beside her, deciding the question was unnecessary. Of course, something was wrong, people didn't look so despondent and cry when everything was all right. I was sure Angela heard the "How are you?" question multiple times a day since her health took a turn for the worse.

"How can I help you?" I draped an arm around her shoulders.

She glanced up, fixing a tearful, hopeful gaze on me. "Norman just called me. He's going to be late picking me up. Can you drive me home? Or to Norman?" She glanced around then leaned toward me and started to whisper. "Lately, Norman's been dropping me off to visit friends a lot. He didn't want me home alone all day while he was sprucing up Santa's sleigh and helping at Harmony Baptist. I get the feeling sometimes I'm overstaying my welcome in some places. I'm becoming a burden to my husband and my friends."

I started to argue but Angela looked pointedly at the empty seats beside her. Her friends had left for lunch without her. "I'm sure they didn't mean to leave you."

"They have plans. The facility lets me participate in some events, but they can't feed me every day. I don't live here. And..." Her face flushed, and she clasped her hands together.

And money was tight for her and Norman with all the medical bills. She couldn't afford to take an Uber and eat out every day. What would happen if Norman was having memory issues? I hated making it more real by giving it a proper diagnosis. Could they afford to move to Season's Living? Would their children offer to have them live with them in Florida?

Should I mention it to Angela? Was it fair to worry her about Norman when she had her own health issues? Besides, I wasn't sure I was right. It was best to talk to Norman first.

"What's wrong?" Angela rested a hand on top of mine.

"Nothing." I pasted a smile on my face. If Norman refused to see his doctor, then I'd tell Angela what I noticed Friday night.

"I can tell something is troubling you." She squeezed my hand. "Is it about the meeting Norman is having with the mayor?"

"A meeting? About what?"

Her eyes widened. "You didn't know. Norman told me he'd be delayed because of an emergency meeting the mayor was calling. I figured it had to do with the parade. Since..." She trailed.

Since Jenna was murdered in Santa's sleigh. Though, I knew there was another reason: the embezzled money. Was the mayor planning on telling everyone that my deceased ex-husband—husband—was responsible? I had to go there and be a voice for Samuel.

I stood. "How about I take you to Norman? The mayor has a comfortable waiting room."

"I'd like that." She grinned, a little girl smile. "Hopefully, I can talk Norman into taking me out to lunch. I'm so tired of being cooped up in either the house or Season's Living. I want to get out and live a little while I still can."

TWELVE

Loud voices carried down the hall from Mayor Vine's office. I made out two people: the mayor and Norman. Either the other city council members weren't present or no one else wanted to say anything. Whatever was the topic, it wasn't pleasant. The voices were growing angrier with each word. I couldn't grasp them all but enough that I knew the budget, or rather the missing money, was the topic.

Angela paused, fear growing on her face. "Maybe you should take me home."

"We're here now. Besides, it might be best if I break it up." I hooked my arm through hers and continued down the hallway, taking small steps as not to drag Angela whose pace had slowed down.

I opened the main door to the office and stepped inside.

"Merry..." Norman said.

I was about to return the greeting when I realized I wasn't being acknowledged but talked about. The private office door was shut. No one knew Angela and I were here.

"Has no need to know," Mayor Vine said.

"She'll learn."

"You can't tell her." Mayor Vine's voice was angry, almost threatening.

"She already knows about the money," I said.

Mayor Vine and Norman grew quiet.

Angela moaned and sank on the couch. She buried her head in her hands.

"Are you okay?" I knelt beside her, instantly feeling remorse at insisting we barge into the conversation. Tense situations were not good for her heart, and I forced her to come along to this one. I should've asked her to stay in the car or had left when she mentioned it.

"He's not going to be happy," she whispered, eyes wide with fear. Her whole body shook.

Before I could ask her which man because I'd never known Angela to fear Norman, the door banged open and Mayor Vine charged out of the office. There was a spot darkening on his cheek.

"What are you doing here?" He glared at me.

I rose and moved in front of Angela. Peering into the office, I spotted there was only two people in the room—him and Norman. "Angela needed her husband. How come you're having an emergency meeting without all of the city council members present?"

Vine's face turned red. "Where did you hear that?"

Norman pushed past the mayor and went to Angela, concern clear on his face. "Sweetheart?" He gathered her hands to his heart, wincing as his fingers flexed. There was a slight bruise on his enlarged knuckles.

Angela kissed her husband's hands. "I'm fine, my love. I was just missing you."

"Who told you?" The mayor stared at me, narrowing his eyes.

I shrugged, not wanting to tattle on Angela and raise the Mayor's ire toward her, as Norman and the mayor already came to blows once. No need to create a repeat performance. "Does it matter? I also heard about you wanting to drag Samuel into a town issue."

Without a word, the mayor stomped into his office and slammed the door. I spent years dealing with a teenage girl, a slammed door didn't stop me from getting answers. I marched right into his office.

"Why are you telling people that Samuel embezzled money from the town?" I demanded. "Don't even try and tell me that you haven't said that. I have it on good authority."

"What would make you believe that person over me?"

I crossed my arms. "Because this person was rather pleased to fill me in on the information. It also explains why the security guard was looking at me like I was an unpleasant person. He just met me. The only thing I wanted to do was talk to you about the parade. You told him."

"The guard shouldn't have said anything to you." The mayor slapped his hands on the desk. A picture frame toppled over, the mayor's family was now face down on the dark wood surface.

"Actually, he didn't. Someone else did. So, you've been telling a lot of people Samuel took the town's money. Why blame him?"

"Because that is who the evidence pointed to."

"What evidence?"

The mayor sat and leaned back in his chair, placing his feet on the desk. He was much calmer than a moment ago. Either the evidence was irrefutable, or he thought saying that put me into a corner.

Well, I wasn't buying it. I didn't believe for one moment, Samuel would be given access to the town's account. And the only time he'd get his hands on the information was during a city council meeting about the parade. There'd have been too many people around for Samuel to take that type of chance—which I doubted he ever would.

"Blaming the dead guy," I said. "How convenient. It won't work. Samuel didn't have access to the town's money."

Norman entered the room and shut the door. He gestured toward a chair. "Why don't you have a seat, Merry? Maybe, there's a simple solution to this problem."

"It sure is. The mayor has to stop accusing Samuel of something he didn't do and tell everyone he's told he was wrong. Samuel didn't steal the money."

"The fact is there is money missing from the account." Norman sat down and using his foot, scooted a chair closer to me. "Let's try and calm this conversation down. The less people who know the better. It wouldn't be good for rumors to get out. Harder to clear up what might just be a simple misunderstanding. It's possible the money was moved into another account and we just noticed it once we went over the books again after Jenna's death. It's natural we'd take another look at the accounts once the treasurer died."

"As I've already said, Norman, there is no way to keep this quiet." Vine leaned back in his chair. "It's already getting out. The town will soon know one hundred and fifty thousand dollars is missing from the coffers."

My eyes widened. That was a lot of money to misplace in another account. "When was this noticed?"

"A few weeks ago," Mayor Vine said.

"Before or after Samuel's murder?" I asked.

The mayor stared up at the ceiling as if waiting for the universe to give him the proper answer.

If it was before, I was positive the police would've looked into it as a motive for his death. Now with Jenna's death—it was a likely cause. "Have you told the police about the missing money?"

Norman and the mayor glanced at each other. The mayor broke eye contact first. I was taking that as a no.

The mayor steepled his fingers under his chin. "Norman wasn't sure that would be the most prudent choice."

My mind flashed to the bank slips Nancy had dropped. "Someone might have killed Jenna because the money is gone. They might have thought Jenna embezzled the money. Being the treasurer, she'd have the easiest time moving money over into another account."

The mayor tsked. "Shame on you. Blaming a dead person who can't defend themselves."

I narrowed my eyes. "I wasn't blaming her per se, just mentioned it would be a motive for someone to kill her."

"Why would someone kill Jenna for embezzling money?" the Mayor asked. "Seems kind of strange to commit a worse crime because you're angry about one someone else did. Murder is worse than stealing."

I hated to admit, even to myself, that the mayor had a point. Why kill Jenna because she stole money? It was better to rat her out to police and watch her suffer in prison. "The police aren't going to be happy that information was withheld from them."

"We were trying to spare you any ill-feelings the community might have over your husband stealing the money. He is still your husband. Correct?" The mayor struggled with holding back a smile.

The man was very pleased about being able to point the finger at Samuel. I wasn't sure if it was because Samuel was dead and couldn't defend himself, or because Samuel had shown himself to be somewhat of an unsavory character and people would believe it, so no one else's reputation would take a hit. Except for mine. Not that I was responsible for whatever my husband—ex-husband—had done. But some people liked to judge others by the company they kept, even if at the end you had tried to get rid of that company—by divorce not murder.

I heaved out a sigh. "It appears that way. My attorney is working on that matter for me."

"We want to keep this quiet for you." The mayor forced out a contrite expression.

Norman patted my hand. "We'll protect you."

I stopped myself from rolling my eyes. How was I going to get out of this? My attorney. Brett dealt with a lot of different types of cases. I bet he'd know what I could do about the mayor trying to pin the embezzling on Samuel, or if he didn't, he was partners in a law firm where one of the other attorneys would know. "I'll get my attorney's advice on this issue also."

A nerve twitched in the mayor's jaw.

"Is that really necessary?" Norman leaned forward and rested a hand on my knee. "We really don't want word getting out. This isn't about shaming anyone. All we really want is to find that money and put it back. Right, Mayor? Would that be acceptable? If the money was returned, we can have this all go away. It's not like

Samuel could steal again."

I opened my mouth to state, yet again, it wasn't Samuel and decided to not waste the words. Something pointed to Samuel having committed the crime and the men weren't going to change their minds. Samuel was the easy answer.

The mayor pulled a notebook onto his lap and started jotting down notes. He crossed through a sentence, wrote a new one then circled it. "It has the potential to work. We just have to have a good reason why we're not pursuing this matter legally."

"We made a mistake," Norma said. "The simplest reason is always the best one."

"Except the security guard and the pastor might not buy it," I said.

Mayor Vine's eyes widened. "Pastor Heath told you about Samuel."

Oops.

"Security guard?" Norman asked.

The mayor cringed.

Sadness welled up in me. I doubted Norman hadn't been introduced to the man as a city council member he'd have known about the hiring. "Yes. Tall guy, dark hair, beard. Has a tattoo. He goes along with the metal detector installed near the front door."

The mayor glanced at his watch and jumped up. "I have an appointment at the other end of town. We'll wrap this up for today and continue this conversation later."

Norman looked at me oddly. "The metal detector was installed here because the court house has to be closed for a few weeks due to asbestos. Court cases are going to take place in the large reception room. The city didn't hire a security guard."

"That's who he said he was."

"I'm sorry, but I have to go." The mayor reached for my arm.

I drew my arm against my body and glared up at him. "Not until we clear this up. You said he was a security guard. You lied to me."

"Now, Merry, all I did was not correct you. You said he was a security guard and I felt it best to let you believe that," the mayor said. "I can promise that if we can get the funds back into the town's account, who he is won't matter."

"And how is that going to happen?" I asked. "Samuel is dead. He can't give you back the money, especially since he didn't take it. You better not be thinking about going after Cassie."

"His daughter isn't inheriting his ticket," Norman whispered. His cheeks reddened, and he looked away from me. "I know you don't want to believe *this* worst about Samuel, Merry. I hated doing so also, but Samuel borrowed the money from the town. He said he'd return it once he cashed in the lottery ticket."

My stomach plummeted, and a familiar anger churned in me. I couldn't believe Samuel outright stole money from the town, but I could see him sweettalking a loan out of someone, though I was surprised Jenna agreed to it. But Jenna was the one who was willing to bend the rules for the right price and I was sure Samuel offered her a nice monetary incentive.

"Do we have a deal, Merry?" The mayor held out his hand. "You pay back the money and this will go quietly away."

I tucked my hands under my arms and slipped past the mayor. "First, I want to have a conversation with someone."

"Merry, wait." Norman followed me out the main office door into the hallway.

I ignored him, heading for the exit. Rage was pulsing through me. I was afraid of lashing out at Norman. How could he believe Samuel would steal from the town? He had known Samuel—the thought stopped me in my tracks. Yes. He had known my husband for years. Longer than I had. And while Norman had congratulated us on our engagement, it had been reserved. I had always wondered why but discounted it as Norman's personality rather than concern that two people he knew and cared about were about to enter into a marriage that suited neither...and might break one of them.

I stopped and turned toward Norman, trying to will away the building tears. I had told myself weeks ago I was done crying because of Samuel. And yet, I found myself near tears more now that he was gone than when we were divorcing.

"Do you think Samuel embezzled—borrowed—the money?" I asked. "That he was that type of man?"

Norman let out a long, pained breath. "I think anyone can be that type of person. Samuel was somehow, once again, in a financial bind. Jenna shouldn't have loaned money, but she did. We know how persuasive and charming your husband could be at times."

My face heated. "Where is that money? When the police were investigating Samuel's murder, they would've been suspicious about that sum of money showing up in his account."

"No one knows what Samuel did with the money. The community will suffer if it's not returned." He clasped my hands. His speech was halting, like he was struggling to remember words. "Once the money is back into the account, this can all go away. I'm truly sorry you're wrapped up in this Merry, but without being able to find the money Samuel borrowed, you're the only hope for this town."

"Are you okay?" I asked.

Norman drew back. "Why do you ask that?"

"Your forgetfulness." I blurted it out before I changed my mind.

In a flash, Norman's expression changed. It went from open and pleading to closed off. "I have no idea what you're talking about."

"You weren't dressed as Santa. You forgot about the parade."

Without a word, Norman spun away and trudged down the hall. But he had faced me long enough for me to have seen the fear, anger, and shame in his eyes. The same look my mother had on her face when I first questioned her about her memory lapses.

I wanted to chase after him. Make him confide in me. Convince him to see the doctor. But I knew Norman was done talking today. I'd try again later to help Norman face the truth. Now, it was time for me to face the truth about what Samuel had done. There was one person alive who had the potential to know the deal Samuel made with Jenna—Eric.

THIRTEEN

There was an eeriness pulling into the Wilcox's driveway. The area around the house appeared dark and gloomy even though the sun was shining and there were no leaves on the trees to block the sunlight. Today's newspaper was still on the porch. The curtains were drawn tight.

Every instinct in me said to turn around. Leave. Instead, I ignored the warning in my brain and parked right next to Eric's truck. He was the only one who'd know the truth about Samuel having any deals with Jenna. I knew I was taking a big risk coming here, but the even bigger risk was not getting the answer before I either brought Brett into this new trouble—or made a deal with Mayor Vine. I didn't want one of Samuel's other bad choices haunting me, already had one to deal with. More importantly, I didn't want it to affect Cassie's life.

Cassie had been raised for most of her life in Season's Greetings. She needed her community right now. Her father had died, her mother was in prison, and her grandmother was dying. I didn't want the eighteen-year-old to feel like she had to flee the town she loved because of a mistake her father made. If Samuel had borrowed money from the town, I would pay it back.

There was a chance Eric wouldn't tell me, but I'd convince him it was just as much for his best interest as mine to resolve this issue. Jenna wasn't innocent in the matter as she'd have been the one to hand Samuel the money.

I slid out of my SUV. The ground was firm beneath my feet, having dried out since my earlier visit. The place was quiet. No birds. No hum of farm equipment. No animals. Total silence.

No one was here, and I wasn't sure that was such a good thing. Where was Eric? Had the police taken him in for questioning? Before, an entourage of cats had greeted me the moment my foot touched the ground. Had the police rounded them up because there was no one to care for them? Uneasiness settled over me. I wasn't sure if it was because of the lack of a sign of life, or the fact the police might already know about Samuel's loan. Someone had killed Jenna. What if the killer thought Eric knew something and silenced him? Or, what if Jenna had been murdered because she witnessed her husband being killed? I had thought I had seen him last night. But, why hadn't he come to find me to ask about Jenna?

The barn door was open. Bits of hay was scattered on the ground from the barn to the house. Someone had been in there recently. I trembled. If something terrible had happened to Eric here, the police would've found him. This would be the first place they'd have looked for him to notify him about Jenna.

"Eric? Are you in there?"

No answer. I walked over and peered inside. No one. The float was dismantled. The tarp was shoved into a corner, wood and metal rods were tossed around the area. The large naughty list was gone. Did the police take it as evidence? Slips of paper were torn up and scattered over the area. I stepped further into the barn. Something seemed off about the scene. The police would've been careful not to destroy anything. Why not take the whole float instead of just the sign? Had someone else come and taken it?

The stench of body odor and alcohol wafted from behind me. As I turned, a metallic click caused my blood to run cold.

Eric glared at me with bloodshot eyes. Dirt was smeared on his face and clothes. Sweat coated his face. It didn't just look like he slept in the outfit but had fought a demon in them. His body was ram-rod straight. He was sober. I wasn't sure if that was good or bad.

"For some reason you just can't stop snooping around." Eric pointed a gun at me. "Let's go."

"I was looking for you. I wanted to ask you a question. I'm thinking now isn't a good time." I inched away from him. I should've told the mayor or Norman where I was going. Or better yet, not come. This was a really stupid idea.

"Let's go talk." He grabbed my arm and dragged me onto the porch. My winter coat stopped his tight grip from bruising me. The railing and old steps rattled as Eric stomped up, pulling me up to the rickety porch. "Now."

I tripped over the top step. It was time to fight. Ducking, I swirled and hooked my ankle around his, hoping to bring him down without hurting myself. For my valiant effort, I found myself pressed into a column with the gun against my temple. His hand shook. I wasn't sure if it was fear or detoxing causing Eric's reaction. Either way, it could result in me getting shot.

"Here's the thing, Merry. We're going to talk. How nasty this gets depends upon you. You can willingly go into my house or I'll have to get someone to persuade you." Eric hauled me away from the porch column and shoved me into the front door.

I shot out my arms, stopping my face from connecting with the door.

"And I'd rather not get Cassie involved. Do you?" Eric asked.

A sob escaped me. Shaking my head, tears cascaded down my face. I was so stupid. I put myself and Cassie in danger.

"Open it. It's unlocked. You probably already know that. Bet you've been inside snooping around."

I shook my head. "No. I was only in the barn. Nobody had seen you, so I thought maybe something happened to you."

"Like you care. How often did you stop by when Jenna was alive?"

"Once."

"Right, once." He spun me around. His hands continued to shake and sweat coated his face. The man was not doing good. "The day before Jenna was killed. Why the sudden interest now in my well-being? Or is it to clean up after yourself. Did you leave something you don't want the police to find?" The muzzle of the gun was firmly pressed into the base of my spine. "Get in the house."

I obeyed. There was a chance I could get away and reach Cassie before him—if the man didn't shoot me during an escape attempt. The way to get out of this alive, and keep Cassie safe, was to talk to Eric. Reason with him.

I opened the door and a cold blast of air hit me. Either Eric forgot to pay the electric bill, or he was the Snow Miser. Eric shoved me inside and slammed the door shut. This was the first time I ever stepped foot in their house, and either Jenna and Eric were minimalists, or they planned on moving soon. The living room was almost bare. Two chairs: a ratty recliner and an old rocking chair with an end table beside it. Crushed beers littered the floor around the rocking chair. No coffee table. No wall décor. Not even a Christmas tree. In the corner was a stack of books. A mix of fiction, non-fiction, and cookbooks. The walls were beige. No photographs. No art. Nothing.

I was surprised by the color choice, considering Jenna was a flashy woman. She dressed—or had dressed—to the nines and had an expensive car. Had the couple been redecorating or were they fleeing? There weren't any boxes or packing supplies. Maybe they had packing materials in another room in the house. I doubt Eric was going to give me a tour so I could find out.

"Sit down." He waved the gun toward the chairs.

A bottle of vodka was on the counter. An idea popped into my head. Could I get the man drunk enough, I'd be able to escape? "Can I get some water?"

"Get me one too." With the back of his arm, Eric swiped sweat from his forehead. "Remember, no trying to run out or I'll have to stop by and visit your stepdaughter at work."

I fisted my hands. I didn't like that he knew where Cassie worked. I didn't ever recall seeing Eric in the bookstore, but it wasn't like I was on the lookout for the man. There had been no reason for him to be on my radar. Sneaking a peek at Eric, I made my way into the kitchen. It was always a good idea to know where a person who wanted to shoot you was at, especially when you're about to try and get them drunk instead of just hydrated.

Like the living room, the kitchen was bare, only the bare minimum on the counters, a toaster and a coffee maker. No packing materials. Carefully, I opened the refrigerator. There was no food inside. I was leaning toward the Wilcox's had planned on sneaking out of town soon—with a nice sum of Season's Greetings money.

"Plastic glasses are in the cabinet by the refrigerator. Instead of water, get me something stronger."

"Are you sure that's a good idea?" I forced myself to ask. Didn't want to be too obedient and clue him in that I was up to something. Hopefully, drinking a partial bottle of booze would knock him out, if not I might just have to hit the bottle against his head.

"I'm so sick of nagging women." He swiped his arm across his brow. "Get me a drink."

Since he insisted. I filled a cup half way with water and the other one with Vodka. I grabbed the bottle and brought it with me. I placed the bottle and Eric's beverage on a side table near the rocker, opting to take the recliner myself. It was closer to the door and I hoped the swaying motion of the rocker would put Eric to sleep.

"Why were you in the barn?" Eric sat on the edge of the rocker. He downed half the glass of vodka, took a breath then finished it.

I eased myself onto the recliner, also choosing to sit on the edge rather than get comfy. "I wanted to talk to you. The mayor said that Jenna loaned Samuel some money from the town's treasury. The only other people who might know about this transaction are the spouses. And it could possibly be related to Jenna's death." Okay, it was a fib big enough to put me on Santa's naughty list, but I needed Eric to believe we were in this together. Bond with him by being a possible suspect because everyone knew the spouse was automatically added to the list. "Then there's the pastor's wife who's trying to find a way to blame me for Jenna's death."

He snorted and poured another generous serving of vodka into his glass. "Why would she do that?"

"My guess is she's trying to steer the blame away from her husband. The pastor had told me he visited you and Jenna on Friday." Rather, he visited with Eric as Jenna never came to the door.

Eric sipped at his drink. "Ya. That's right. The pastor was here. Saw Jenna's car. A couple minutes past the time he was supposed to be home and she'd called, wanting to know his whereabouts. His wife keeps him on a tight schedule. Surprised she didn't put a GPS tracker on him."

"I didn't know Sarah was the controlling type. How long were you and Benjamin friends?"

"Can't say that we were."

"How do you know so much about their relationship?'

"Can't say." Eric flushed and chugged down the drink.

"At least the police believe us that the pastor was here. Sarah is going to tell him he wasn't."

"I don't know if they'll believe me. I haven't spoken to the police yet." Eric poured another drink.

A chill raced through my body. Eric hadn't reacted when I mentioned Jenna's death. He knew even though he hadn't been notified. How? From Facebook or—I stopped that train of thought. I couldn't think about that right now. I had to stay calm and collected. *Think, Merry, think.*

"What kind of host am I? Let me fill you up." He dumped some vodka into my water.

At least I had been upgraded from hostage to guest. Hopefully, I'd be able to sneak out of here soon. I pretended to sip the drink, letting the liquid touch my lips.

"The pastor. Never thought of him." Eric closed his eyes and leaned his head against the back of the rocking chair. He placed the gun on the table beside him. "Makes sense. He tried to sweet talk

Jenna and she didn't fall for his perfect pastor routine."

"What was he trying to sweet talk her into doing? I didn't know he was friends with Jenna."

Maybe Pastor Heath was the one who borrowed the money from the town's coffers and once Samuel died decided my ex-husband was the perfect scapegoat. What better way to know what was going on in the mayor's office than having your wife work there. I thought it was odd Sarah would take on that part-time job during the Christmas season. It was the busiest time for the church.

Eric snorted, eyes remained close. "He was friendly to everyone he needed something from. He'll become your best friend soon, considering your wealth."

"My what?" I leaned forward. The glass slipped from my hand and pinged off the floor. The water and vodka soaked into the carpet.

"Your winnings. You had to know everyone would find out." Dangling his arm down, Eric snagged the bottle of vodka and instead of using a glass, chugged straight from it. He swiped his arm across his mouth and grinned at me. "And some people will want a portion of it. Maybe even feel they're owed it."

Was that what this was about? Eric needed money to escape from Season's Greetings. You'd think he'd have enough with the money stolen from the town. Well, he was out of luck. One I didn't physically have the ticket on me, and two, no bank was going to hand over twelve million dollars.

Eric continued to grin at me. I stayed still, trying not to let him know it unnerved me. His eyelids started to droop. I continued to look back at him. His lids fluttered closed, and body slumped to the side. His arms relaxed and dangled by the sides of the chair.

The bottle clattered to the ground. A strangled snore came from Eric. I sat still, barely even breathing, making sure Eric was soundly asleep. A few more snores erupted from him. Yep. Out.

Still, I carefully rose to my feet, leaning forward and taking hold of the gun. Paper crinkled in my hand. I tiptoed backwards, keeping my eyes on Eric and kept a tight hold on the gun and papers. I held an arm out behind me, searching for the door. Good thing there wasn't any décor in the living room. Nothing to trip over and wake the slumbering beast.

The door creaked open. I held my breath. Eric was motionless. I ran down the porch steps, yanking my keys from the pocket.

Almost to my car. I threw a panicked look over my shoulder. No Eric. I pulled opened the car door and climbed inside, stashing the gun in the glove compartment. The papers fell to the floor. It was almost over. Hurry. Get somewhere safe and call the police. I had no idea how long Eric would be out or if he'd follow through on his threat of hurting Cassie. My gaze rested on the paper. A bank slip. Other bank receipts flashed in my mind. Four deposit slips for twenty-five thousand dollars. Each one a different bank. Two located in Season's Greetings. The other two in neighboring towns. All from last week. I highly doubt Jenna and Eric earned one-hundred thousand in cash from their business ventures. Jenna also had Nancy depositing money for her on Friday.

Was it so the tellers didn't always see her? Make it seem like real business expenses because she had someone else depositing money?

Jamming the gear shift into drive, I floored it, turning the wheel toward the barn and driving through the yard, around the building. I wasn't the best at backing up and wanted out of there pronto. I glanced in the rearview mirror. Eric wasn't on the porch. I wasn't sure if I should be relieved or terrified. There was a back door. Going out the front wasn't the only way.

The pastor's visit with Jenna. The lottery ticket I wasn't so sure I should claim as my own. Jenna being best friends with Nancy—the town's biggest gossip of others' secrets, real or fake. If I added up all the bank slips, it was less money than what was stolen from Season's Greetings, but the Wilcoxes wouldn't earn six figures from their legal business ventures in a week, especially in cash. Though, a side hustle of blackmail would generate quite a bit of cash. Were the names on Jenna's naughty list the people she'd been blackmailing?

I wasn't sure how long Eric would remain unconscious, and once he came to, he wouldn't be happy. I had to get to Cassie and warn her. Protect her.

What had I been thinking going to see Eric? Saving myself. That was what I had focused on and trying to make sure I wasn't on another suspect list, I put Cassie in danger. I'd never forgive myself if something happened to her. I had to find a safe spot to pull over and call the police.

My foot pressed the pedal harder. The SUV picked up speed. The next turn almost sent me skidding into a ditch. A truck rumbled out from a side road. I jerked the wheel, avoiding the other driver with inches to spare. The back tires slid and skidded on the rough surface of the shoulder. Rocks pinged against the vehicle. A low hanging tree branch smacked the windshield.

I winced and ducked, hoping the windshield didn't crack. I maneuvered the SUV back onto the road and slowed. I'd do no one any good by injuring or killing myself. Expect for Sarah Heath. She wasn't overly fond of me right now.

On second thought, I'd head to One More Page and call the police once I got there. This way, I'd be able to protect Cassie from my very stupid mistake.

FOURTEEN

I whipped into a vacant spot in front of One More Page and dug out my cell phone. All looked quiet here. For now. I punched in 911.

A dispatcher picked up. Before he finished his "greeting," I launched into my explanation of what happened at the Wilcox farm. "When I left, he was passed out drunk."

"Who was ma'am?"

"Eric Wilcox. The man who threatened to hurt my stepdaughter if I left his house. He wanted me to stay there. My stepdaughter is working at the bookstore. He might show up here."

"Units are on their way to the residence. An officer will also go to the bookstore. Where is your location?"

"I'm at the bookstore."

"An officer will be there shortly to talk to you."

"I'll be inside." Even knowing it was best to stay on the line, I hung up and slid out of my car. Almost choking myself with the seatbelt in my haste to get inside the store.

The bell jingled as I yanked open the door of One More Page. I scanned the store for Cassie, desperate to see her blonde hair or hear her laugh. I had to know she was okay. People were milling about. Most smiling as they browsed books and consulted lists. Rachel had three large chalkboard placards listed with the top ten books in a wide range of genres. Off on the side was a wrapping station where customers could wrap their purchases. A little girl was taking advantage of the gift-wrapping station and swaddling a baby doll in a red and green plaid paper.

Christmas carols floated in the air, classic songs from years gone by. The soft tones and gentle voice of the singer had a soothing effect on me. My heart rate slowed. The scolding voice in my head quieted. The scent of sugar cookies and pine, the smells of Christmas, wrapped around me. Everything seemed calm. Normal. As if nothing bad could happen in the store.

Neat stacks of books were piled at the register, each with a name. Rachel must have an option for customers to leave their purchases to be wrapped for them. Shop owners were always adding new services to help increase the profit margin. I didn't know when Rachel would find the time to wrap presents and run the store.

"Welcome to One More Page," Garrett greeted me. An elf hat was on top of his head, not quite on as it was too small to pull down. He pointed at it. "Cassie's idea."

"Where is she?" I tried to keep my voice light and breezy, instead it came out squeaky and forced.

"Picking out a story for story time. We're a little behind as we had to redo the display window."

In place of the naughty and nice signs were books depicting Christmas around the world. I should bring over some of the glass blocks I made, the one with Santa flying over houses would be perfect.

At that moment, Cassie stood and carried an armload of books to a plush chair in the corner of the children's section. She settled into the seat and flipped through the books. I heaved out a sigh.

"When the story's over, Rachel holds a mini craft class. This week it's Christmas ornaments." Garrett showed me a table filled with sealed boxes. "We're behind and haven't had time to set up the crafting stations."

Perfect reason for me to stick around. "I can help. I'm good with crafts. I can sort out the items while you take care of the customers." There was a line growing at the register.

"Thanks. I was starting to hate people buying books. But, if no one bought, I'd be out of a job."

A shadow passed in front of the window. A black jeep pulled into a spot out front. A man jumped out and quickly yanked open the passenger door. A doll flew out and landed on the hood of the car next to the jeep. A stuffed dog followed, resting on top of the doll. Either the child had great aim or had plenty of practice throwing items. Just what Cassie and Garrett needed, unruly kids coming to attend the craft event. Good thing I showed up when I did. I just hoped the wild one didn't interfere with me keeping an eye out for Eric.

The bell jingled. I spun to the door. The mayor's security guard, or who I'd been led to believe was a guard, and three little boys and a toddler girl, entered. The kids ran toward the children's section while the guard flopped into a chair near the windows. The little girl, about two, screeched and pointed at a book out of her reach. One of her brothers handed it to her. The toddler looked at the cover then clunked a different brother on the head with it.

"Quit it." He snatched the book from his sister and tossed it.

"Books are for reading. Not throttling," the exhausted dad said.

The toddler flashed a sweet smile at her dad. She picked out a larger book and smacked a different brother with it.

"Why did I agree to take them for the whole day?" He groaned and draped an arm over his eyes.

The foursome continued to pull books from the shelves and drop them on the floor or hit each other with them. The boys were nice enough not to retaliate against their baby sister who was doing most of the thumping.

"You might want to stop that before you leave with a huge bill. They're going to ruin the books." My voice was a little judgier than I intended. Or maybe not. Books were expensive, and the children were going to destroy quite a bit of them. Rachel couldn't—and shouldn't—take the loss because the father "quit" parenting.

He moved his arm, allowing me to see the terrified look in his gaze. "I'll pay for the books. Stopping enraged people from visiting the mayor was easier than getting those four to listen. Especially the youngest. How will I explain to my sister her princess is a terrorist?"

So, the children were his niece and nephews. I didn't feel quite as judgmental knowing the man wasn't used to taking care of children. And four were a handful even for people used to wrangling kids.

"You just need the right tools." I gasped and raised my voice. "Look at that, Santa has his camera running."

All the children in the store grew quiet. Oops. I had no choice. On with my show. I pointed at the security camera located near the door and aimed toward the register. There was a red-light blinking. Business must've picked up as Rachel renewed the security service, or after Jenna's death it was worth going into more debt. "I better make sure to put back the stuff I was looking at or Santa might skip my house. Don't want to be on the naughty list this year."

The nephews' eyes widened. One by one, the boys ranging from five to nine years old, picked up the books and placed them back on the shelves, each sneaking a peek at the camera.

"Thanks." The uncle said, giving a thumbs up.

"Invoking Santa's name works about 75 percent of the time."

"What do you do the 25 percent of the time it doesn't work?"

"Bribery."

He nodded toward the children who were cleaning up. "That is what bribery got me. I told them if they'd eat their lunch without smearing it on each other, we'd take a trip to the bookstore and they could pick out a book. I had no idea the youngest thought that meant choosing one to use as a club on her brothers."

"There's always one child you need to be a little more specific with."

He smiled. "I'll keep that mind. Thanks, Merry. I'm Jack."

We shook hands. His grip was firm and warm. The sleeve of his flannel shirt retracted, and I saw the end of a tattoo. I was about to ask him if he could clarify his job title as the mayor and Norman seemed to differ on it when Garret walked over and interrupted the conversation.

"Cassie said no more than six crafters at a time. She tried eight and the kids were too crowded."

My face flushed. Oops. "I offered to help with the Christmas craft since that's kind of my thing."

"What is? Christmas or crafts."

"Both."

"Let me give you a hand. I'm sure the four I brought will be over there soon to participate."

Cassie ran over and hugged me. "Thanks so much for your help. I wasn't sure we'd be able to pull off the craft. We keep getting slammed."

"Where's Rachel?" I was surprised she wasn't in the store today. The day after the parade was usually a big day for the store.

"She had some errands to run and will be in later."

"This is usually one of the biggest days. I'm surprised she's not here considering not all her employees are reliable." I kept my voice low not wanting Garrett to hear me. Right now, he was slowly meandering back to the register. No wonder Cassie was zipping around, the boy moved slower than a naughty child walking up to Santa.

Cassie's eyes filled with tears. "Did Rachel say something about me? I've been trying to stay focused."

Shame rippled through me. The poor girl. She thought I was talking about her. I was sure Cassie hadn't been her bubbly and productive self at work lately. "No, sweetie, I'm sorry I said that. I'm just protective of you and Rachel mentioned Garrett not showing up on time yesterday. That's why she was late to the float staging area."

"He came to work early yesterday because Rachel had to leave for a family emergency."

"I'm sorry. I must've misheard Rachel. It was chaotic last night with half the floats arriving late and around the same time." I busied myself with sorting out the craft kits.

"It's okay. Last night had to be so stressful for you. I'm going to get on my elf costume. Children listen better if they think I'm Santa's elf." Cassie gave me a one-armed hug and ran back to her stack of books.

I knew what I had heard. Rachel had lied to me about Garret. Why? Or was it that she hadn't wanted to confide in me about her family issues? Her relationship with her parents was strained and she rarely talked about them. What had happened that Rachel was so ashamed of to not even want to ask her friends for help?

"That's what I need," Jack said. "An elf costume."

"I'm surprised you had the day free to spend with your nephews and niece. I'm sure the mayor had a lot of people to contend with today. I'd think he'd want his security guard there." I stole a look at Jack, wanting to see his reaction. Was he going to fess up?

Jack shrugged. "I'd have thought so too, but he called me this morning and told me he longer had a need for my services."

What had the mayor hired him for and then no longer needed—right after Jenna was killed? Maybe Jack wasn't a security guard, but the Mayor's private bodyguard. Had Jenna been blackmailing the mayor? The bank slips. I had tossed them in the trash at One More Page yesterday. The police would need those.

I placed a plastic ornament onto the empty paper plate. "Can you make sure this table gets sticker sheets to decorate? I misplaced something yesterday and just remembered I tossed it in the trash when I was here. I'm hoping I can dig it out before it's collected."

"Good luck finding it. You might want to wear gloves in case there's moldy food or dirty diapers." Jack shuddered. "I've made that mistake before."

Gloves first. I walked down the hallway and entered the women's room, certain I'd find a pair of cleaning gloves underneath the sink. At the golf course, I made sure that each bathroom had a pair of gloves in the vanity. There was no way I'd clean without wearing a nice pair of plastic gloves to have a layer of protection between me and whatever I had to clean. It was the one thing I hated about the job, cleaning up after people.

The storage area of the vanity was filled with cleaners, extra toilet paper, and soap but not gloves. I moved the items, hoping they were hidden behind all the bottles. Nope. None here. The door to the men's room was closed and I didn't want to invade it. I knew Rachel kept general office supplies in her office. I hoped she didn't mind that I went in there to find some gloves.

I tapped on the door. It creaked open. There was a soft glow coming from the computer monitor and an image was flickering, like there was a moving image on the screen. Cassie and Garrett had said Rachel was out on an errand. Had Garrett been watching a movie in the office? Was that why they were behind in setting up for the craft and story time hour? Cassie loved her job. She wouldn't have been back her goofing off with a ton of work to do.

The young man seemed to have just floated into town. I knew nothing about him, and Rachel didn't seem to know much about him either except he attended the local college and needed a job.

For some reason, on her limited budget, Rachel decided to hire him. Of course, she did, I scolded myself, she had a soft heart. I knew that about her, and it wasn't too hard for other people to figure that out either. It was also why her business just barely stayed afloat, Rachel was willing to look away when she noticed books walking out the door if she knew someone was struggling. Books were hope. Everyone deserved to have hope in their hands. Rachel was always the first to volunteer to help and to give people the benefit of the doubt.

Like you had at one time. The errant thought caused a sadness to well up inside of me. That was true. A few months ago, heck weeks ago, I had been the type of person who searched for the good in everyone around me and downplayed all negative qualities as just minor annoyances I'd learn to ignore or accept. Samuel's murder had changed me. Now, I saw deceitfulness lurking in people and it made me leery and second-guess people. I wasn't liking this new characteristic.

Rachel's open heart was why I adored her, and I overlooked

her one annoying trait: her gossip without gossiping. Rachel collected a lot of secrets as people usually forgot she was around and were a little too open within her earshot, but she never repeated anything without someone doing some prodding...and usually that came with a big hint from Rachel that she knew something you should know. That was also the difference between others' gossip and Rachel's. She only passed on the information to the people who needed to know rather than making it common knowledge.

I roved my gaze over the shelves on the back wall. No gloves. I glanced over at the wall where the plaque had hung. Frowning, I walked closer. There was a nail hole in the wall where the plaque had hung. It was smooth. I ran my finger over it. The nail hadn't come loose, and the wooden plaque clobbered me on the head. Someone had removed it.

Who had been in the store that night and wanted to hurt me? Or have me not see something? There had been so many people in the store that night. Had it been Eric who snuck up on me?

"Can I help you, Merry?" There was a tinge of anger in Rachel's voice.

"Sorry for coming back here without your permission. I was looking for some gloves to dig through the trash."

"You were what?"

"I threw something away yesterday I should've kept."

"Why are you staring at the wall in my office?"

"Because I think someone knocked me out last night. The plaque didn't fall off the wall. Someone took it off." A sudden rush of tears filled my eyes. I swiped them away, a little scared about the sudden onset of emotions. I wasn't a bottle-everything-up type of woman, but I also didn't wear my heart on my sleeves. I wasn't sure who I was anymore and that scared me. I doubted people. Distrusted me. And now allowed everything to bring me to tears.

"You're not making any sense." Rachel led me to a chair and forced me to sit down. "How about you start from the beginning and tell me what's going on. You've been acting so strange the last two days. I thought it was your argument with Jenna and then finding her body, but it's something more. Isn't it?"

I explained what happened Friday night. "I swore I heard someone behind me before the pain in my head. When I came to, Cassie was in the room and showed me the plaque that was on the floor. It made sense. Except for the computer monitor was off and the naughty sign was gone."

Squeals came from the store. The craft and story hour had begun. Cassie needed help and here I was trying to figure out if the pastor was a suspect. Either I needed to head back to the front and get to crafting or search through the trash.

"Do you have any plastic gloves? I need to look through your trash and don't want to touch anything icky. Nancy was running errands for Jenna and some bank slips fell out of her purse. One-hundred-thousand-dollar worth of deposits split between four banks. And I just found another receipt." I refrained from saying where I found them. I didn't want Rachel knowing I made a risky—and stupid—decision to go to Eric's house. Alone.

Rachel's eyes widened. "You're sure about that."

I nodded. "I think Jenna was blackmailing people."

"That's a good reason for someone to kill her."

"That's why I want to find them and give them to the police. There's your motive."

"Absolutely." Rachel dug around in her desk and withdrew a pair of driving gloves. "Use these. I just put all the trash in the dumpster this morning. I'd help but I need to get up front and help Cassie and Garrett."

"Thanks. Tell Cassie..." I trailed off, unsure how to explain my absence after I agreed to help her. "I had promised to do the craft."

"Don't worry. I'm sure you'll come up with something if she asks. I'll say Brett called you."

I hugged her and snagged the gloves from the desk. "Thanks. Let me go get those slips before something happens to them."

"Be careful. Sometimes feral cats get into the dumpster. Don't want one to attack you."

"Thanks for the warning."

Rachel turned off the computer and headed down the hall into the store while I went out the back door to play in the dumpster.

I approached it cautiously, studying it. The door wasn't too high off the ground and a quarter of the way opened. There was a small bag, like from an office trash can, right on top. I'd start with it before climbing inside. I leaned forward and sniffed the air a few times. The stench wasn't too bad. I might not have to rush home and fumigate myself after searching for the bank slips and the sign.

The dumpster door squealed as I pushed it open. The kind of sound that grabbed onto your spine and made you grit your teeth. Donning the gloves, I grabbed the handle and pulled. The bag didn't budge. Part of it was hooked onto a metal edge of the dumpster. Nothing worth doing was easy. I tugged again. Still didn't move. Using booth hands, I yanked and lifted at the same time. The bag burst into pieces. Pieces of paper floated in the air, some landing on the ground others inside the dumpster.

I picked up the slips of paper on the ground. Customer receipts. No bank slips. Great. I was going to have to go in. Holding onto the frame of the door, I hiked one leg into the dumpster then the other. The smell was worse standing inside. My feet squished on something. I shuddered.

What was I going to do with the paper I looked at? I should've devised a more thorough plan than dig through the dumpster. I dropped the slips of paper onto the ground, vowing I'd pick them up after I was done looking. More receipts. I checked a couple of the dates. The slips were from yesterday, so I shouldn't have to dig too far down to find the potential evidence.

I stepped on something hard. It was about the size of the board I used for the Santa lists. Had Rachel thrown out the nice list or Garret? Cassie would've brought it to me if Rachel no longer wanted it.

Carefully, I reached down and brought out the board. It was a sign I made. Coffee grounds and shredded paper were on it. I was a little sad that my hard work went into the trash. If Rachel hadn't wanted it, she could've returned it to me or passed it on. A bright color piece of fabric was underneath a trash bag.

Shaking the board, I reached for the fabric and pulled it out. The slips of paper fell off the board. Once the fabric was in my hand, I recognized it. It was Sarah's scarf. My gaze went from the scarf to the board. It was a sign I had made—the naughty list. And instead of Jenna's name on the bottom, it was now Eric Wilcox.

FIFTEEN

Why was Eric's name now on the sign? Was he in danger? *He threatened Cassie, why should you care?* I was a little ashamed by my thought, but also agreed with it. Why should I worry about Eric's safety? He wasn't showing concern for anyone else. If Eric had been the one to assault me and steal the sign, he might have changed it and threw it away, hoping someone would find it and make people think he was in danger. Or that someone killed Jenna as a way to get even with him.

But, if that was the motive, what had Eric done to upset someone? The man did have a bad habit of drinking and driving, though he seemed to be careful enough not to ever get arrested for it. I knew it was a source of frustration for the officers in Season's Greetings. They knew about it but could never catch him in the act. Had someone finally gotten fed up with the lack of justice and decided to get rid of Jenna who covered for her husband and now planned on taking out Eric?

You're stretching there, Merry. I had to agree with myself. The simple answer was usually the correct one. Eric was trying to divert attention from himself being the killer by portraying himself as a potential victim. I examined the sign. The "E" and "i" in Eric's name overlapped tiny pieces of stickers. Someone had removed Jenna's name and added his.

There were footsteps in the alley, heading toward the dumpster. A shadow grew closer. My heart hammered. The person wasn't making a sound. I was sure they were able to see me. I hadn't been trying to hide myself or the mess I was creating right outside the dumpster. What if it was the person who altered the sign?

I remained still, holding my breath and hoping whoever was in the alley left.

The steps grew closer. I raised the board over my head, the only weapon I had to protect myself.

Officer Orville Martin looked in the dumpster.

I lowered the sign. "Thank goodness it's you. I found—"

"If you're about to say evidence, stop. Don't say it and don't touch anything else."

Orville grabbed hold of my arm and practically hauled me out of the dumpster, and not too nicely. The sign thumped the side of the dumpster.

"I'm just trying to help." I shook off his grasp. What was with him? The police didn't know about the evidence in the dumpster. "Nancy dropped some bank slips with Jenna's name on it."

"Why would they be in the garbage behind the bookstore?"

"Because Nancy didn't take them back and I didn't want them, so I threw the slips away."

"And now, for some reason, you realized it would be a good thing for you to have."

"No, I thought they'd be good for you...the police...to have."

Orville heaved out a breath and crossed his arms, centering a what-am-I-going-to-with-you look on me. It was like I was a wayward teenager who needed a scolding. Heck, I was a year older than the man.

"I don't want to consider you a suspect in this murder," Orville said. "You ain't making it easy. I should take you in for questioning instead of talking to you out here."

"I'm a suspect."

Even I heard the lack of a question in my voice. I wasn't surprised. This wasn't my first time dealing with a murder, and I had to admit I made a good suspect. Argued with the victim the morning before she was killed; showed up at the victim's house the morning after she died to snoop around. It was my word against Eric's on who was the aggressor.

"Let's lay everything out. You had words with Jenna at her house on Thursday. No one has seen or heard from Jenna since your visit. She's texted and called a few people, hanging up before anyone heard her voice. Doesn't look good for you. This morning you decided to go visit the widower, who you said held you at gunpoint and threatened Cassie. Now, you conveniently find evidence pointing to Jenna having large sums of money, I'm presuming, which somehow tie into her murder. Anything I'm leaving out?" He crossed his arms and glared at me.

He wasn't going to like this. Neither was I. I was looking pretty guilty. "In the dumpster, I found the naughty sign with Eric's name on it." I gave it to Orville.

He held the sign, staring at it. "Ah yes, forgot to mention that you found the sign with Jenna's name on it and someone took it from you, and now here it is. In your possession with Eric's name on it."

Orville's voice had grown cold. I trembled. He was officially putting me on the suspect list. "What did Eric tell you about my visit?"

"Nothing. The man wasn't there."

Oh God. I shouldn't have left. I should've stayed there and seen what Eric wanted from me instead of getting him drunk and escaping. The man must've just fallen asleep and took off once he saw I was gone. He could show up any minute. Cassie was in the store. Unprotected. I raced for the door.

Orville stepped in front of me, blocking me. "Settle down before you run in there. No sense upsetting the girl. Nothing is going to happen to her in the store. There's an undercover officer in there. A squad car is out front. I doubt Eric will walk in knowing we're here."

Tears rushed into my eyes. "He threatened to go after Cassie. You don't believe me. You think I've made all this up because I had something to do with Jenna's death."

"I believe you, Merry."

"It doesn't seem that way."

"Because I have to keep an open mind. I have to come to terms that someone I know, someone I like, someone in this town is a murderer."

The sadness in his voice shook me. This wasn't easy for Orville or any of the officers in Season's Greetings. The person who killed Jenna was likely someone they knew, liked, possibly even loved.

"We're not going to let him harm that girl," Orville's tone had grown softer. "If he gets anywhere near her, we'll stop him. We want to find him. There are a lot of questions he needs to answer, and it doesn't look good that he's avoiding the police."

"What about the sign?"

"I'll show it to the chief and see if we can get any prints off it."

"Mine and Rachel's will be on it. Also, Cassie and Garrett. They might have adjusted it in the window." My mind went back to last night. "And the people who decided to take selfies with it. Who do you think killed Jenna?"

"Can't really say. We just go where the evidence sends us." Orville walked over to the dumpster. "Be aware of your surroundings and let Cassie know to keep an eye out for anything unusual, but don't scare the girl."

He was right. I wanted Cassie protected and aware but not terrified. How was I going to manage that? She was going to her grandmother's tonight for dinner. A house that was off the main road and tucked into a quiet wooded area. A perfect place for someone to sneak up on an ailing older woman and her teenage granddaughter. I should finagle myself an invitation.

"She's going to be at Helen's tonight. What if he goes there?" My voice hitched.

"We'll keep everyone safe. Though it's a lot harder to do if you're going around antagonizing people."

I was about to defend myself and decided my best defense was to keep my mouth shut. Also, because there was little to argue against. I was riling people up. Though, I shouldn't be too surprised that Sarah wasn't happy that her husband was tied to Eric and Jenna at this moment in time. Right now, the pastor also made a good suspect and church goers weren't going to be too forgiving about that.

"Sarah Heath was the one who showed up at my front door acting like a hen wanting to peck my eyes out."

Orville drew back and relaxed his features, trying to wipe away the shock that had flashed on his face. "Mrs. Heath spoke to you this morning?"

"She came to my house. Basically, she wanted me to stop telling the police stuff that made her husband look bad."

"Interesting."

I was glad that Orville thought it was too. "The pastor told me he went to Jenna's to talk to her Friday morning, but she wasn't there."

"He told you that?" All expression vanished from Orville's face.

I nodded. "He told me he went to talk to Jenna about some city council stuff. Since he's the vice mayor."

"Anything else?"

I talked myself right into the topic I had wanted to avoid—the loan or embezzling, depending on how you viewed it.

Orville placed his hands on his utility belt. "Merry, you have to tell me. You can't keep withhold information that's important to this case."

"What if it's a rumor?" My heart thudded in my chest.

"You didn't have a problem sharing earlier."

My cheeks heated. He was right. Some of the information I already passed on could be deemed rumors. I trusted Orville. He wouldn't spread gossip. "The pastor mentioned that the mayor was saying that Samuel had stolen money. I've been trying to find out the truth. That's why I went to Eric's."

Orville heaved out a sigh. "The better thing to have done would've been calling the police and let us determine who's doing the lying. You're going to get yourself hurt."

The fact that he didn't ask me to clarify my statement told me that he already knew about the town's missing money. Giving the town money wasn't going to stop the truth from coming out. "I'll be careful."

"You're going to stay out of this, Merry."

"I feel responsible. There's something in my head. Something I'm missing."

"Call me." Orville pulled out a business card and jotted down a number on the back. "That's my personal cell. If you remember something, call me and I'll help you talk it through to see what you can remember."

"I don't want to waste your time."

"I'd rather my time be wasted than have another murder to investigate. Don't put me in a position of having to call your kids and tell them something terrible happened to their momma."

Using my kids was low but if he wanted to shock me, it worked. I didn't want my children receiving a call that something happened to me because I was being nosy. I wanted to know who killed Jenna, I felt responsible. I was there that night. How could I have not seen or heard anything? Trying to assuage my guilt wasn't going to put a protective bubble around me. Whoever killed Jenna wasn't going to want anyone to find out. They killed one person, killing a second was probably easier after you had done it once.

"I'll call you. Can you ask an officer to keep an eye on Cassie and Helen? Drive by their houses and check on them tonight."

Orville patted my shoulder. "I'll do what I can, Merry. It's time for our annual food drive so I'll have someone stop by tonight and check everything over. Helen is a smart woman and she'll know something is up if an officer stops by."

"You don't think it'll be a good idea to tell them?"

"Tell them what? Everyone in town knows that someone killed Jenna and the person hasn't been caught. Either they don't think the person is a threat to them, which is good, or they don't care. The last thing Season's Greetings needs is a bunch of vigilantes running around town, or even a slew of amateur sleuths."

I went back into the store, trying to ignore the feeling that once again I was missing something, forgetting a detail.

Rachel was helping one of Jack's nephews place some stickers on an ornament. The niece was sitting on the reading circle carpet, a brother on either side, as Cassie read *The Grinch Who Stole Christmas*. The little girl was thumping her feet on the circle. Her small booted feet nearly crushing her brothers' fingers. The boys had quick reflexes and were able to move their hands away in the nick of time. I had a bad feeling that was the point of the game.

I brought two chairs over for the boys. They offered me a grateful smile. The niece stared up at me, tears welling in her big blue eyes. Her lower lip trembled. I squatted down and fixed my best momma-don't-play-that-game smile on her. "Want a chair too?"

She shook her head. "Brothers down here." She patted the two empty spots on the carpet beside her.

"Now you can dance your feet all you want without smushing your brothers' fingers. Santa wouldn't want you doing that."

Her eyes widened. Tears pooled. "Brothers here. By me."

"I think it's best your brothers sit on the chairs." I stood and planted my hands on my hips, giving her my stern momma look.

She narrowed her eyes on me. The tears drying instantly. This was a child that was used to getting her way no matter what. She crossed her chubby baby arms and turned away from me.

Cassie pressed back a smile as she continued to read.

I walked over to the crafting table and started cleaning up. A mother walked over to the counter, carrying an armload of books and some craft kits. Messy canvas kits would be easy to assemble. Couple tubes of paint. Sponge paint brushes. Small canvases to make it easy to mail. And have a couple choice of decals. I had a color printer and could put together an easy to read direction sheet with color pictures.

Tugging out my phone, I quickly messaged the idea to Bright. We'd been thinking of a way to expand our handcrafted Christmas and this was perfect for us. Craft kits that allowed children and adults to create their own handcrafted items for their loved ones. We might lose a little bit of business for the items we handcrafted, but there would always be people who preferred to buy the handcrafted look and now we could branch out to those who preferred to do their own crafting but wanted the ease of a kit.

"Thanks for bailing on me," Jack said, dropping silver glitter into the clear ornament. "Hope whatever came up was worth ditching me. I'm not really the crafty type and could've used some help." He capped the ornament and held it up. Lopsided stickers spelled out "let it sow."

"Let it sow? Interesting phrase for a Christmas ornament." I tucked my phone into my back pocket and snuck a look at the picture window. There were some people lingering outside. None of them Eric.

"Well, the terror wanted mine to say let it snow but my sheet was missing the letter 'n.' Hard to write snow without an 'n.'"

"Why didn't you take one from another sheet?" Leaning over, I peeled an "n" from a discarded sheet and carefully peeled up the "s" and moved it over. "There you go, you can now let it snow."

"It was the only sheet missing letters, so I took it for me. My niece insisted I craft with her and I discovered it's quieter if you just do as she tells you. She got bored five minutes into the project and went to listen to the story."

Or rather to torment her two brothers who tried to escape her. "Unless you always want her to boss you around forever, you have to learn to say no."

"Didn't seem the time or place."

I wonder if his niece was solely responsible for the squealing Rachel and I heard earlier. The doorbell jingled. I glanced over. Nancy entered. No Eric.

"It's never the time or place to say no to her," one of her brother's muttered casting an evil eye on his uncle.

Jack ruffled the young boy's hair flicking a concerned gaze in my direction. "Uncles are supposed to be the fun guy. Besides your sister is still a baby."

The little boy scrunched up his nose. "Two isn't a baby. I wasn't allowed to hit people when I was two. You're just scared of her. Like Dad and Mom are. She always gets her way."

As if to prove the little boys point, the two brothers on the chair pushed them back and sat by their sister, putting their fingers back at risk of being stomped on by her. The little girl caught me watching them, she stuck out her tongue and smiled.

Jack and the girl's parents sure had their hands full. "You're going to have a fun-filled rest of the day and evening."

Jack shook his head, a look of terror crossing his face. "I'm done in an hour. I told my sister I could babysit until three."

"You never know. Stores are more crowded. Could take them longer to get their errands done." Again, the bell jingled, and I whipped my head in the direction of the door. A group of teenage girls. Garrett hustled over to help the giggling bunch. I should move to the other side of the table before I gave myself whiplash.

Jack turned and stared at the door for a moment before returning his attention to the pile of stickers in front of him. "Are you okay?" He picked up a sheet, counted letters then put it back down.

"Sure. Why wouldn't I be?" I asked, stopping myself from checking out who was now coming in the store. Traffic was picking up at One More Page.

"You seem to be interested...or should I say terrified...of whoever might be coming in the store." Jack pulled a capital "w" off the sticker sheet.

"I had a run-in with a creep earlier and he made a comment about visiting the store." I tried to keep my tone light and breezy. It didn't work. My voice broke and a tremor shook each syllable. "What are you adding to the ornament?"

"The cute little terror's name. I expect by tomorrow this one will be in pieces and she'll try and snatch one of her brothers'. How in the world will I fit Wilhelmina on here?"

"I can do it." I knelt and took the ornament from him and gathered a pile of sticker sheets. There had to be enough letters in the castoffs to spell the child's name.

"Explain it all to me." He made himself as comfortable as possible on the child-size chair and patted the one next to him.

"It's a long story." I moved from the floor to the chair. "I probably won't come out looking too good."

He looked me up and down then grinned. "I find that hard to believe."

I narrowed my eyes. "I wasn't looking for a compliment."

"Didn't say you were. You just seem too friendly and happy to be trouble."

Little did he know how my life was going lately. "You'd be surprised. My ex-husband, or maybe not my ex-husband, was murdered a few weeks ago. People think he won a load of cash and because our divorce wasn't exactly finalized, it means I'm a very rich widow."

"Someone's trying to shake you down for money and is threatening those you care about to get some." He nodded, a been-down-that-block-before gesture. "There will always be people who think extortion is an easy and viable way to make money."

"It's not quite like that. Just trying to let you know my life is complicated and not the sipping on cocoa, watching Christmas movies all day lifestyle you assume I have."

He rolled his eyes. "What is it about people with generally good lives always wanting them to be more drama filled. Having a topsy-turvy life shouldn't be a goal. Calm is good. Boring is good. Nothing wrong with happy."

He had a good point. My life wasn't quite the kiddie coaster I was used to with small hills and downward plunges, but it hadn't totally jumped the tracks.

"The thing is that I've been asking a few questions and it's irritated some people. One person mainly. He made a comment about going after Cassie if I didn't do what he wanted. I want to make sure she's safe. I don't want someone hurting her because I've been trying to find answers to what's going on in this town. That's why I want to know whose walking in here."

He cupped his hand over mine. "Who is it? It'll be better if more than one person is on the lookout."

"You can't sit here with me until her shift is over."

"Sure, I can."

"Eric Wilcox." I nodded toward his niece who was yanking more books of the shelves. "You need to keep all your attention on Wilhelmina not look for Eric."

"I can. I'm a multi-tasking kind of guy. Besides, someone shared a great parent tip with me." He cleared his throat then called out, "Santa's watching you, Wild One."

The little girl turned and stuck her tongue out at him.

"Interesting nickname." I sorted the sheets by color. Wilhelmina's name might end up being a rainbow of colors.

"When she was born, two of her brothers had trouble saying her name. It sounded like wild one and stuck."

"Was that before or after her personality showed itself?"

"Are you hinting that her behavior is a result of the nickname?" Jack's phone buzzed. He glanced down at it and grinned. "My sister will be back early. She's in the area, so she can pick up the kids here rather than at our uncle's house. I know he'll appreciate that."

I went to put a half-sheet aside and paused, staring at it. An "x" was gone. My mind flashed to the naughty list that had Jenna's name on it. These letters were similar.

The "w" was also missing. Jack had said the sheet he had was missing an "n." The other sheets had two "n's" on it. Jenna. Wilcox. I couldn't think of a Christmas word with "x" unless one of the children put Merry X-mas on their ornament. That was possible.

Stop it. The command interrupted my excuses, stopping me from ignoring what was right in front of me because I didn't want to think—see—the worst about a friend. It wasn't a coincidence that an "x" was gone from the sheet of stickers. The box had been sealed when Garret showed it to me.

The security cameras were working today and also last night. I had seen an image on the screen. I was certain of it. And I hadn't seen a movie playing on the computer, it was movement in the store. The cameras were working. Rachel lied to me.

The books. The Wilcox home had looked wiped out except for the few pieces of furniture and lots of books. Almost a small library worth of books.

Rachel. Rachel had added Jenna's name to the sign and lied about the security camera. Thursday night, Rachel had an emergency. Friday, she was late to the parade. Lied about Garret not showing up on time. Today she left the store again. To run an errand. I had almost run into a truck leaving Eric's house.

Had Rachel been involved in Jenna's murder?

SIXTEEN

No, it couldn't be. Tears filled my eyes. Hastily, I swiped them away, not wanting Cassie to see. Poor Cassie. Rachel was also her friend. Her employer. A mentor. How would she take the news? I hoped I was wrong. The top wish on my Christmas list was Rachel not being a murderer.

How could I prove myself right or wrong? I should know for certain before I called the police on my friend. Tears dripped down my cheeks. I wiped them away and took in small breaths, hoping to settle down. The computer. I could sneak back to Rachel's office and see if the image on the monitor was footage from the security camera.

Jack paused in gathering up the coats and hats his sister's offspring had scattered around the bookstore. "What's wrong? Is he here?"

"No." I stopped myself from saying nothing was wrong. I needed help in creating a diversion, and Jack had some resources available. "Can you hand me a book? Doesn't matter which."

"Sure." Jack grabbed a book from the nearest shelf and handed it to me.

"I need a diversion," I whispered, discretely placing the letter stickers between random pages. Didn't want anyone getting rid of them while I poked around.

"What?"

"I have to look at something in Rachel's office and need her to stay out here. I also don't want her to see me leave."

"Does this have anything to do with Eric?"

Did it? It was a good question. Maybe Eric had killed his wife and somehow wrapped Rachel into it. The guy had threatened me at gunpoint. There was a likelihood he did the same to Rachel. "Possibly."

"I'll see what I can do for you. I've always been a sucker for a lady in distress." Jack surveyed the room, settling his gaze on his niece. The little girl was in front of a bookshelf, looking up at the top row of books. He grinned. "I think with help from a naughty elf, I can create quite the distraction."

I hoped so. Scanning the store, I spotted Rachel in the cookbook section. Cassie was reading to children. Which meant Garret would be manning the register. Perfect. I picked up the book where I hid the stickers and made my way to the end of the line. It was three people deep. If anyone else got in line, Rachel would open up the other register. Please let everyone else continue to browse.

It would be nearly impossible to sneak into the office if Rachel was at the register. Jack and his niece would have to create one heck of a distraction for Rachel to abandon buying customers.

"That's not what I meant!" Jack bellowed. "Get down from there."

"She's going to die!" A little boy screeched.

"Mom is going to kill you," another little boy announced, a little too gleefully.

I couldn't help it, I turned around to look instead of sneaking my way into the office. My mouth dropped open. Customers gasped. Rachel screeched and ran toward the case the toddler used as a ladder.

Wilhelmina was standing on the top shelf of a ten-foot tall bookcase. "I want this one." She beamed down at her uncle and reached for a book.

For a split second, total terror crossed Jack's face. His distraction plan was out of hand. Shame rippled through me. I couldn't believe I placed a child at risk so I could spy on my friend.

Jack's oldest nephew was sitting on the floor, flipping through a magazine. He looked up and his baby sister then returned his attention to his reading material.

"Call the fire department." Rachel jabbed a finger toward Garrett. He nodded and went to the phone in the corner of the register area, his back toward me. Cassie was busy trying to corral other children from using the bookcases as a jungle gym.

Jack jerked his head backwards. Now was my opportunity.

Tucking the book securely under my arm, I made my break. My heart pounded as I entered the office. The computer was on. The screen was blank. Dropping into the office chair, I pushed the button on the screen. An image popped up. The store. A tightness filled my throat. I was right. She lied. The security camera in the store area worked. And I bet the one in the office was functional as well. Rachel knew who hit me and stole the sign.

Had she done it? Or Eric. Once again, tears threatened. No. Not now. I had to document the proof before something really did happen to the cameras. I was sure Rachel had deleted the recordings implicating her.

I wished I could talk to Rachel. Find out what had happened. Her reasons for lying to me. To the police. Had Eric threatened her? Why did I feel I owed her a chance to explain?

Because you don't like the truth. You want to be wrong. True. I hated it. I wanted Rachel not to be involved. A simple explanation for everything that was adding up against her. Like the security cameras. She had turned them off and after Jenna was murdered, decided it was more prudent to have them back on even if it meant taking on more business debt than she was comfortable. People changed their minds all the time. What seemed like a bad idea became the better choice depending on the circumstances. There was something to be said for trusting and believing in your friends, and quite a few other words to use for a person who refused to see what was before them. Hadn't I already created a problem by going to see Eric?

I allowed my anger at the mayor to overrule common sense and headed straight for Eric's place, the proverbial lion's den. And all for what? To prove that my deceased ex-husband hadn't swindled money from the town because I was afraid Cassie and Helen would be judged by it—that I would be judged.

Using my cell phone, I snapped pictures of the screen and a few of the stickers sheets I placed in the book. Orville's business card. He had given me his cell number. Quickly, I pulled out the card and entered the number into my phone. Before I talked myself out of the truth, I sent him the picture and what I suspected-- Rachel was involved in Jenna's murder.

The office door shut. I spun around. Rachel locked the door and braced herself against it. "What do you know, Merry?"

The tone of her voice told me what I needed—but didn't want—to know. She had lied to me. "The security cameras work. You lied about canceling the monitoring service."

Rachel continued to grip the doorknob, back pressed against it. Her complexion was pale and her body trembled. "Yes."

"Why? Someone attacked me." I stood, figuring it was better to be on my feet than sitting down if things ended up getting rough in here. I wasn't much of a fighter but could defend myself. Or at least I hoped so. "Was it you?"

Tears snaked down her face and she shook her head. "I thought you had only saw the sign, and someone snatched it before you got it. I didn't know you were hurt."

"Jenna's name had been added to that naughty list. It was important for the police to find out who took the sign. The tapes might help the police solve the case. But you didn't want the police to know who altered the sign...because it was you. The stickers I saw spelling out Jenna's name were very similar to the ones for today's craft."

Slowly, she walked toward me.

I fisted my hands. The store had been crowded but not so much that someone wouldn't have seen a person altering the sign. After Jenna's murder became public, someone would've stepped forward. No one stepped forward because the sign wasn't changed during store hours. It was done in secret.

"You didn't want the police seeing you take the sign out of the window, go back to your office, then place it back into the window. That's why you lied about the security camera. Or you know who hit me and took the sign." I braced myself for a fight.

Instead of attacking me, Rachel collapsed onto the chair, drawing her feet onto the cushioned seat. "Both."

"Why?"

"Because someone had to threaten her. It was the only way."

The images of stacks of books floated into my brain. Eric's house. An empty house beside some basic furniture pieces, a few random kitchen supplies, and books. Random titles. I thought Eric or Jenna were eclectic readers. Instead, it was random purchases to have a reason to stop at the bookstore and see Rachel.

"The only way to protect Eric," I said. "You've been sleeping with him. That's why you got upset when I was asking question about your guy."

She shook her head, tears tumbling down her cheeks. "No. I wasn't just sleeping with him. I love him. He asked me to help. I don't know what I was thinking. Why I thought—" Rachel lowered her face to her knees and sobbed.

"Are you saying you killed her?" Had she been so desperate for love she killed her rival?

"No. She was already dead when I arrived at their house. Eric called me, said he did something stupid. We couldn't see each other anymore. I went over and..." Her remorseful gaze sought something from me. Forgiveness? Understanding?

I felt empty. "You helped him move Jenna's body. You put her in Santa's toy bag. You two tried to pin her murder on someone else. Norman or Pastor Heath could've been blamed."

Rachel shook her head, her hair swung wildly about her shoulders. "No. I didn't do that. All I did was let him use my car to move her."

"All you did?" My voice rose into a high-pitch squeal. "You lied to the police. You're covering up a crime. A murder."

"Please, Merry, I need you to understand."

"I can't understand this." I started for the door.

Rachel jumped up and snagged my wrist. "You can't tell anyone. I won't let you."

I narrowed my eyes on her. The anger churning through kept my tears and despair at bay. "What are you going to do? Kill me also?"

Stunned, Rachel let go of my arm and took a step backward. "I didn't kill her. I didn't hurt anyone."

"What about our town? Whoever else the police are investigating in Jenna's death? You don't think they've been hurt. You have to tell the police everything that you know."

"I can't do that. I'll go to jail for helping him."

That was something she should've considered before she loaned her car to a murderer. "Fine, don't. But I will."

Rachel tried to step in front of me. I knocked into her, sending her sprawling onto the floor.

She drew her knees up to her chest and rocked. "Please don't, Merry. It was an accident. It was dark. Jenna was leaning against the bottom step of the porch. He only tapped her with his car. He didn't mean to."

"He was probably drunk." Everyone feared that one day Eric would kill someone with his drunk driving. It just happened to be his wife. All those years of covering for her husband ended with Jenna being killed by him.

"You have to help me." Rachel rose to her feet. "Please, Merry. I didn't kill her. I shouldn't have agreed to his plan. But I didn't see any other way out for him."

"He didn't deserve a way out. He deserves whatever punishment is handed to him. He killed his wife. Whether or not it was premeditated, he still killed her because of his actions." How could Rachel not see that? Could love really be that blind? I unlocked the door.

"You have to, or I'll tell everyone that you let Eric put Jenna in

Santa's bag. Everyone knows Christmas, and the parade, are your babies. No one will believe that you didn't have a clue." The threat trembled from her.

With my hands fisted at my side, I took a step toward her. "You'll do what?"

The door creaked open. "Merry, I need you to back away from her," Officer Brianna Myers said.

Rachel smiled at the officer. "It's okay. We're just having a small disagreement. It's all worked out now. Right, Merry?"

"No. Eric killed Jenna. And Rachel—"

"I heard everything." Brianna removed the handcuffs from her utility and walked toward Rachel.

As I hurried out of the office, Brianna reciting the Miranda warning and Rachel's sobs mingled together.

SEVENTEEN

Where was Cassie? I scanned the crowd. I wanted to explain to her what was going on with Rachel before Brianna marched out the store owner—our friend—in handcuffs. Through the window, I spotted a police car in one of the front spaces and a fire truck was in the road. The store wasn't just filled to capacity because of holiday shopping but because of plain nosiness. Everyone wanted to see the "show."

And they were going to get a good one in a few minutes. I heaved out a breath. Even though I was angry at Rachel for her stupidity and aiding a killer, a tiny piece of my heart went out to her. She had wanted to help—save—the man she loved. It wasn't a choice I would've made but I knew the heart could lead a person astray.

Jack was holding his niece and talking to Paul McCormick. The little girl was lightly smacking her uncle's cheeks and bellowing for him to look at her. Jack continued to speak to Paul, shifting the little girl so only one small hand reached his face. A volunteer firefighter, wearing gear, was carrying a ladder outside, having saved the little girl from her climbing expedition. The McCormick family's hardware store was a few streets over. Paul likely ran straight over after learning of the emergency.

Paul smiled and nodded at me.

"I should know by now not to take my eyes off this one for a second," Jack said, glancing over at me and smiling slightly.

Not what I had in mind for a distraction, allowing his niece to climb the bookshelf and put herself in danger, but it had work. Though, I do wonder how Jack's sister would feel about his "lackluster" babysitting skills. I had a feeling he was going to find out soon as a woman raced into the store, a long scarf flying behind her. Her gaze was scattering around the store and finally rested on him and the child. A slight look of relief settled over her face.

"Mommy, I climb." The little girl beamed and held her arms out to her mother.

The mother groaned and plopped into the closest chair. "What did she do now?"

There was a long line at the register. Garret was checking out customers as quickly as possible. Nancy was the next in line, tapping her foot as she glanced at her watch. The pile of travel books in her arms nearly slipped from her grasp.

"I didn't think when I told her to pick a book, she thought it meant I was giving her permission to climb the bookcase to retrieve one from the top shelf." Jack deposited the child into his sister's lap.

Cassie was placing books back into the bookcase. She must've sensed my stare as she turned. Her smile faded, and horror filled her face. She gasped and the books in her hands slipped to the floor.

"What's going on?" Garret's voice shook.

Glancing over my shoulder, I saw Brianna leading out the handcuffed Rachel. It was too late for me to explain first.

Nancy rushed for the door, placing her pile of books on the nearest display table. It wouldn't be long for word to spread around town about Rachel's arrest. But did Nancy know it was tied to Jenna's murder, the embezzled money, or something else? There was one way to find out what Nancy knew, head over to Yule Log where Nancy had a standing dinner date with her friends and eavesdrop.

But there was a more pressing need. Cassie and Garret would be left with the task of closing the store tonight and answering questions regarding Rachel's arrest. I walked over to Cassie who appeared frozen at the shelf. Her eyes were wide and shimmered. I wrapped an arm around her shoulders. She leaned into me, still holding the book as if it was a lifeline.

"You used that girl. For this." Rachel jiggled her cuffed hands. Tears streamed down her face. "I can't believe you'd do this to me, Merry."

"I've already advised you of your rights." Brianna's tone was compassionate. "Reconsider saying anything else."

A low buzz filled the area. Whispers were zinging around. Three words were in every comment: murder, Jenna, and why. I remained silent. It wasn't my place to answer the question. The town would learn soon enough. My heart struggled with the emotions reeling through me. Anger, disappointment, and sympathy. In her desperation for love, Rachel made a horrible decision and was now going to pay for it.

"What did you do?" Cassie pulled away from me.

"I didn't do anything." Though, I was snooping and that was something, but my actions weren't why Rachel was arrested. It was her own that had her in the police's custody. "I had to tell—"

"You went in the back," Cassie cut me off. "The police came and arrested her. Why?"

"Not here," I whispered to Cassie. People were inching toward us and I didn't want to supply the truth to everyone. "We can talk in the back. First, I'll finish cleaning up the crafting table."

"No, I'll do it myself." Cassie stomped over. "I want you to leave."

I gaped at her. Was she serious? "Cassie, what's going on?"

She threw plastic ornament bulbs into the box then jammed the remaining stickers inside. "Go, Merry. Don't you have a business you should be taking care of?"

"Yes. But I'm not going to leave you and Garrett to handle stuff around here on your own. You need help."

"I don't need yours."

I turned my head to look at Garrett. He was Cassie's friend.

Maybe he knew what caused her to snap. The young man shrugged, confusion and fear flashing across his face. I wasn't sure if he was worried about Rachel or Cassie's attitude. The girl was livid. It had been awhile since I dealt with a teenager's temper tantrum and I had to say this was a doozy. But usually I had a small clue on what it was about. This time I was lost.

Jack trailed his sister out of the store, helping to herd the four children toward her car. Two of the boys were thrilled about their baby sister's antics, while the older one complained about the fact she wasn't getting in trouble since he got into super trouble when the fire department was called because of him.

Cassie yanked the box off the table, bumping into my shoulder as she took the long way around to the stockroom.

That was it. I had enough. I reached for her arm.

"Maybe it's best for you to go." Paul snagged my hand, twining his fingers through mine.

The heat radiating from his skin started to calm my frazzled nerves. "And leave them to close the store tonight on their own? I can't do that."

Cassie glared at our hands. "I've closed the store on my own before. I don't need you." She stomped away.

I slipped my hand from his grasp. Was that why Cassie was angry? She thought Paul and I had something going on between us. Samuel and I had only been divorced—or I thought we had—two weeks before he died. I understood how it would be too soon for Cassie to consider someone she loved and had filled the mom role was moving on so quickly. I wanted to tell her that Paul and I were just friends but there were too many people around and I didn't want to hurt Paul by proclaiming a lack of feelings with a large audience hovering nearby.

Plus, it would be a lie. I did like Paul.

"I'll help them ring out the last few customers and close the store," Paul said.

"I have a feeling she isn't happy with you either." I tucked my hands underneath my crossed arms. "Rachel might not like someone else handling her business affairs. At least we're friends. Or were."

A rueful smile played at his lips. "I don't think Rachel has the ability to veto anything right now. As for Cassie, I'll talk to her and explain Scotland has asked me to keep an eye on you. She's been friends with my baby sister since kindergarten. She'll listen to me."

"I can't leave her." The words flew out in a panicked whisper.

"What's going on?"

"I irritated someone, and they made a comment about causing problems for Cassie." I didn't know if I was too scared or ashamed to tell Paul the whole truth.

"I promise I won't let that happen."

Nodding, I left, trying to ignore the "doomsday" fluttering in my stomach. Was it worry over my plan on talking with Nancy or disappointed in what Paul said—his interest in me was because of a promise made to my son? Or was the feeling confusion because I cared about what he said.

If there was someone I trusted it was Paul. I didn't know what it was about the man, except that he was a close friend of Scotland's, that instantly made me trust him. Or it could be the guy always treated me with respect. He asked for my opinion, never tried to talk me out of anything or brush off my concerns. When I had called him with my concerns about Norman, he didn't try to convince me that Norman wasn't having a stroke. He came to help. Based on my words. No judgment. No admonishments later because I was wrong.

Holding my head up high, I headed down the street. Even though Jenna wasn't killed because of money, there was still a large amount of cash gone from the town's budget and the mayor planned on making me liable for it.

Plus, it gave me something to focus on beside my friend being arrested for aiding and abetting a murderer.

EIGHTEEN

Yule Log was hopping even though it was nearing dinnertime. The diner was usually crowded for breakfast and the start of lunch, especially if homemade cinnamon rolls were on the menu. I'd never seen a long line stretching outside the door this late in the afternoon. Either rolls were added to the lunch menu or the gossip was awesome today. There was a lot to talk about: the parade, Jenna's murder, and Eric's disappearing act.

Everyone in town was here for the same reason, find out what Nancy knew about Jenna and Eric. And soon the residents would also be interested in why Rachel was arrested, though it shouldn't be too hard to guess it had to do with the murder—or the missing town money if that had leaked out. I was thinking not as no one had approached me about it yet. If for no other reason than to ask me to donate some money to cover the shortfall.

The jingle bell above the door tinkled as a group of diners came out and another patch went in. A very long wait to go inside. The line was orderly, and everyone waited patiently for their turn as not doing so resulted in a person being banned. Yule Log had the best food, atmosphere, and prices.

Sharon Dell, the owner of Yule Log, had a well-established system. There was a line for singles, giving you a spot at the counter when a stool was vacated. And don't even think about jumping from the line of parties-more-than-one to snatch some stools if your required number of spots just happened to become available.

Sharon would toss you out. You had to pick to either be a single or a party, and once you choose, you were stuck with that decision.

Sometimes, couples took the risk of standing in the single line that they'd be able to wrangle side-by-side seats. Single diners were usually quicker as most of the time it was hunters, those heading to work, and the people who disliked talking to anyone. They were at Yule Log for a good, cheap meal, not to socialize.

Waiting diners were staring at the cell phones or reading the newspaper. The front window had been washed and instead of Santa's sleigh filled with toys, there was a greeting wishing everyone a safe holiday season. My holiday spirits dipped. I hated seeing the change to the whimsical window display. Sharon's nephew was an amazing artist and had a folk art mixed with Norman Rockwell style. The drawings always reminded me of simpler times and expressed a timeless Christmas. The only reason I could think of the change to the window décor was people heard about Jenna's final resting place.

"Up on a Housetop" played from my phone. My spirits plummeted a little more. Scotland. I doubted he was calling to check on how the flow of the RV was working for me. One, he wasn't much of a caller, more of a texter, and two, he was a police officer. I'm sure a murder, at a Christmas parade, popped up on his radar and was the reason why Paul was asked to "keep an eye" on me.

"Good afternoon, son, are you off today?" Knowing darn well his shift had started at three, I hoped the reminder kept this call short. I really didn't want a lecture from my child. I was surprised he was allowed time to call me.

"Mom, what the heck is going on?" His tone was a tossup between angry and fearful. Whether I liked it or not, I was getting a talking to. "Why didn't you call last night to say you were hurt? When did it happen? Was it when you found the body?"

No reason to ask me since he seemed to already know everything. Being a parent of an adult child was hard. Things seemed to be shifting where my children felt an almost motherly responsibility to me while I was warring with the need to mother them against the reality that I had to let them spread their wings. Some days were better than others and I hated to admit, it was easier to let them adult when they were an hour and half drive away. If they had stayed in Season's Greetings, I'd have been all up in their business—and them in mine.

"I'm fine. Just had something bounce off my head at One More Page. Aren't you supposed to be working?"

No need to tell him that I thought it was deliberate. I was still the mom in this relationship, and I didn't want my son to worry and rush home. I wanted him to visit just not because he thought I needed a keeper. That was why he continually dropped hints about his friend Paul liking me, an easy way to keep tabs on his mother.

"This constitutes as an emergency. My supervisor said I could make a quick call and check on you. Someone was killed during the parade you organized."

"No one was killed during it," I corrected.

Waiting diners swiveled in my direction. I hurried away, tucking myself into a small alcove between two buildings. The sun was setting, and the light started to fade. I hoped we wrapped up the conversation soon. I was getting a little spooked standing in the small space that wasn't entirely closed off. There was a small walking path leading from the back of the stores. Perfect opportunity for someone—like the still missing Eric—to exit from the back door of a store and grab me.

"Mom. What's going on?" Scotland sounded frantic.

"Everything is fine. Trying to find a private spot to talk to you." I lowered my voice not wanting anyone to overhear the conversation. All the conversations of the people waiting had ceased. They were interested in what I was talking about. Couldn't blame them. I'd have been eavesdropping too.

"Mom, what aren't you telling me? Where are you?"

"I was waiting for a seat at Yule Log and left the line. From your bossy attitude, I have a feeling you already know what's going on in town."

"Mother, I'm not a child anymore. You should be able to turn to me and Raleigh for help."

Which meant a lecture was coming from my daughter—and even worse—either a call or visit from her father, my ex-husband Brett. He had found reasons to visit Season's Greetings every few days and this would give him another one. I couldn't complain too much as he was helping with my divorced-or-not issue and the ticket.

"Jenna Wilcox was murdered before the parade. She hadn't shown up with her so-called float, so I went looking for her." Actually, I went after Norman as the man had been acting out of sorts. That detail didn't need to be passed on to my son. I didn't want to start a rumor about Norman's health. Though, I should find a way to chat with his wife. She might have noticed Norman's confusion and memory lapses though with her health problems, Angela might not be aware of her husband's declining health.

"Oh God, Mom. You didn't find her?" He sounded sick.

The corner grew darker for a moment. I eased out of my spot and scanned the sidewalk. No one was walking away. Had anyone heard me? The setting sun was at a spot where a large Christmas display on the roof across the street had blocked the light. No one over heard me. I didn't want someone targeting Norman because they thought he knew who killed Jenna or passing on the information to a lurking reporter who'd make it front page news. Chief Hudson would not be happy about that.

"I'm meeting someone for a late lunch, early dinner. I have to go." Deliberately ignoring my son's last question, I didn't want to lie to him—or say yes.

"Who you meeting?"

"A friend. Hope you have an easy day at work. Stay safe. I love you." Scotland tried to interrupt, I talked right over him. Sometimes a mother had to assert herself. "Tell Raleigh I love her, and I'll see you guys soon. I'll head up to Morgantown next week if you guys can't make it to Season's Greetings."

While I had talked to my son the line had grown longer. By the time I got to the front, Nancy and her friends might be done eating and moving on to their next Saturday activity, bingo at the fire hall. I had to get in there. I was terrified of cutting in line for two reasons: the crowd and Sharon. Sharon did not put up with line jumpers. The last person was banned for a month. I turned off my phone, not wanting to be interrupted or hear a lecture from my other child.

With Christmas season upon us, I didn't want to get banned. Sharon made the most incredible cinnamon rolls. The rolls were a Christmas tradition for my children, and I didn't want to disappoint them and explain I wasn't able to purchase any because I cut in line. They'd never let me forget.

I stood on my tiptoes. Still couldn't see how many diners deep I was in line. I jumped up, nearly colliding into the man in front of me.

He turned and narrowed his eyes at me.

"Sorry, I'm hoping to get in before Nancy leaves. I have to talk to her."

Sharon was making her way toward me.

I wanted to shrink into a speck of dirt. "She's probably not even here." I started to slink away.

Sharon looped her arm through mine. "No, Nancy's here. And I think you should have a word with her. She's talking like you're kind of responsible for what happened to Jenna because you organized the parade."

I drew in a sharp breath and willed away the brewing tears. It was one thing for me to chastise myself, but quite another for someone else to do it. Someone I liked. I should've seen or heard something, but I hadn't because I was wrapped up in hosting a perfect Christmas parade. Visions of recent past dealings with the police flashed in my mind. I did not want to be a suspect again, or for people to consider me one. Organizing an event where someone was murdered didn't place a person on the most-likely-to-have-committed-murder list, and shouldn't because the best friend of the deceased couldn't refrain from gossiping for one day.

My anger let me forget for a moment—one small moment—that I had come because I hoped Nancy was gossiping about what she knew about Eric and Jenna. I just hadn't ever considered I was part of it.

I dropped my arm to my side, releasing me from my connection with Sharon. Patrons standing in line at the register parted, giving me a clear shot to Nancy. The woman looked like she was holding court rather than mourning her friend. The diner at the register waved off the waitress rushing over to ring her out. She wanted to stay because it appeared the feature show was about to begin.

A mother tugged a high chair closer to the table as I marched over to Nancy. Forks stopped clinking on plates and conversations hushed.

Nancy sat at a round four-top table with three women. Her entourage was hanging on every word, leaning forward with their elbows on the table, wicked glee gleaming in their eyes.

"Two bodies," Nancy said. "How many people find one much less two? Seems so unusual. Unless..." she trailed off and took a large bite of a BLT.

"Slander is a crime." I started to place my hands on my hips then decided to shove my shaking hands into my pocket. At the widening of Nancy's eyes, I took my hands out, slapping them on the tabletop. I didn't want anyone thinking I was about to whip a weapon from my pocket.

The wreath at the register was tilted at an angle as the diners vied for a good vantage point of what was turning into a come-to-Jesus talk with Nancy rather than a fact-finding mission. Focus. You're here for information not a cat fight. No matter what Nancy was saying.

"Slander?" Nancy's expression was full of innocence. "That is a harsh accusation to throw at people for stating basic facts of someone's life."

The three women excused themselves, exchanging glances that said Nancy was right about the possibility of my involvement. My show of temper wasn't helping me.

The fight had gone out of me. I didn't want to fight with Nancy. She had just lost a friend and was hurting. She wanted to know—needed to know—what happened and was trying to puzzle it all out. Jenna wasn't a nice person but didn't deserve to be killed. I had those same feelings after Samuel was murdered.

I sank into a chair. "I'm so sorry for your loss, Nancy. Jenna was your best friend."

A waitress ventured over to us. Her hesitant steps told me she was reluctant to do so. "There are a few cinnamon rolls left if you'd like to order one."

"I'll take one and a cup of coffee." I'd be up half the night now, which would be a good thing since I still had orders to complete. Spent a lot of time sleuthing rather than crafting.

Nancy and I sat across from each other, neither of us making eye contact or talking. People grew bored and returned to their meals and conversations. The waitress placed my order on the table and walked off, shooting confused looks at us. It had to be strange. One minute, Nancy is a chatterbox and I'm about to tell her off, now we're both mute.

"I'm sorry," Nancy whispered. "I was trying to hint that you were responsible. The only time people listen to me is when they think I'm revealing dirty secrets."

I placed my hand on hers. "You need people today and all anyone wants is gossip about your friend. To be honest, that was my intention. I feel like I have to find out what happened to Jenna. You knew her best."

"Why Jenna?" Tears filled Nancy's eyes. "I've been asking myself that all day. Did I tell her something that caused it? I was starting to think she was using some secrets I told her as a...bargaining tool."

"Why do you think that?"

Nancy shrugged and dragged a fry through ketchup.

"Was it because of certain errands she had you go on? Like to the bank." The only reason Jenna would allow Nancy to make the deposits for her was that she held something over Nancy's head—like being the source of the information she was using as blackmail.

Nancy stared at me, mouth open.

"You dropped some slips at the bookstore. I tried to give them back to you."

Her lips trembled. "Do you still have them? I need them back."

I shook my head. "I threw them away."

"We have to get them." Nancy waved for the waitress. "Check and to-go boxes." Her voice was shrill.

"The police would have them by now."

Nancy paled and collapsed back into her chair.

I jumped up. "Are you okay?"

She motioned for me to sit back down. I took a seat beside her, scooting as close as I could. People were once again staring at us.

Tears cascaded down her face. "It's too late. I wanted to protect her. Her memory."

"She was blackmailing people?" The expression on Nancy's face told me I was correct. "You have to tell the police."

Nancy shook her head. "It doesn't matter anymore. No one needs to know what she was doing."

"Of course, it matters. You don't—"

She glared at me defiantly. "If you do, I'll deny it. I'll say I don't know what you're talking about. You're lying."

"Someone killed your friend. Do you want them to get away with it?"

She shook her head.

I leaned closer. "Then why won't you talk to the police? Are you afraid people will blame you for what Jenna was doing?"

"I don't care about that."

"Then why? Jenna deserves justice."

Nancy rested her head on mine. Her whispered words were full of terror. "Because she was blackmailing almost everyone in town. I don't know who I can trust."

NINETEEN

Everyone in town. Nancy's words filled every space in my head as I drove home fighting the instinct to turn around and go to the police station. The thing stopping me wasn't my fear that a police officer was involved, but the fact that Orville warned me how my meddling was putting me on the suspect list, and a slight part of me didn't want to know what was happening with Rachel right now.

What should I do? I pulled into my driveway, sitting there as sadness settled over me, pushing down on my spirit. The heaviness sapped my energy. I didn't want to leave my vehicle. Go into my house. I just wanted to sit and focus on the guilt eating at me. I pulled my phone from my purse. The screen was dark. I had forgotten to turn it back on when I left Yule Log.

I switched it on. Multiple messages from Bright popped up. Either we had a crafting emergency, or she was tired of waiting for me to fill her in on the parade and contacted me for details. I was sure it was all over the news. It wasn't every day that a woman was murdered in a Christmas-named town right before the annual Christmas parade.

I was right. Bright wasn't a beat around the bush kind of person. She got straight to the point.

Please tell me the police didn't wrap you up in this murder.

Not formally. I messaged back. *Though I'm doing a good job of putting myself on that particular list.*

Talk.

In as few characters as I could, I typed out my suspicions, having to go back a few times to correct words. It would've been easier to type everything on the computer, but I had to get it out of me. Christmas surprise secrets were the only ones I liked keeping. This was too much for me. For Nancy. She got it out by entrusting it to me, now I was handing—sharing—it with Bright.

I closed out of messenger. Bright would help me figure out what to do. I knew she wouldn't judge me. She'd understand my reluctance to go to the police but also why my conscience demanded I do so.

Slipping out of the car, I noticed the plastic mail bin by my front door. My mail person was a gem. She'd leave my packages and regular mail in a bin if it didn't fit in my mailbox, saving me a trip to the post office during my busy season.

I balanced the box against my hip, opened the door, and then flipped on the light switch that would bring my inflatables to life. The bright, happy Christmas beings and critters always brought me joy. I needed it in abundance tonight.

Ebenezer whistled, shrill and angry from his habitat. He didn't want to stay in there one minute longer. Balancing the box in one hand, I placed the ramp into Ebenezer's area. Better for him to use some of his energy figuring how to get out than me lifting him out. He'd tear through the house. I didn't want him knocking the safety gate into the Christmas tree and bringing it down.

I carried in the box and placed it on the dining room table. Who was Nancy afraid of? Who in town could make her afraid of going to the police? One of the officers? The police chief? Or Mayor Vine. She had worked for him. It was possible the mayor "borrowed" the money from the town and Jenna discovered it, promising to keep quiet if he paid her off. For the plan to work, they'd need money added back into the town's account. The best solution was tying the missing money to Samuel and having me pay it back in order to protect myself, Cassie, and her grandmother.

But, the only way to keep a secret was to make sure only one person knew about it. It was a secret the mayor wouldn't want anyone else to know...and now I did. Did that put me in danger?

While I waited for Bright's advice, I pulled up the picture of the naughty list sign Jenna had made. Besides the names being city council members was there anything else in common? What sort of secrets could Jenna have on them? The only name out of place was Eric. The ugliest thing I knew about him was his drinking and driving problem. That was something everyone in town knew. Why would Jenna add him to her sign?

Had she included him for another reason? Or she thought it best to add a non-council person's name to the list?

The council members all had access to the budget numbers. Did they know about the missing money? Was everyone keeping it quiet from the town? Or was Jenna blackmailing the mayor for something else and one of the other members stole the money. Norman. Pastor Heath. Rachel. My stomach tightened. Another motive for Rachel to have committed the crime. Had Rachel been telling me the truth on how Jenna was killed?

I'm going to the police, I messaged Bright. I'd hand over the receipts I found at Eric's house, let them sort it out. It was better to let the police find out and announce to the town who was a thief. Or more accurately, I didn't want to discover that it was one of my friends.

Good. Because now I don't have to try and convince you that's the right thing.

Which was what deep down in my heart I had wanted: Bright, my partner, the one person whose advice I'd follow, to tell me what to do. I hadn't wanted it all on my shoulders. Having someone to bounce ideas off, to lean on, was what I missed most about having a husband, a companion, a life partner. It was lonely and stressful to always rely on yourself to make huge decisions.

That was what I wanted from Brett, to take some of the responsibility of the decision regarding the winnings, and it wasn't fair. I was keeping him at arm's length, friendship wise, yet was waiting for him to tell me what to do with the money. Not because he was my lawyer, but because I didn't want to make the decision myself. The *wrong* decision myself.

Which was what I had to do. Decide. Myself. It was time to stop using others as an excuse for not making a solid decision or waiting for them to do it for me and then getting a little snippy. Either I was responsible for my life or I wasn't.

I'm asking an officer to come here. I messaged.

What will the neighbors think?

That the police are watching me.

I called Orville's cell phone.

"Talk."

Since Orville preferred brevity, I complied. "I have some potential evidence. Was told Jenna was blackmailing people."

"Where are you?"

"Home."

"Be there in fifteen minutes."

Fifteen minutes didn't give me enough to work on any order. Though it was plenty of time to work myself into a knot of worry. Who else knew I had this evidence? Nancy knew I had the bank slips but threw them away. Had she believed that the police had them now? The diner had been packed. Had anyone overheard us?

Eric. He had to know by now that along with his gun, I took the bank slips that were on the table. Would he come here looking for the items? Or go straight for Cassie?

Cassie is safe. I reminded myself. Repeatedly. Paul was keeping an eye on her. He wouldn't let anything happen to her. Soon, she'd be at her grandmother's house and not at home alone. There was safety in numbers.

Bonnie. Bonnie would be home alone.

The doorbell rang, and I almost jumped out of my skin. I peeled back a corner of the curtain and peeked out. Orville.

I whipped open the door. "Have you found Eric?" Please, please, say yes.

He shook his head. "We're still searching. Matter-of-fact, I have to make this quick. There was a possible sighting of him. You should stay home tonight. We have reason to believe the man is armed."

I grimaced. Not anymore. "The items I have are in my car. And I wouldn't worry about Eric being armed." I walked over and braced myself against the passenger door of my Traverse. He wasn't going to like this one bit.

"Merry, what do you have?"

I opened the car door and stood on the other side, thankful for the physical barrier between me and Orville. "Eric's gun."

"You have what?" His eyes grew two sizes.

"Eric's gun that he pulled on me this morning. When I grabbed the gun from the table, I also picked up bank slips. I didn't think it was a good idea to let him keep the gun. He had threatened Cassie."

"Where is it?" Orville sounded old. Drained. I feared I might be the death, or at least the loss of sanity, for the poor guy.

"In the glove compartment."

Orville retrieved it.

He shut the car door. "Can you do me a favor and stay home?"

"I'll try."

Not very hard. I had to warn Bonnie.

TWENTY

I pulled into Bonnie's driveway and left the engine on. The two-story house was dark. It would be invisible against the night sky if not for the Christmas lights on the houses on either side. What most people hated about winter, the early darkness, was what I loved. The stars shone earlier. Christmas lights were brighter. I hadn't noticed before tonight that it also brought out loneliness. Grief. Cassie's house was devoid of Christmas. There were no decorations on the porch, in the yard, on the house.

Emotions crashed over me, threatening to pull me into an abyss of pain and longing. Lies. Dreams. Secrets. Hopes. All of it was mixed up in the time I spent with Samuel, dating him and then married to him. There were some good memories mixed in with the not so good, I hoped in years to come I'd remember those a little more and have the bad ones fade. I hated feeling so much animosity for a dead man. Cassie would need me, and it would be hard for her to come to me and trust me if she sensed the anger toward her father that was rooted in my heart.

Taking in a deep breath, I slid out of the car and went to the front door. It had been months since I had lived there, and yet it felt like almost a decade. So much had happened to me since I divorced—or thought I had divorced—Samuel: finding him dead, betrayed by a friend, threatened in my own home, almost shot. I wished I could still be that same happy, woman with a child-like attitude of believing and expecting the best from everyone. My life had its ups and downs, but a circumstance had never changed me.

Until now.

I rang the doorbell, hearing it echo though the house. The darkness started making me antsy, conjuring up visions of eyes peered at me from the bushes. I slipped my cell phone from my pocket and clutched it in my hand. I rang the doorbell again and followed it with a knock. My cold fingers felt the word "Waters" that was etched on the knocker. I shoved my hands into my coat pockets. There wasn't a sign of movement in the house. The porch light remained off.

Was Bonnie not home? My mind slipped into judgmental thoughts. How could Bonnie stay in the house of the man who might not have been her husband? Deceived her? Didn't she feel betrayed by him? Or she didn't care because she had loved him? Had I ever truly loved Samuel or had I loved the fact he needed me, and I was once again a mom? In my head I knew that just because my children moved out didn't take away my mom status. My heart had said differently. I had been lost and alone.

Samuel understood what it felt to be left even though our circumstances were different. And later I discovered that Samuel's behavior contributed to women leaving him. The person I felt sorry for was Cassie, a girl who so desperately wanted a mother. I had hoped to fill that need for her. During our tumultuous divorce, I had felt it was best for me to pull back. For my sanity, I needed as little to do with Samuel as possible.

I still had my children. I had people I was connected to—a family to claim and to claim me. With Samuel gone, Bonnie was alone. Her parents had passed away years ago and she had no siblings. No children. And at her age, mid-forties like me, the chance she would find someone was dwindling away. Bonnie and Cassie could become friends, if not a makeshift family for each other. The two had never gotten along though they had declared a truce and treated each other like roommates forced to occupy a living space at a college dorm. I hoped the living situation continued to work out for them. Cassie was only eighteen. Too young to live alone.

Sighing, I walked back to my car and got inside, placing my hands in front of the heater vents. What if I was still married to Samuel? Did that make the house mine? My gut clenched. Could I sign it over to her? Was there still a mortgage? How would Cassie pay it? I had been so wrapped up in the parade and my business, I hadn't even thought about how Cassie was doing financially.

I pulled out my phone and called the one person who could relieve a few of my worries. Brett.

He answered on the second ring. "I still haven't heard anything, Merry. The courts are a little slow with the impending holidays. It is the weekend." He sounded weary.

No greeting. No how was I doing or asking about holiday plans with the kids. Just straight to business. Was I only calling him now when I had a problem? When was the last time I called him to invite him over to share lunch or dinner with me and the kids? Or just to thank him for all the work he was doing to help me straighten out my life? When had I asked about how he was doing? He and his wife had recently separated.

Shame flickered through me. I was handing off a lot of burdens to Brett. He and I had remained friends after our divorce, not just for our children's sake but because we truly liked each other. We made great friends. Lousy married partners. And I wasn't being a good friend lately, I had turned into a me person.

"Sorry. I guess I have been a little pushy." I had wanted to say that I wasn't calling about my issues, but I was tired of dropping little white lies here and there.

"Anything wrong?"

"I'm fine."

Brett and I remained connected, neither of us talking.

"It's been a long week. I didn't mean to make you feel bad if you called to ask a question. I'm your lawyer."

I cringed. That was what I had said I wanted, a professional relationship between us. Lawyer and client. "I miss us also being friends. I feel bad the only reason I call is because of a problem."

"It's not like you're going to call to arrange dates for birthday parties. The kids didn't invite me to either of their last ones."

"Me neither. And I have a feeling it's better that way." From what I heard, Raleigh's last birthday party involved a trip to a casino to see a male revue show. I wasn't up to seeing my daughter put dollar bills in some man's thong.

"What can I help you with?"

I told him my concerns about Cassie's house. "Is there anything we can do?"

"Sign the lottery ticket and pay off the mortgage. It'll be a safe investment for Cassie. She could rent out a room to Bonnie and that would give Cassie some money for monthly living expenses. The majority of the money would remain in a trust account for her and gain interest. The only issue would be going against Helen's wishes. Helen is adamant about not giving Cassie the money."

"I know, she thinks it will ruin Cassie's life. I think I could convince her this is a good idea. Helen's house is falling apart. I might also get Helen to agree to move in with Cassie and Bonnie. There is a bedroom on the first floor."

"Helen's health is declining."

I nodded, even though Brett couldn't see me. "Cassie hasn't noticed yet."

"Maybe she has."

"She hasn't said anything to me."

"Because that would make it real."

I stared at the dark, blank canvas of the house. Samuel's Christmas display had rivaled mine. It was also what drew me to him. I had always told myself if I got married again, it would be to a Christmas man.

Cassie loved Christmas as did her father. It was sad to see the house dark and not one strand of light on the house. It had to be hard for Cassie to want to decorate the house when it was a father-daughter tradition. I should see if my children or Paul could come down and help me decorate it. I was sure he'd lend a hand if asked.

As would Brett.

"What are doing the next few days?"

"Why?"

"There's a house in Season's Greetings that could use some major Christmas cheer."

"I'm free tomorrow."

"Perfect."

Bonnie and I were still navigating our new relationship with each other and weren't at the point yet where we exchanged phone numbers. The only option of finding her was to check out the places she normally frequented, and the only other place I knew was Season's Living. It was likely she picked up extra nursing shifts at the assisted living facility. It was lonely going home to an empty house that had once been filled with love and hopes for the future. I should see what she was doing for Christmas. I hated the thought of her being alone. Her only vice was having fallen in love with Samuel.

Visiting hours were over in about thirty minutes. The parking lot was deserted. The security lights casted a faint orange glow around the lot. I chose the closest spot to the main building, staying in my car for a few minutes and searching for anyone lurking about. Eric knew my mom lived here. I'd be vulnerable at this time of night walking the few yards to the building. No one was out and about.

Stop scaring yourself. I opened the door, tugging on my winter coat. There was a cold bite to the air. My breath hung in little clouds as I walked to the front door. Lights swept across the parking lot. Good. Someone was coming to get in a quick visit. Some of the residents had sons and daughters who always arrived within twenty or so minutes of the ending of visiting hours. They always feigned surprised at having to leave so soon after arriving.

Since I was here, should I stop by my mom's apartment? Usually, I visited on Friday, but the parade had kept me busy and this morning my mom didn't know me. Tonight, I really needed my mom. My heart clenched. Tears welled in my eyes. I couldn't bear it tonight if she still thought of me as the nice lady who taught crafts.

An engine revved. Shielding my eyes from the light, I continued toward the sidewalk, making sure I didn't trip on anything. For some reason, the person in the car was shining their lights on me like I was on a stage and needed to be back lit. The high beams flashed on. The motor revved again.

Panic started to set in. You're fine. You're fine, I told myself, hoping I'd soon believe it. I picked up my pace. The sooner I was in the building, the better I'd feel.

The tires squealed. Rubber stench filled the air as the tires spun on the asphalt. They were going to run me over. I ran for the sidewalk, praying someone else pulled into the lot before the maniac hit me. I heard the car bearing down on me.

I leapt for the sidewalk, hoping it offered me some protection from the car. I landed on the ground, my heavy coat taking the brunt of the impact. I rolled like I was on fire, trying to put as much distance between me and the parking lot.

The car sped away. I stood up. Had it been Eric? A chill raced through me and my legs almost gave out. Get into the building. They might come back. The thoughts spurned me forward. I pulled out my cell phone, clutching it to my heart as I ran for the door. I yanked it open, fumbling to tap in my password so I could call the police.

Angela was sitting in a visiting area nearest the window. She smiled at me. "Coming to see your mom?"

I gaped at her. Hadn't she seen the car? "How long have you been here?"

"A few minutes."

I sat down beside. "Did you see the car in the parking lot? It tried to run me over."

"I saw a car pull to a stop and someone got in. I didn't see you in the lot. They might not have either." She scanned my outfit and frowned. "I don't know why they say no white after Labor Day, a white winter coat would be so much easier to see at night.

Especially with how early night comes."

I checked out my attire. I was wearing jeans and a dark purple coat with a matching stocking cap pulled low on my head. Had my mind conjured up a murder attempt? Was my imagination getting the best of me? I had been thinking about murder all day.

"Are you visiting your mom tonight?" The night receptionist walked over to me, an anxious expression her face. I knew what that meant. My mom was in the past and if her present showed, demanding to be known, it would send my mom into an emotional tailspin the nurses would have to deal with tonight.

"No. I wanted to talk to Bonnie." I sat on the couch next to Angela. "I'll wait here with Angela. I thought you had plans with Norman for the rest of the day."

"After talking to the mayor, he said he had more matters to deal with and it was best I wasn't home alone. He took me to lunch and dropped me back off." She heaved out a sigh. "Our town is becoming so different from what I remembered. It's not the same place I raised my children."

"It's a good place to raise children. It's why I moved here thirteen years ago." I started listing all the pluses of Season's Greetings.

She patted my hand. "Don't feel the need to defend it. All towns grow and change because the people change. Attitudes of the time change. Sometimes for the better. Sometimes not."

"Jenna's murder?"

She nodded. "Never happened before now. Everyone has too many personalities nowadays. Who they are at work, online, church. They're someone different in each place."

"Not everyone," I said. "I'm always the same person. So are my children."

Angela twisted to look directly in my eyes. "Are you sure? You don't act different when talking to customers than friends? Scotland isn't more formal when he's wearing his police officer uniform than hanging out with his mom at home?"

Okay, she had me there. Scotland had to be a different version of himself when he was on duty. But he was still the same person. Still respectful. Still devoted to truth and justice. Still helpful and caring. In his heart, he was the same person. Just a little more formal and with more rules to abide by when he was a police officer.

"Hi, Merry, heard you wanted to talk to me." Bonnie's white coat was draped over her arm along with a bright blue scarf. A few weeks ago, I wondered why Bonnie wore a white coat during winter, now I knew. It was really dark in the parking lot and the bright white coat made her easier to see.

"It was nice catching up with you." I hugged Angela.

"It was nice having someone to chat with." Angela squeezed my hand, her eyes sparkled. "I loved being able to craft again. Those signs were so much fun. I had wanted to make a couple more."

"You're a natural." An idea popped into my mind. "I could use some help catching up on Christmas orders."

"Really?" Angela beamed and clapped her hands.

"Really. I can pick you up at home on Sunday. How does two sound?"

"That would be wonderful." Angela settled back against the seat, smiling and eyes twinkling. With her white hair and the rosy glow in her cheeks, she resembled Mrs. Claus.

Bonnie and I walked a few feet away. "It's nice seeing Angela so happy. She's been rather sad lately."

"It has to be hard knowing you're coming to the end of your life."

"True. And she does spend most of her time in her thoughts. It was nice seeing her take part in the crafting class. I take it you're here about the letter." There was hope and fear and in her blue eyes.

"Letter?"

"Yes. I got a letter from the court in yesterday's mail." With shaking hands, Bonnie pulled it from her coat pocket. "I'm terrified to open it. I was trying to guess by your demeanor if it was good or bad."

"I haven't checked my mail in the last couple of days. I have a bin of it to sort through when I get home."

Bonnie's eyes narrowed. That was the woman I knew. "You might not care if you were married to Samuel, but I do."

It had to be hard, wanting and believing you were married to the man of your dreams, only to find out you were either a bigamist or never married to him. "It's easy for me to ignore my mail since Brett is handling the matter for me. He'd have called if there was major news."

Bonnie's shoulder slumped forward, and she plastered a smile on her face. She shoved the letter back into her pocket. "The mortgage company is questioning the ownership of the home. With no will, everything is in question. I was hoping it was over with."

My heart went out to her. All of Samuel's assets were frozen while the judge sorted through the mess Samuel created with his deceitfulness. "Does Cassie know about any of this?"

Bonnie shook her head. "It didn't seem like something a teenager should be burdened with."

"Do you have anything—note, email, text—where Samuel said he divorced me? That could help. I have plenty of messages where I told people I was divorced."

Bonnie smiled. "I might. I'll send them to your attorney if you think it might help."

"I doubt it would hurt."

"Thanks, Merry." Bonnie slipped on her coat. "What are you doing tonight? Would you like to come over? It'll be nice to have someone to hang out with."

The receptionist walked over to Bonnie and whispered something.

Frowning, Bonnie nodded then came over to me, pulling her phone from her coat pocket. "I have one more task to see to before I head home. I'll give you a call when I leave."

"Everything okay?" I asked even knowing from the expression on Bonnie's face something wasn't all right.

Bonnie patted my arm. "It's not your mom. She's becoming a little more aware of "when" she is. I bet she'd love to see you tomorrow."

I recited my number to Bonnie and then added hers to my contacts.

"I told Norman about my new part-time job." Angela dragged her husband over to me.

"That was a nice offer, Merry." He tilted his head to the side and stared at me.

The scrutiny was making me a little uneasy. Had Orville told him I was concerned he was showing signs of his memory slipping? I hated giving it a more technical term, making it more real. I knew the path that he and Angela might find themselves on. It was a hard road. Stressful. Was Angela healthy enough to handle it?

"Friends help each other out." I smiled at them.

Norman breathed out a sigh of relief. "I'm glad that things are okay between us."

"Why wouldn't they be?" Angela wrung her hands together, her voice taking on a tinge of panic. "Is it because of the fight this morning in the mayor's office?"

"It wasn't a fight, my love, just a slight misunderstanding." Norman patted her hand. "The mayor thought Merry might have been responsible for something but realized she wasn't."

"It didn't help that he had told a few people," I said. "It's over with." I hoped.

Angela tsked. "The mayor shouldn't go around talking bad about people. He's not going to get reelected doing that."

Nor would he once it got out that money was missing. No matter who took it, it wasn't going to bode well for the mayor—which gave the mayor a good motive for murder. Where had he been the night of parade? I didn't remember him being there. The mayor attended every year. Even finding a way to ride on whichever float was likely to be the town's favorite, besides Santa's sleigh. Only Santa was allowed on it.

I was sure the police would find that highly interesting. I made a mental note to pass it on to Orville, not so much believing the mayor had a motive for murder but that I hadn't seen him at the parade. Maybe the key to finding the murder was pinpointing who hadn't been there that night. The person who committed the crime would want to be as far away as possible.

"The mayor has spoken with the forensic accountant and everything should be cleared up shortly."

"With who?" Why did Norman think the matter was resolved if a forensic accountant was involved? No one could just put back money. The accountant would know. What had I been thinking even contemplating going along with that plan? I'd be trying to cover up for a crime, maybe not as bad as having embezzled the money but it wouldn't be seen as a positive thing.

"The man the mayor hired. You mentioned meeting him."

Jack. Why hadn't Norman mentioned that in the mayor's office?

"I have to go." I spun toward the door, my mind tumbling with unkind words I wanted to scream at Jack and excuses to give Bonnie on why I was bailing on our plans.

TWENTY-ONE

I jumped into my vehicle and started the engine. Leaving it in park, I snagged my cell from my purse and called Bonnie. "I have to cancel. But I need you not to go home alone. Cassie and Helen are having dinner tonight. You should join them."

Bonnie drew in a sharp breath. "Why? Where are you?"

"In the parking lot. I don't have a lot of time to explain. Just please stay somewhere else tonight."

"I'll be at your car in two minutes. Don't leave or I'll call the police and tell them you're in trouble."

Heaving out a breath, I slumped against the car seat. This wasn't going the way I planned. I wanted to keep Bonnie safe not drag her into this mess like I had Cassie. I should've listened to Orville and stayed home.

There was a light tap on my window. Bonnie pointed at the car lock. I unlocked the doors and Bonnie slid onto the passenger seat. Turning sideways, she dropped her purse onto the floor and settled into the seat. "Start from the beginning."

"That will take a long time."

"At least tell me why I shouldn't go home, and what is going on with Rachel. I heard you were there when she was hauled out of One More Page in handcuffs."

The incident was getting around town. "I went to talk to Eric Wilcox and it didn't go well."

Her eyes narrowed. "Merry, what aren't you saying?"

I was churning up some reasons in my mind and stopped, settling on telling the truth. I needed to share with someone, and Bonnie loved Samuel. There was no way she'd pass this on to anyone else. "Mayor Vine told me that Samuel had borrowed money from the town with the intent of paying it back from the lottery winnings. From what I understood, Samuel made the deal with Jenna."

Slowly, Bonnie shook her head back and forth. "No. He wouldn't have done that. It's not true."

I kept my opinion to myself. While I had defended Samuel against stealing, borrowing I could see him doing. "That's what I went to find out and when I didn't see Eric, I looked around a bit. Eric caught me and forced me to go inside and talk to him."

"Forced." Anger tinged her voice. "Did he hurt you?"

I shook my head. "He threatened to go after Cassie if I left. I was able to leave, and I'm worried he'll try and come after her...especially now that Rachel's been arrested. I didn't want you alone at the house."

"Why would that—" Bonnie covered her mouth with her hand, eyes widening. "The police think Rachel and Eric are somehow involved in Jenna's death."

"She is," I whispered, holding back a sob.

Bonnie pulled me into a hug. "Honey, I'm so sorry. I know how close you two are. Your poor heart just can't get a break lately."

"Now, Cassie is mad at me."

"She'll get over it." Bonnie leaned back, keeping her hands on my shoulders. "Cassie's world has been turned upside down again, and she's mad at you because you're her safe person. She knows you'll forgive her and move past it."

Was Bonnie right? Cassie saw me as her safety net? "I don't know..."

"I do. Cassie adores you. Even if she's forgets it from time to time. It's the same thing I see with my patients. When they feel overwhelmed by their situation, they lash out at the people they know won't turn away from them." Bonnie buckled up. "I'm ready.

Let's go."

"Where are we going?"

Bonnie shrugged. "Your house or mine. It doesn't matter. You don't think I should be alone, and I don't think you should either. I'd start driving before someone wonders why this car is hanging out in front of Season's Living and calls the police."

That was definitely something I didn't want and from the resolve on Bonnie's face, she wasn't getting out. "The first place Eric is liable to show up at is my home."

"Then my place it is."

"I don't think that's a good idea." The words choked out of me. My heart started to race and sweat broke out on my forehead.

"Where else do you suggest? It's either my house or yours. Unless you want to crash Cassie's dinner with Helen."

I shook my head. Where were we going to go? I shifted the vehicle out of park and pulled onto the road, hoping a place popped into my head. The fact was it was either my place or Bonnie's. Neither one seemed like the best choice.

"You don't want to go inside my house." Bonnie placed a comforting hand on my arm. "You don't have a lot of good memories there."

Not many. I had some. And they were all wrapped up with Christmas. Actually, the majority of my happy memories in this house was of Cassie. Being her mom. Having her blossom as my daughter.

"I had good ones." I choked out. "I allowed myself to forget. I focused on the negative. I—"

"Left a man who didn't love you. There's nothing wicked in that. You couldn't stay in the marriage for Cassie."

"I could've kept being her mom." I tightened my hold on the steering wheel.

"I wouldn't have allowed it."

"You didn't stop me." I flicked my gaze toward her. The look in her eyes told me to listen.

"I would've. There was no way I'd have let you be a part of

Samuel's life. Reminding him of what I lacked. I'm not a mothering type. I knew that from a young age."

"You mother the patients at the nursing home."

"I like old people. Never liked babies. My grandparents raised me and then my younger siblings. My mom passed us off once we were no longer at the baby stage. My mother loved babies. Wasn't so fond of children."

"I'm so sorry." I hadn't known that about Bonnie. Actually, there was so much I didn't know about her. I had narrowed down her identity to Samuel's new wife who didn't like her stepdaughter. There was so much more to her. She had deep hurts that affected how she related to people.

"It's the past." She tried to brush it aside.

"It's also in your present," I said. "It's why you're having trouble bonding with Cassie."

"She's eighteen, Merry. She doesn't want another mother. The girl has had worse luck with them than me."

The light turned red. I looked at Bonnie. Her face was full of sadness and regret. "How about her friend? There's still a chance to have a relationship with her."

Bonnie tilted her head to the side, holding still for a long moment before nodding. "A friend. I can do that."

"How about you order pizza for pick up, and we can do some Christmas decorating. At your house. I'll just need to swing by my place first and pick up Ebenezer. I don't want to leave him alone all night."

"Sounds good. I'm so glad the new pizza place has an app. I hate making phone calls." Bonnie tapped on her phone. "I've been wanting to decorate the house but haven't because I start wondering if it's too soon for Cassie. Christmas was her and her dad's thing...that they shared with you. I didn't want to intrude. What if I'm wrong? What if she didn't want to ignore Christmas but didn't know how to start and thought I didn't want it?"

The light turned green and I headed for the pizza place. The first year after a loss was gut-wrenching. It was hard enough to remember to breathe, trying to celebrate something—anything—could make you feel like your lungs were being crushed. That first Christmas after my father died was a blur for me and my mom. We had carried on, went through the motions of decorating as it had been our special time. The holidays were when I was brought magically into their lives. My mom didn't want to lose that. Said she needed it, to celebrate that happiest of days that had brought her and my dad so many more.

Just because the sightings and sounds of Christmas filled my spirit and eased some of my grief and turmoil, didn't mean it did the same for everyone else. I wanted Cassie to love the season again, not grow to hate and associate it with bad times.

Samuel had always been the one to orchestrate the holidays for him and his daughter, until last year when I was part of their life. It had then been us. The only really "us" thing between me and Samuel. I shouldn't have put so much stock in that area, shelving our relationship in the perfect category because we did Christmas amazing together. Because of that one thing, I had ignored all the non-us moments, all the differences of opinion we had on most other topics. Cassie needed Christmas. Needed good memories of her dad.

"Cassie was pilfering through my Christmas t-shirts today to find the perfect one to wear to work," I said. "She took a couple of extras also."

"That has to mean she wants to participate in Christmas."

I nodded. "She was reading Christmas stories to the children and looked so happy. Also, she was wearing a hat with elf ears and made her co-worker wear one as well."

Bonnie smiled. "I do believe we can do with some Christmas magic in the house. Let's pick up Ebenezer and decorate the night away."

"First, the pizza since it's on the way." I flipped on the radio and Elvis Presley singing "I'm Dreaming of a White Christmas" flowed from the speakers. The sound of his deep voice sent a calmness through me. It characterized strength, steadfastness, and optimism. Everything I longed for.

Bonnie sighed and settled back against the seat. "That's how you sing Christmas."

I reached the small stretch of road where it appeared that you were leaving Season's Greetings. For almost a mile, there were trees on both sides of the road and no businesses. It was a like a forest sprang up in the middle of town, an undecorated forest as it was the only section of town with no Christmas decorations. It was also deer central. Most accidents between deer and cars happened on this small stretch of road. Residents had petitioned for lights, but it was always vetoed. To the east of me, the trees blocked the view of Jingle All the Way, the local dive bar. Something most people in town appreciated, the ones who didn't want it known that it existed and those who didn't want people knowing of their comings and goings from it. On the west side was a small apartment complex. The renters on the backside of the complex feared the lights would keep them awake and also encourage the deer to migrate into their yards.

"I see some movement by the trees." Bonnie pointed toward the wooded area on the passenger side.

I slowed down, alternating my gaze from the road in front of me to the tree line. In the distance, on my right, a large shape moved from a small patch of grass on the side and went across, now moving toward. What was it? A huge deer? Bigfoot? Headlights flashed on. A car.

I hoped it wasn't a drunk driver. There had to be some reason the vehicle had pulled off the side of the road and turned off its headlights. Or it was someone trying to figure out how to turn them on. But why pull back on the road before they turned on the headlights?

"What were they doing?" I asked.

"Who knows. People behave strangely at night," Bonnie said. "Might be someone trying to find the small dirt road leading to the bar as they don't want to use the main entrance."

"Hopefully they find it on the next pass or figure it's better to go home rather than trying to sneak into a bar."

"I wonder..." Bonnie trailed off.

"What?"

"Could it be Eric?"

"I'm sure he knows exactly where that road is," I said.

In a way I hoped it was Eric because if he was on this road, he wasn't near Cassie and Helen. Was he trying to track me down? Had he guessed I'd go to talk to Bonnie, and was waiting for me and planned on turning around and getting behind me? But wouldn't it have been easier to wait until I passed? Unless they planned on hitting into the side of my vehicle, though he'd need a larger car than his two-door truck to knock my Traverse into the trees. Or so I hoped.

The vehicle heading south was almost beside me. It was a white twelve-passenger van. Large enough to damage my car. I clenched the steering wheel.

"Look out!" Bonnie jabbed a finger toward the passenger side window.

A dark shape tipped toward the road.

I swerved, almost directly into the path of the van. The object hit the side of the car. The van sped up, inching toward the soft shoulder and zipped around me.

"It's a person!" Bonnie screamed, grabbing the handle above the door. "Stop!"

Tears rushed into my eyes and I slammed on the brakes. My car slid into the other lane. I fought with the wheel, trying to get back on the correct side of the road and not hitting the person again. My legs were shaking. I went for the brake—and hit the gas instead. Trees loomed before us. I tugged the wheel away from the trees, spinning my car in a half-circle.

Bonnie screamed. I pumped the brakes, coming to a stop a few yards away from where the person ran out into the road. My heart was hammering. My vehicle was sideways, though back in the lane that would've taken me home.

"Are you okay?" I faced Bonnie and unbuckled my seatbelt.

She looked into the rearview mirror and then at me. "They're not moving."

Bonnie bolted out of the car. I turned on my hazards, jumped out and ran to the figure laying in the middle of the road.

Bonnie was kneeling beside the person, fingers pressed against their neck.

"Are they okay?" I wrapped my arms around myself, the cold seeping through the fabric of my coat.

Bonnie stood, trying to block the person from me. "Call 911."

I froze in the middle of the street. An overwhelming scent of alcohol wafted toward me. Laying on the ground, face up, was Eric. A dead Eric Wilcox. Clutched tightly in his left hand was a Christmas-hued scarf, gold fringes splayed across the asphalt.

Red and blue lights swirled around in the night, dancing across the asphalt, giving almost a cheery dance club vibe to the horrible scene. Orville was placing flares in the road while another officer directed traffic, which had picked up since the accident. An ambulance was pulled to the side of the road. The back door was opened, and the stretcher remained inside. There was nothing the paramedics could do for Eric.

A sheet was draped over Eric's body. The lights bounced off and around him. Every time I looked away, my attention returned. My emotions battled each other. Relief that Cassie was safe was followed by shame for feeling something other than sadness at a man's death.

Brianna was blocking the looky loos who lived in the apartment building from checking out the deceased. A couple of people had cell phones ready to be the first to post the news to the town's social media page. A shiver worked its way from my head to my toes. I wanted to throw up. I leaned against my vehicle, wrapping my arms tightly around myself.

Standing near the shoulder where Eric had emerged, Chief Hudson was talking to Bonnie. She pointed toward the spot where

Eric had stumbled out into the road.

"I didn't hit him that hard." My words were barely a whisper.

Keeping my hands tucked against my side, I walked to the front passenger side of my car. The headlights were still on. There wasn't a crack in the headlight. There wasn't any damage to my car. How could I have killed him? Tears ran down my face. I didn't. I didn't kill him. I knew it deep within me. Eric had been dead before he hit my car.

Shame rushed through. Eric was dead, and I was blaming him for it. Why had he stepped out into the road? Especially knowing a car was driving by. It was dark. He had to have seen the headlights. Or had he been hoping to get hit? If Eric knew Rachel had been brought in for questioning, he knew it was only a matter of time before he was arrested for his wife's murder. My mind returned to the fact that my car had no damage. I hadn't killed him.

What had happened to Eric?

I closed my eyes, forcing into my mind the minutes before impact. "He fell into the road. He didn't walk out into it."

"Are you sure about that?" Orville asked.

I startled, jerking forward and banging my leg into the bumper. "Yes. He kind of tipped into the road, toward my car. I bet he was at the bar. Surprised you guys didn't go looking for him there."

Inching his head slightly to the side, Orville stared at me, face devoid of expression. I read him loud and clear. It was such an obvious place, they had looked for Eric there, and had instructed the owner to call them when Eric showed up.

"I'm sorry. Of course, you did. This doesn't make any sense to me." I swiped away the fresh tears running down my face. "I didn't kill him. I know I didn't kill him."

"Aw, Merry, it wasn't you fault. Eric probably tied on a good one at the bar. It's dark. The guy walked out right in front of you. You didn't see him." Orville patted my back. "Don't you worry about this. No one is arresting you."

"I. Didn't. Kill. Him." I said each word loudly and as clear as I could with my voice shaking and tears clogging it. He had to understand. I needed him to understand that. "Look. There's no damage to my car."

Orville inspected my car. "It was likely his head slamming onto the asphalt that killed him."

The coroner van pulled up.

"You and Bonnie can leave," Orville said. "If we have any more questions, the Chief or I will get a hold of you. Would you like me to call someone for you?"

"I swear, Orville, he fell into the road and hit the side of my car."

Orville sighed. "I understand this is upsetting for you. You don't want to carry around a burden like this—"

The van. "There was—"

He held up his hand to silence me. "It was an accident, Merry. Go home. I can have someone take you if you'd like. I want you to leave while we finish processing the scene. You don't want to stick around while we do that."

He was right. I didn't. "Can someone drive Bonnie home? I just want to go my house. Crawl into bed."

He smiled at me softly and patted my shoulder. "Sure can, Merry. You just go home and tuck yourself in. If you need anything, give me a call."

I nodded, not trusting myself to say anything. Orville might pick up on the fact I knew something was wrong. What the scene of the crime was portraying wasn't the truth. Eric didn't stumble out into the road and die after getting hit by a car. He was lying face up, a couple feet away from where he tripped into my car. Eric hadn't died on impact. He crawled to that spot.

Orville paused, turning back to look at me. I held in a breath. He knew it too.

TWENTY-TWO

The inflatable ménage in my front yard cheerfully blinked, waved, or stayed still while lighting up the neighborhood. Even the sight of all the decorations didn't pick up my dwindling spirits. This was one of the worst Christmas seasons ever. Found out I wasn't divorced. Cassie was angry at me. Samuel was murdered. Helen was dying. Jenna was murdered. Rachel helped hide Jenna's body. Eric was dead, someone killed him and had hoped to cover it up by shoving him in front of my car.

Tears tumbled down my face. For the first time in my life, I desperately wanted the holidays over. All the happiness and cheer made the horror and sadness worse. No wonder some people hid from the holiday.

"Rachel, why?"

She knew what I went through being wrongfully accused of Samuel's murder. How could she do that to someone else? Love was supposed to make you a better person—not worse. There were a lot of good men in Season's Greetings. Why pick Eric? Someone else's husband and a man known to love his alcohol a little more than his wife. While I wanted to let Rachel fend for herself in her legal matter, there was something in me that couldn't write my friend completely off. It wasn't her livelihood that was at stake, it was her life.

There was something stirring in my mind, making me feel like I was missing something. It weaved in and out of my overloaded brain. Or it could just be I wanted to be missing something so the truth was no longer the truth. I hated the truth. I hated that one of my best friends helped conceal a murder. A murder her married paramour tried to pin on someone else.

I pulled into my driveway. Why Norman? Had they hoped Norman would also be blamed for the embezzling, allowing Eric to sneak away with the money? Or had Eric wanted to implicate someone else—Pastor Heath and Sarah—but it was easier to place the body into the sleigh. The pastor likely kept the church's vans locked. Van. A van had driven past me. A white twelve-passenger van. Just like the one Harmony Baptist purchased.

Hammy blinked on and off. The curtains across the street peeled back and then fluttered close. Cornelius was shooting me one of his death stares. If there was one thing he hated more than a large inflatable creature, it was a large inflatable creature that blinked and was directly across from his window.

I smiled over at his house. The brief moment of merriment ended the moment the black jeep parked in Cornelius's driveway registered in my head. A similar car to the one Jack drove. Carefully, I made my way to the edge of my driveway and squinted, trying to make out the tags. I couldn't read the numbers, but it was an out of state plate. I was certain it was Jack's vehicle.

Why was the forensic auditor at Cornelius's house? Spying on me?

Sharp whistles floated out to me. Ebenezer had escaped and was at the front door, either trying to protect the house from intruders or hoping to make a break for it once the door opened. I couldn't leave Ebenezer alone, who knew what chaos the critter would cause now that he was free, and I was at my threshold for chaos.

There was an oblong shaped package leaning against my door. What had I ordered? This was not only the season of joy, love, and goodwill toward men but shopping for presents and inventory items. It was either more vinyl or the new makeup mirror I bought my daughter Raleigh.

I grabbed the package and opened the door, using my feet and the box to block Ebenezer's escape route. I flicked on the light that controlled the inside lights. My Christmas tree cast a flickering of green, red, blue, and yellow light around the room. The line of glass blocks glowed. The event that should've brought some pride for a job well done now filled me with sadness. I placed the package down and unplugged the blocks, darkening the representations of the floats.

Quickly, I disassembled the line-up and shoved the blocks into a corner of the living room, at the last moment grabbing an afghan and tossing it over the bunch. I'd deal with them in the morning. I picked up the package and froze. My mail had been delivered earlier. This hadn't been left by the mail carrier. I stared at the package. There wasn't a return address on the box.

Where had it come from? With trembling hands, I carefully opened the box. I gasped. In the package was a naughty list sign—with my name last on the list.

The one that had Jenna and Eric's name was with the police. Evidence. Where did this one come from? It looked exactly like the one I made. The original one I had made for Rachel had been stolen. Eric? Had he left the sign at my door before he drank himself to oblivion—which resulted in his death.

There was one person who'd know for sure. Cornelius. There were two things the old man enjoyed about life: spying and tattling. He'd have noticed who dropped off the package.

I tucked Ebenezer under my arm like a football. "Come on, buddy, we're going to visit a neighbor."

Ebenezer wasn't so much of a protection animal more like an early warning system. He hated most people and made a horrific sound, a cross between a high-pitched whistle and nails on the chalk board. If the critter sensed someone nearby, he'd sound his ear-piercing alarm. I should've listened to it when Sarah Heath showed up at my doorstep.

His furry body tensed. Ebenezer sputtered out small hissing sounds. I spun, crossing my other arm over Ebenezer to protect him. A fiber optic scarf blew gently in the wind. I planted a kiss on Ebenezer's head. "I guess you don't like eight-foot tall hamsters. Don't worry. Hammy won't hurt you."

I had a feeling Ebenezer doubted it. His body didn't relax until after we crossed the street. I knocked on Cornelius's door.

The curtain moved. Cornelius peered out, green eyes glaring at me. "Can't you tell it's dark outside?" He yelled through the closed door. "Decent people don't come visiting at this hour."

"I'm not visiting. I'm here for information. Did you see who put a package at my door?"

"I'm not your doorman." The curtain fell back into place.

"Someone put a naughty list with my name on it at my door."

A barrage of deadbolts clicked out from the cylinder. The door was cracked open, showing one of Cornelius's eyes. He looked a little amused. "Now why would someone go and do that?"

"Not sure."

Ebenezer wiggled in my arms, trying to get a sniff at the eyeball peering out at us.

"Let me guess, you've been making someone's business yours that you shouldn't have been."

"This isn't the first naughty sign to show up with someone's name on it. They took a risk stopping by my house. Everyone knows you keep an eye on what's going on around here."

"True. So, that makes this our problem." Cornelius opened the door wider, motioning for me to come inside. "This is what I get for deciding to live near a nosy woman. I hadn't heard anything about a sign. I'd have kept a better watch if I'd known those were being placed around town."

I decided not to remind him that I had moved in second. "Don't tell anyone I told you about the sign. The police wouldn't be happy with me. It's not common knowledge."

"Lately, they don't ever seem to be happy with you. Orville looked downright miffed when he was at your place earlier." His eyes widened. "Was it another sign?"

"Other items related to the Wilcox case."

His mouth twitched, fighting a smile. "You a suspect again."

"No." I squealed as Ebenezer wiggled himself, behind first, from my grasp and plopped onto the floor. He scurried down the hallway.

"You brought a rodent into my house." Cornelius took off after Ebenezer.

"He's a guinea pig."

"Makes him a rodent. Look it up." Cornelius shouted at me.

"Great. Now he's under there."

I followed after Cornelius, stopping just before I stepped fully into his living room. I gawked. I felt lightheaded, giddiness rushed through. His living room was a Christmas spectacular. There were multicolored Christmas lights strung up on the wall. A wooden handmade creche with wooden handmade nativity figures was under the Christmas tree. White lights were attached to the roof and inside the manger, twinkling a heavenly glow around the Holy family.

Every inch of the room had an ode to Christmas, whether it was a Santa figurine, a miniature Christmas scene, or a wireless musical decoration. The room looked like the most amazing Christmas store ever. I didn't know Cornelius had this type of over-the-top, every inch full of holiday charm, Christmas bedazzled at the finest, in him. I was kind of in love.

Ebenezer's furry head poked out from behind the creche. His eyes glowing evilly from the effect of the lights above his head. Gazing up at the lights, Ebenezer rose and opened his mouth, ready to gnaw on the tempting wires.

"He better not bite it." Cornelius glared at my furry sidekick, who was taking an interest in the lights on the tree.

"I'll get him." I dropped to my hands and knees. Ebenezer's eyes lit up and he wiggled his nose and scampered out, hiding behind the presents located near the wall. "We're not playing hide and seek, you rascal. Get out from under there."

Flattening myself to the floor, I shimmied underneath. Ornaments jingled and jangled. The branches swayed.

"You better not break anything."

"Ebenezer, you're not being a very good guest." I moved presents out of the way. For someone who didn't like Christmas, Cornelius sure did complete a lot of shopping this holiday season. He wasn't quite the curmudgeon of Christmas that I pegged him for.

"Why did you bring that creature with you?" Cornelius voice came from up above.

I glanced up. Cornelius had moved aside a branch and was glaring down at me. "Because he's not that into people."

"Well, I ain't that in to him."

Neither was I at the particular moment. The critter was taunting me. Ebenezer cha-chaed a few inches from my fingertips, moving closer than farther. "It was dark and if someone was trying to sneak up on me, he'd let me know."

"Why would anyone do that?"

"For the same reason they left a naughty sign with my name on it."

"You brought a rodent into their house too."

"No. It was...never mind." Why did I think talking to Cornelius would get me any information? The man was about as cooperative as Ebenezer. A door started to open.

I froze. Jack. I had totally forgotten about his car being outside. What if he had left the sign by my door? Not one motive popped into my head. A huge change for me as lately I was good at thinking of reasons for people to be added to a naughty list.

Ebenezer whizzed past me.

"Stop him." I wiggled out, doing everything in my power not to knock over Cornelius's Christmas tree. Long, muscled arms snagged Ebenezer before he made it out of the living room.

"Uncle Corn, why is there a woman under the tree?" Jack asked.

I scooted backwards as fast as my knees allowed. Watching me with amusement was veteran, former bodyguard of the mayor, and forensic auditor, Jack—Cornelius' nephew.

"I didn't know you had a nephew." Or a niece and grand nephews and nieces. Though, I did see the family resemblance in the behavior shared by Jack's niece and his uncle.

Jack's brows quirked up and he turned toward his uncle. Ebenezer tried to break out of Jack's firm hold. With what sounded like a defeated sigh, Ebenezer relaxed his body, feet and head dangling down. He looked like a floppy, stuffed toy.

"What are you doing here?" I narrowed my eyes on Jack.

"I thought we established that." There was a twinkle in Jack's eyes. "Visiting family."

Okay, he had me there. He wasn't over here for forensic auditing business. "You lied to me."

His brows quirked up. "Excuse me."

"You. Lied. To. Me. You said you were a security guard."

Cornelius snorted.

"No, you thought I was security guard and I just went along with it. Seemed better to have a cover, and it was a valid reason for searching items and asking questions."

"You had no right to go through my bag. What would you have done if you had found something? It wouldn't have been allowed as evidence in a court of law."

"The mayor was more interested in getting the money back than charging anyone with the crime." Jack sounded disappointed. "He was certain you'd hand over the cash."

"I had nothing to do with it." I stared at Cornelius with desperation in my gaze. I couldn't stand for anyone to think I was a thief and in cahoots with Samuel. Who I was almost certain hadn't borrowed or stolen the money. The police had gone through Samuel's finances when he was murdered. They'd have found a large chunk of money that showed up in his back account without a job attached to it.

"That's what I told him. Kids don't listen too well these days." Cornelius righted the tree I had knocked askew. "The mayor only brought you and your maybe-husband into it because of the money. But apparently someone else feels differently."

"What does that mean?" Jack asked him.

"Someone left the lady a sign with her name on it."

Jack's features scrunched up in confusion.

"A naughty list. The last—" I stopped talking. I probably shouldn't share the last two people whose names I saw on a naughty list were now dead. And one of them was my first choice in having left the sign. Maybe, Jack saw someone. "Did you see anyone by my house? Or a package by my door when you arrived?"

"No. I went over to your place right after I got here and there wasn't anything by your front door. I've been in the attic dragging down Uncle Corn's outside decorations."

He had outside decorations? Since I moved in, Cornelius had never placed even one string of lights on his house. Focus. Cornelius newfound Christmas love was not any of my concern. Could simply be his great-niece loved Christmas and he didn't want to get on the child's bad side. "What time did you stop by?"

"About twenty minutes ago."

It wasn't Eric. Twenty minutes ago, I was talking to the police about Eric stumbling into the road. Who had left the sign?

"Are you okay?" Jack asked, stepping toward me.

Ebenezer flung himself toward me, like he sensed I needed some comfort. I opened my arms and caught Ebenezer as he managed to escape Jack's grasp. Ebenezer placed his front feet on my shoulders and cuddled into my cheek. My daughter had been right, getting a pet was a good idea. I stroked his soft fur.

"It wasn't Eric," I croaked out.

"Who put the sign at your door," Jack finished the sentence.

"How can you be sure of that?" Cornelius asked. "The man doesn't like you."

My legs felt shaky. I sat on the ground. "Because he was dead."

"What's going on?" Jack squatted beside me.

"Twice I've found a sign that had additional names on it. Both of those people are dead."

"What?" The men stared at me.

"After Norman and I found Jenna's body in the bag, the

naughty sign in One More Page's window had her name on it. This afternoon, I found the same sign—that had been taken from me—in the garbage with Eric's name on it." I swallowed the lump of fear growing in my throat. "Twenty minutes ago, Eric was being removed off the asphalt after having fallen onto the road in front of my car."

"Now your name is on it." Jack frowned. "I don't like this."

Neither did I.

Cornelius headed for the kitchen. "I'm calling the police."

"Do you have any idea who could've left the sign?"

I shrugged. The person I had really ticked off was now dead and the other one—Rachel—was in jail. "Maybe it doesn't mean anything."

"Do you really think that?"

I wanted to.

I sat on Cornelius's couch, a sleeping Ebenezer in my arms as Orville collected evidence—the wrapping paper and sign—from my house. It was not being taking lightly. I had asked him numerous times about Rachel and the investigation into Eric's death and received no response. Not even a stop asking me.

What now? Or rather who? The only other person I had irritated was Sarah Heath. She wasn't the leave a passive aggressive threat on someone's door, more the barge into the house and confront them type.

The image of a van flashed into my head. I hadn't told Orville about the van. He had cut me off when I tried to earlier, probably thinking I was once again going to say I didn't kill Eric.

Jack and Cornelius, who were whispering in a corner, stared at me. Neither man looked pleased. Probably had overstayed my welcome. All my presence had done was involve them in a possible threat to my life and allowed Ebenezer to taste-test a few of Cornelius's decorations. I had wanted to leave but decided this time to follow Orville's directive and "stay put" until after he retrieved the items from my house. I had borrowed a jacket from Cornelius, zipped it up hallway and placed Ebenezer into the makeshift pouch. So far, it had contained my little buddy, and Ebenezer was snoozing away.

The front door opened, and Orville stepped inside scanning the room. "Everything's clear. You can return home."

I rose and jostled Ebenezer. He snorted and resettled into the jacket pouch. "I just remembered that a car drove by right before Eric fell into the road. A twelve-passenger van."

"We should discuss that elsewhere." Orville glanced in Jack and Cornelius's direction.

My face heated. "They know about Eric dying."

Orville pressed his lips together. He was avoiding looking at me. There was something he wasn't telling me, and he wished he could.

Jack was watching both of us. "With Jenna having been killed, and now Eric dying, the mayor isn't going to be able to keep the missing money under wraps. There are a few members in town who already know about it."

Orville sighed. "I know. You. Cornelius. The pastor and his wife. Norman. Rachel. Merry."

"And Nancy," I added.

"People are going to bring Merry's name into it," Jack said. "The mayor isn't going to take the blame for it. He's made that clear to me."

Orville faced me. "It might be best if you stayed somewhere else tonight. Just until I find out who left the sign there."

"I have a good guess...the person who was driving the twelve-passenger van."

"There are a lot of places someone could've been or heading to besides your house."

My face heated again. It was either the start of hot flashes, or my conscience giving me a physical scolding. It wasn't nice to throw the pastor or his wife out as a suspect based on the fact Sarah was rude to me. "I'll be fine at home."

"That's not a good choice," Jack said.

"If someone is after me, I don't want to put anyone else at risk." Already did that once today and it wasn't a burden I wanted to carry again.

"You can stay here," Cornelius said, a little begrudgingly. "I have a couch."

I was shocked that he offered. Though, I have a feeling his nephew pressured him to do so. "While I appreciate it, I don't want to put you and your nephew at risk."

"He doesn't stay here," Cornelius said. "I doubt your rodent will let anyone sneak in here."

"I will stay here tonight." Jack crossed his arms. "I won't leave the two of you alone."

"Likely a smart thing," Orville said. "Those two don't get along too good."

"Cornelius and I are present."

"I'm not saying anything that isn't the truth," Orville said. "Maybe you can visit your kids in Morgantown."

There was no way I was going to bring whatever trouble I might have stepped into to my children. "No."

"Come on, Merry, be reasonable. You need to be somewhere safe or where the police can keep an eye on you. I can't really stay here all night," Orville said. "And Brianna has been pulling sixteen hour shifts since the murder. Heck, we all have."

I felt bad. For someone who didn't like to cause strife, I sure was contributing a lot of it to my friends' lives. How could I relieve their concerns and mine? The RV. I grinned. It was perfect.

Orville groaned. "I don't like that look."

"It's perfect. Trust me."

Orville rolled his eyes.

"My RV. I can stay in it tonight."

"How's that going to help?" Orville crossed his arms over his barrel chest, courtesy of muscles and a bullet resistant vest.

"I'll park in the police station's parking lot."

TWENTY-THREE

When I bought the RV, I had envisioned many places I'd stay overnight: campgrounds, RV parks, schools, even Walmarts. A police station never entered my mind. I knelt on the couch in the main living space of the RV and peered out the window. What was going on in there? There were a couple of police cruisers parked in front of the station, and I could see lights shining from the windows but no movement. I was parked at the farthest end of the station, facing it in a spot where I didn't block the entrance and wasn't too much of a spectacle.

Ebenezer squealed and scratched at the couch. I leaned over and lifted him up. "Nothing going on. See?" I held him up to the window.

There was nothing going on. Or at least nothing I could see. I should just go to sleep, there wasn't much else to do besides spying on the police station, as I hadn't retrieved any of my cutting machines or laptop from my house. I had wanted to show Orville I was going to be safe and snagged the keys from my house and jumped into the RV. Also, forgot about bringing a change of clothes. Fortunately, my holiday attire was quite comfortable.

I could turn on the television and find a Christmas movie to watch. Hallmark played them 24/7 this time of the year. There was enough gas in the tank to keep the generator operational overnight. We'd be relatively warm and entertained. I'd feel better sleeping on the couch then tucked into the bedroom in the back of the RV.

The parking lot turned brighter. A beam of headlights lighted the way to the police station. I leaned closer to the window, my nose almost touching the glass. A dark colored jeep parked in front of the station.

Jack? I ran to the craft area and stared out the window across from my work station, hoping to get a better look at the person entering the station. I couldn't tell, though I was pretty sure it was Jack. Was he coming to the station to turn in evidence regarding the embezzling?

There was one way to find out, ask him. I made coffee and a bowl of popcorn. After snagging a blanket from the bedroom, I made my way down the step, raising up my glasses as the cold air fogged them up. I settled on the bottom step, tucking part of the blanket underneath me to ward off the chill and being careful not to spill the mug of coffee in my other hand. The popcorn bowl was beside me. The haze started to leave my glasses. It was the one thing I really disliked about winter, going from the warmth of a house or car to the outdoors usually blinded me for a few minutes.

From inside the motorhome, Ebenezer made noises of displeasure. Either he was missing my company or irritated that I was out while he was trapped inside. Or he wanted to eat my snack. I popped some kernels into my mouth. I felt safe sitting outside as the back of the RV faced the road leading to and from the police station. Someone would have to drive into the lot or walk around the RV to get to me, either way I'd see them. I stretched out my legs and hid my hands under the blanket for a few minutes before I snuck one out to grab another handful of popcorn.

After I'd eaten half the bowl of popcorn and drank my cup of coffee, a figure left the police station. They stood underneath a security light and stared in my direction. Jack.

I waved. "Hello, neighbor. Care to sit for a spell?"

Jack jogged over. "I don't know how Officer Martin would feel about you sitting out here at night."

"No one will be able to sneak up on me. Besides, who's going to take the chance of doing something to me while I'm in the parking lot of the police station."

"A person who's already killed two people."

I gaped at him. "What?"

"Let's go inside where it's warmer and safer." Jack gathered up my snack while I hitched up the ends of the blanket.

Opening the door, I held out the blanket, hoping Ebenezer thought it was an impenetrable barrier. "What do you mean two?"

"From what I gathered, Eric didn't die because of the car accident."

"How do you know this?" I was right. I hadn't killed him—even by accident. Did Eric have a massive heart attack or something—or was he murdered before being pushed in front of my car?

"I overheard some officers discussing it."

"Overheard or eavesdropped?"

Jack poured us some coffee. Sitting down, he handed me a cup. "Both."

"Why did you come to the station tonight?"

"It was past time for me to give the police all the information I had about the embezzled money. At first, I agreed with the mayor that it was best to keep it quiet; the police had been informed there might be an issue with the town budget and that a forensic accountant was taking a look at it. The mayor was worried that the town's image could be damaged if word got out right before the Christmas parade about the missing money."

"Visitors might decide not to come and that would hurt all the businesses in town."

Jack nodded. "Yep. There was something shady in a town where a quarter of a million dollars—"

"How much?" I screeched. Ebenezer scurried down the hall and clawed at the bedroom door. I had scared the poor critter half to death. I sprang up and picked up Ebenezer, cuddling him.

"Two hundred and fifty thousand dollars."

"That's not what Mayor Vine told me. He said it was one hundred and fifty thousand." The figure Jack said was more than the amount of the bank slips I found. Either Jenna had more accounts, or she didn't have the money.

"If Jenna took it the police would know soon," Jack said.

My stomach tightened. Or Jenna had nothing to do with the stolen money and it was given to someone else for safekeeping. Eric might have been able to hack into the town's account and steal the money and give it to Rachel.

"I'm thinking Jenna was blackmailing the embezzler," I said. "Maybe Eric found out who it was and tried the same thing."

The house had been packed up. But the books were left unpacked. My guess was Jenna knew about the affair—the reason Rachel's name was on the naughty list—and Jenna wasn't taking the books with her and Eric. Unless, Jenna hadn't planned on Eric relocating with her.

"Once the police are able to get all the bank records for Jenna and Eric, they'll be able to know more about it. One of the things Uncle Cornelius told me when I took this job was not to trust anyone on the council. Jenna had been plotting since the day she was born. Even as a child, she never did anything without a motive. The world was all about her. No one wanted to cross that woman. She was dangerous."

"The whole town wasn't afraid of Jenna Wilcox. Someone killed her."

"Uncle said the only person who would stand up to her since Christmas was affected was you."

"One other person would," I said. I had thought it was strange that Sarah Heath would apply for the secretary job at the mayor's office, considering the Christmas season was the busiest for her church. One thing would have Sarah agreeing—protecting her husband, the vice mayor of Season's Greetings. He wouldn't come out unscathed. The pastor had access to the accounts and with his wife working in the mayor's office, he'd know exactly how close the mayor was coming to figuring out the truth. "Sarah Heath. I'm certain she'd do anything for her husband."

"Including kill a woman?"

Sarah's scarf had been in the dumpster with the naughty list that had Eric's name on it. And a large van—a possible church van—had driven by right before Eric fell into the road. What if they had braced him against a tree, knowing eventually he'd fall into the road and get run over?

"Sarah confronted me about what I told the police. She said I was accusing her husband. All I did was answer their questions with the truth. Do the police believe that Samuel was involved in the embezzling?" I asked.

"The police are looking at every angle. I know you and Samuel didn't have anything to do with it. Adding his name into the mix was just a way to try and get some funds back into the account."

"The mayor knew I'd cave."

He stared at the ground, hands clasped in his lap.

"Jack?"

He looked up at me, a sadness in his eyes. "Everyone agreed that you'd pay the money to save Cassie and Helen additional heartache."

"Everyone?" My voice was shaky. Was I now only a source of money to my friends?

"Mayor Vine. Jenna. Norman. Pastor Heath. Rachel."

My friend hadn't decided not to tell me the whole truth, instead she had agreed to the plot and involved me by telling me about Jenna's naughty list float theme.

"Are you okay?" he asked.

"It's hard finding out your friend and the people you trust are plotting behind your back. I can't believe they were all willing to lie about Samuel. He wasn't the best guy out there but doesn't mean a crime he didn't commit should be blamed on him just because he's dead. The man can't defend himself."

"I don't think they thought it all the way through. To them, they were doing the easiest thing to save the town."

Something occurred to me and I jumped up, fisting my hands at my sides. "You went along with them."

"Wait a minute." Jack held up his hands. "I originally thought that Samuel was involved and was agreeable to their plan of keeping matters quiet if the money was returned. It was their town.

It seemed like a nice thing to do for an ailing, elderly woman who just lost her son and a young woman who just lost her dad. I hadn't realized they were creating a scenario in order to save themselves."

"You think one of the city council stole the money?"

"Yes. The problem is who. My prime suspect was Rachel Abbot."

My eyes widened. "Rachel?"

"It was why I agreed to take my nephews and niece to the bookstore. I wanted to look around and knew I'd be able to create a distraction or two to get a peek at her records."

"That doesn't sound legal."

"With Jenna having been murdered, I was willing to venture into questionable tactics to get to the truth."

Couldn't say I blamed him. "Why Rachel?"

"She was always nervous and not really forthcoming with information. I could tell she was hiding something. And the way books were altered told me it was someone who was familiar with accounting procedures. She owned her own business."

"The fact that she was sleeping with Jenna's husband was what she was worried about everyone finding out. Do you still think Rachel stole the money?"

"I'm starting to doubt it. That was one of the reasons I stopped by to speak to the police tonight. I wanted to know what they found in her financial records. Nothing. If Rachel was hiding money, she's really good at it."

"That leaves the mayor, Pastor Heath, and Norman."

"The mayor's accounts have been gone over multiple times. He was the one who asked my uncle for advice on the matter. It would be stupid to bring in a professional that would unearth everything."

"I wonder who does Harmony Baptist's books."

"What are you thinking?"

"I'm sure the pastor keeps tabs on the financials of the church and with it being a small congregation, they probably don't have a lot of employees. Strange how Sarah took a job at the mayor's office during a busy time for the church. I've been meaning to go back to church. Tomorrow morning is a good day to start."

Jack smiled at me. "It's a date."

TWENTY-FOUR

Before the early church goers and breakfast diners were out and about, I pulled out of the police parking lot and headed for home. My overnight RV trip had been uneventful, except for Jack's visit. He was stopping by my house in forty minutes and I wanted to shower and dress before he arrived. There was no way I wanted to get ready with him in the house. I could send him over to his uncle's house, but I wasn't sure I wanted Cornelius in our business. The odds were even for him either lending a helping hand or calling the police on us.

Ebenezer stood on the passenger seat, enjoying the view out the window. Or at least I believed he was able to see outside. I'd have to see if I could rig up something for traveling that kept Ebenezer safe and allowed him to look out the window. One of the reasons I adopted Ebenezer, besides his utter cuteness, was to have a traveling companion. I wanted him to enjoy the experience but couldn't risk people's safety over a belief that he'd stay put and not run under the pedals, and I didn't want to squish my pet.

"See anything interesting out there?"

Ebenezer plopped down onto the seat. I took that as a no.

There weren't that many drivers out and about. Good thing because the RV was lumbering along this morning, I wasn't sure if it was from using the generator last night or I was being a little more cautious since my traveling buddy was free to move about the cabin. I was thankful I didn't have to drive past the spot where Eric died. My attention was already split between driving and my little buddy, no sense adding a third. I flipped on the turn signal and was back on the main road leading home.

"Oh Holy Night..." I sung. There was something about hearing or singing Christmas carols that made it impossible for me to think unhappy thoughts.

The rest of the drive, I alternated my view from the road to Ebenezer. Fortunately, he was content to sleep the morning away. I pulled into my driveway with twenty-five minutes to spare. Plenty of time to shower, dress, and apply some makeup. My makeup routine was minimal: foundation, blush, and lipstick. I usually forgo eye shadow and mascara as half the time shadow irritated my eyes and I always managed to get mascara on my glasses.

Right on time, there was a knock on my door. Just in case Sarah decided to pay me another visit, I rose on my toes and peered out the peephole. It was Jack with a box from Yule Log and a drink carrier filled with six to-go foam cups. He was dressed in a button-down light gray Oxford shirt with the sleeves rolled up and top two buttons undone, red t-shirt underneath, jeans, and combat boots. Eclectic wardrobe choices that were very fitting for the man standing on my doorstep.

I opened the door. "Good morning."

His gaze traveled up and down my body, doing his best to hide his surprise at my attire. "You're festive this morning."

I had put on my Sunday Christmas best: a black, full skirt that fell to my knees with tiny images of reindeer in different states of flight, a white sweater with small beaded wreaths on the neckline that rested along my collarbone, and deer earrings and a matching brooch. The only part of my outfit that did not have a Christmas image were my calf-high dress boots. "It's how I do this time of year. How many people are joining us this morning?"

"Just me and you. I wasn't sure your morning beverage preference, so I brought a few."

"Coffee with a Christmas flavor." I stepped aside so he could enter.

"For some reason, I'm not surprised about that. There's one marked sugar cookie. You might want to tone down your outfit. You'll be easily spotted." Jack headed for the dining room table. "Hard to do a clandestine mission when you're trying to resemble a Christmas decoration."

"Trust me, I'll blend in." I shut the door, sneaking a glance over at Ebenezer who had decided to enter his habitat himself. He was eyeing Jack warily. The critter seemed to have loved Jack last night, now he was standoffish. Usually, my sidekick liked or loathed people, I'd never seen him neutral.

"This is going to be an interesting morning." Jack placed our breakfast on the table. "Before we head out, we have to devise a battleplan."

"Battleplan. That sounds a little ominous."

He grimaced. "Sorry, occupational hazard."

"And just what was your occupation before forensic accountant?"

"Basically, a hodge-podge of military duties related to keeping people and the nation safe. It's all I'm at liberty to say."

"The old if-you-told-me-you'd-have-to-kill-me line?" I brought plates to the table.

"Nothing that drastic. Discretion is important. It's part of my life. Part of who I am."

"Runs in the family." Cornelius was the most private person I knew. Heck, I hadn't even known the man had family members.

He grinned. "That is true."

I plopped into the chair and placed a cinnamon roll on a plate. "So, Mr. Discretion, how would you go about our fact-finding mission this morning?"

"First thing is establishing the goal."

"Find out who killed Eric, left the sign at my door, and what role Sarah plays."

"That is three. You're missing one." He held up four fingers. "Who killed Jenna. Who killed Eric. Sign. Pastor's wife."

"It's the same mission, and I know who killed Jenna.

Fortunately, multi-tasking is a skill I have. It's a requirement when you're a single parent of more than one child. You have to keep your attention on more than one thing at a time."

"You know who killed Jenna?" Jack's green eyes zeroed in on me.

I tried not to fidget under the scrutiny. I talked myself into quite a conundrum. I hadn't realized he hadn't picked that up at the police station. I thought by now everyone knew that Eric killed Jenna and Rachel had known. "Sorry, I can't say anything else." Matter-of-fact, I shouldn't have said what I had.

"All right, but it's easier to work with someone if you trust them."

"I trust you," I said, and was a little surprised to realize that I actually did trust him. I didn't think he was involved in what was going on in Season's Greetings. There was something about him that gave off the vibe he was a man who didn't play games. He was a holder of some secrets but was honest about it. "I just can't tell you how. You'll have to trust me."

He picked up one of the to-go coffee mugs and held it up. "Can do."

It had been a few years since I attended church and I felt a little out of my element standing in the small foyer leading to the sanctuary. Of course, my skittish feeling might be more from the fact I was here on a covert mission. I wasn't sure if the odd looks I received was because I brought a guest—Jack—or the fact that I had never attended a Harmony Baptist Church service. It had actually been quite a while since I had been in a sanctuary. I'd been in plenty of fellowship halls for crafting events but not for fellowshipping.

I had attended services when my children were young but as my craft business blossomed, my attendance became sporadic. Vending events were either full weekend events or on Saturdays, and that left me Sunday to catch up on housework and preparing for the week ahead. Hints of sadness pricked at my heart. I missed feeling like a member of a community.

Being a part of a group was what I'd miss most about full-time crafting, at least working at the pro shop and tax preparation kept me out and about in public and connecting with people. My business was a solitary endeavor. I had a partner, but we lived in different parts of the country and our communication style was written. Here was a chance for me to take a step into the general community and I was petrified. I knew everyone, and they knew me. Yet, what did I really know about them? I knew their names, jobs, how many children, hobbies, but other than that I had no clue about their dreams, fears, or what lurked in their hearts they didn't want known.

"You okay?" Jack asked.

I nodded and pushed open the double doors separating the foyer from the chapel. The sanctuary was serene. Simple, faux evergreen wreaths were hung on the ends of the pews. A Christmas tree was on the stage to the left of the podium where I presumed Pastor Benjamin Heath would be speaking from this morning. There were minimal decorations on the tree, small green and red round shaped ornaments and a star at the top.

Members of the congregation were smiling and chatting quietly with each other. Some stared at us boldly while others tried to feign a disinterest in our having wandered into their church. The clothing choices were a mix of formal, casual, and Christmas inspired, with the women being more ode to Christmas than the other two options.

"You're right," Jack whispered into my ear. "You blend in."

I grabbed his arm and sat on the last pew, dragging him down beside me.

He leaned into me. "You don't want to sit closer? Get a better read on the pastor."

"New people usually take the back rows. Don't want to sit in someone's pew and cause a scene." I wasn't quite ready to let the pastor and his wife know I was here.

"No, you wouldn't want to do that."

"For now, we observe."

"You observe from back here, I'll go closer."

I started to argue with him and quickly decided against it, letting go of Jack's arm so he could slip out from the pew. It was a good idea. There was way too much interest being directed our way. One of my daughter's friends was staring at me oddly. She quickly looked away and tapped away on her phone. *Please don't text, Raleigh.* I didn't want to explain Jack to my daughter or her brother.

Fortunately, the service was starting and even though the friend was in her twenties, her mom sitting beside her snagged her phone, glaring at her wayward adult daughter. There were just some places and times when parents couldn't help being parents.

Jack took the first available seat, right next to Nancy. She looked a little shocked and happy that the man was squished into the small space between the end of the pew and her. On the other hand, her husband wasn't too keen on it and shot eye daggers at Jack.

Pastor Benjamin Heath walked onto the stage. A screen lowered from the ceiling and a hymn popped up onto it. Whisperings flowed around me. Sarah stood beside her husband, a hymnal clutched tightly in her hand.

"We didn't vote on that." A woman gripped the man's arm beside her.

"Pastor never mentioned a new sound system either." He tilted his chin up, indicating the viewing area on a second floor that was a fourth of the size as the seating area on the main floor.

There was a youngish man, early twenties, manning a sound board and a laptop. Harmony Baptist was going high-tech, and it was a surprise to their congregation. The murmurs were growing louder and more boisterous. The congregation was building up to a good old-fashioned mutiny.

Pastor Heath started singing louder, trying to drown out the voices of dissent. The hymnal shook in Sarah's hands, her back ramrod straight. Her face was a cascade of emotions ranging from sorrowful to murderous as she took in each one of the congregation members separately.

I felt a gaze on me. I scanned the congregation, Jack caught my eye and placed a hand on his knee, pointing at Sarah and nodding. I agreed. Perfect suspect. Or more likely aiding and abetting her husband. Did Jenna blackmail the pastor over the embezzling? And more importantly did they kill Eric because they believed he was about to tell the world the pastor was an embezzler or because Eric tried to point the finger at them for Jenna's death? The sleigh had been parked not too far from the church van.

Angela stood and began to sing "Silent Night," her voice sweet and pure. The complaints switched over to the song. Some voices sung grudgingly, others happily. The sanctuary wasn't the time and place for a fight. It would be saved for another time.

A shudder quivered up my spine. I shifted my gaze away from Angela and spotted Sarah glaring right at me. I wasn't much of a mind reader, but it was clear to me there was murder on that woman's mind—and I had a strong feeling it was about mine.

TWENTY-FIVE

The pastor had invited everyone to meet downstairs for fellowship and snacks. I had never seen a large group of people move so fast and harmoniously in my life. Either the food served was amazing, everyone skipped breakfast, or no one wanted to miss out on a syllable of gossip. I was in the latter group and quickly discovered I was the majority of the gossip. People clustered together in small packs, sipping coffee and nibbling on pastries as gazes veered my way and then focused on something else. I stood in what seemed like center stage and berated myself for thinking this was a good plan.

The rest of the service had gone well except for Sarah Heath launching death stares throughout the service. Which, fortunately for the pastor, stopped people talking about the newfangled, state-of-the-art-not-wanted-by-the-majority audio equipment and instead had speculations running rampant with what I had done to cause Sarah's wrath. Even now in the fellowship hall, Sarah fixed her laser beams eyes on me.

I was starting to believe the woman didn't care too much about saving my soul—just judging it. There was a simmering temper on the woman that was now visible to all. She was protective of her husband. I had seen it. She was definitely a woman capable of issuing threats and looking darn well like she meant them.

A woman smiled at me softly, her gaze holding sympathy and relief. She was probably the usual target of Sarah's wrath. Raising her coffee cup to her lips, she tipped the cup slightly in my direction. She was either wishing me luck or bidding me farewell.

Jack materialized beside me and handed me a cup of coffee. "The pastor's wife wants to vaporize you."

People milled about us, averting their eyes while at the same time trying to keep us in sight. I didn't know how many people the basement room usually held but it was packed today. It seemed like the congregation had grown to twice its size during the walk down the stairs. I had positioned myself in the middle of the room, near a set of doors leading into the kitchen, thinking it afforded me the perfect spot to watch everyone else. Now, I felt trapped and like I was on display.

Then again, everyone was also curious about the man who rode into town a few days ago, had worked for the mayor, and now had shown up to their church. Things in town had started going a little wayward once Jack Sullivan had arrived. Yep, if I was them, I'd be keeping my eyes on Jack too.

"I don't think she likes my mix of reindeer and wreaths," I whispered back. "She's a Christmas purist. Thinks Santa and all the other secular trappings should be eliminated from the Christmas season."

"I'm sure that's the reason." Jack blew at the steam rising from his coffee.

The pastor excused his way through the crowd of his members, making his way toward us.

"Good morning, Pastor Heath." I had wanted to say something nice about his sermon, but I hadn't paid much attention as his wife's death glare and trying to pick up snippets of gossip consumed my attention.

"Since the service is over, it is the perfect time for you to be on your way." He made a sweeping gesture toward the stairs.

I wasn't sure if I was hurt, angry, or amused by this situation. Was I, Merry Winters, good-girl slash rule-follower who was all about Christmas cheer, really getting kicked out of church? During the Christmas season? It was time to get the pastor's mind off the fact that his wife didn't like me. "I'm enjoying the fellowship. The decorations in the church are quite lovely. I'm amazed at how quickly you pulled it all together. I was here a few days ago for an afternoon crafting event and the downstairs was still decorated for Thanksgiving."

"We had to postpone the Thanksgiving dinner due to the weather."

"When was your Thanksgiving dinner?"

"Wednesday night."

So that meant the decorating was done Thursday. What if Jenna had been placed in the bag Thursday night? No one had actually seen her Friday. But Norman—Sarah and Pastor Benjamin—loaded the sleigh on Friday. Though, Norman had left to take care of Angela, which left Sarah and Benjamin there. Together. Near the sleigh. Had they seen Eric placing Jenna in the bag?

Why not tell the police? Were they afraid Eric would mention the embezzled money if they told the police about him being near Santa's sleigh? Had they decided to kill Eric and try to make it look like a drunk had wandered into the road?

The pastor was looking at me oddly. I blocked out the questions tumbling through my mind.

"Everything is lovely. It's apparent how much you love your congregation. To have this turned around so soon is incredible," I gushed. "Leaves me speechless."

The pastor drew back a bit. I was having a hard time deciphering if his expression was concern or confusion about my over-the-top reaction. I had to settle down.

"A church doesn't run on the service of one person alone. The congregation is a huge help. Without the members on the decorating committee, the chapel and fellowship hall wouldn't have been ready for today's service."

Jack backed away from me and the pastor. I hoped he was going to eavesdrop on a few other conversations or head off the pastor's wife whose laser gaze was zeroed in on me. The woman side-stepped right around him.

She sidled up to her husband, hooking an arm through his and clutching on tight. "Are you not going to protect the congregation? She is here to start trouble for our church."

"That's not true."

"Really." Sarah crossed her arms and tapped the tip of her kitten heel onto the carpeted floor. "When have you ever been in this church?"

"Tuesday." I smiled at her.

She narrowed her eyes. "Let me rephrase that. When have you attended church service? Rather than only entering our building to sell your craft items."

My cheeks heated. I cast my gaze on the ground.

"Nice welcoming you give people," Jack said.

"This isn't the way the bible tells us to treat someone. Merry should be welcomed in this church just like everyone else." Norman draped an arm around me, his voice booming for all to hear.

"She's here to cause trouble."

"Don't we all cause trouble for God time to time?" Norman asked. He squeezed my shoulder gently.

"She's here to accuse my husband of killing that horrid woman," Sarah said, between clenched teeth.

Hisses erupted from all around us and church goers drew in a sharp breath.

"Sarah, I know this has been a stressful time for you but is this really how you want to conduct yourself," Norman whispered. "This will be remembered long after the police have solved the murders. I am sure no one will believe that Pastor Benjamin had anything to do with it."

"Thank you for your help, Norman, but I can defend myself." I slipped away from him.

The pastor motioned toward the stairs. "I must ask you to leave, Merry. The last few weeks have been devastating for you. Your husband murdered. Finding Jenna's body. All that trauma isn't good for the soul. I do have the utmost compassion for you, but I cannot have you distressing my wife and the congregation."

Members started to move closer together. They were closing ranks. Shutting me out.

"Let's go." Jack took hold of my arm.

I shook him off. "I'm not staying. A long time ago, I made a vow to myself not to be where I wasn't wanted."

Nor did I need an escort. My feelings weren't that fragile that I'd crumble into a heap. I wasn't that interested in being liked or wanted by people who were showing a bit of their true colors. The Heaths weren't the loving and welcoming people they always portrayed themselves.

"I'm glad the message was received." Sarah smiled sweetly at me.

Next year, I'd make sure their float went after Santa Claus—if I was still the one organizing it. I wasn't sure I'd want the job and also not sure the mayor would want me back. Holding my head high, I started up the stairs. Jack trailed behind me.

"That was a first for me," I said. "I've never been kicked out of a church before."

"Not for me." Jack placed a hand on the small of my back.

"You've been thrown out of a church."

"Actually, more than once."

For some reason, I wasn't surprised about that. Jack Sullivan was trouble. I just wasn't quite sure what kind he was.

Two church members were tidying up the pews, placing hymnals and Bibles back into the holders, collecting discarded bulletins and other items left behind. I snagged one of the bulletins. There had been a list of the committee members. I might be able to find out when the rest of the decorating committee crew had left.

I stopped in the middle of the aisle and looked up at the media equipment, wondering just how much the new sound system cost. A system the congregation hadn't known about.

"What are you thinking?" Jack asked.

"More not very Christmassy thoughts about a pastor and his wife. I think we should tell Orville about the new sound system.

Where did they get the funds to buy it? The congregation didn't know about it."

Jack looked up at the balcony. "I'm thinking I should get a closer look at it first. Maybe it's new to this church but was a system someone donated to them. The sound guy is still upstairs. He might be willing to talk about it."

I broke my gaze away from the upper floor and stared at the stage. The white lights on the tree twinkled, bouncing off the frosted glass windows. I scooted to the edge of the pew. Could a tree decorator see outside? The sleigh would've been near the window.

A low buzz came from my purse.

"Well, unless you want to face the wrath of the pastor's wife, I'd say you should head out. I'll check out the sound system and meet you at the car."

An unattended toddler in a red and green velvet dress was crawling up the stairs to the stage, eyes fixed on the Christmas tree. Her black patent leather shoes slipping on the carpet. The shiny baubles too much of a temptation for the little girl. I couldn't say I blamed her. While adults might not find the simple, round ornaments eye-catching, to a small child they resembled balls perfect to fit in a small hand, or like giant gumballs hanging from a Christmas tree. A treat Santa left behind just for them.

"I have to stop a catastrophe." I dropped my purse onto the first pew. Where were her parents? The child had made it to the top of the stairs and pushed herself onto unsteady legs. The three tiers of ruffles making up her skirt swung around her legs as she toddled, arms outstretched for the tree. I ran up the stairs. The child was a few inches from the tree, her small hands opening and closing as she neared one of the ornaments.

"My pretty. My pretty." The little girl sang. She reached for a bright red ornament.

I hooked an arm around her waist, swinging up her body and scooping her legs into my arms. The little girl looked into my face, bright blue eyes wide and startled. "You might have knocked that tree over, little one. Where's your mom and dad?"

Her lower lip trembled. She took in a deep breath and let out a roof-shaking wail, flailing her little arms and legs in what seemed twelve different directions at the same time.

"Your grandma is going to tan my hide." A man a few years older than me ran up the stairs. He held out his arms. The little girl leaned toward him, desperate to get to him. "This is where you snuck off to? Thought your daddy or momma was keeping an eye on you."

"She wanted the ornaments." I handled over the wiggly bundle.

"Grandma lets her take the ones off of our tree and the little one just doesn't understand it doesn't mean she can take any she sees." He jiggled the little girl in his arms. She giggled.

"I was afraid the tree might fall over if she grabbed one."

"The pastor secured it to the wall. He knew it would tempt the little ones. I should've known she'd head straight for it." The man carried the little girl away from the tree.

Why hadn't I thought of that? The baby gate I was using to keep Ebenezer away from the tree took away from my Christmas atmosphere. I might be able to rig something up. I walked behind the tree to check out his handiwork.

Four small hooks had been placed at the bottom of the wall and two were near the frosted window. Thin wires stretched taut went from the hook's metal pole in the middle of the faux tree. That wouldn't work. Ebenezer would gnaw the wire in no time. With one hand, I grabbed a few branches of the tree, like a curious toddler, and braced the base of the tree with my other hand just in case the wire wasn't as helpful as the pastor believed. I shook it. It swayed. A toddler could easily bring down the tree.

The pastor sure hadn't tried very hard. There was a section of the window where the frost had worn off and gave a lovely downward view of the area where Santa had parked his sleigh. Either the pastor had been in rush when putting up the tree, or something he viewed distracted him from securing it properly.

"We're a Couple of Misfits" played from my phone. The

grandfather paused, glancing over his shoulder to stare at me. My face heated. I hurried to my purse and dug around for my phone. The song continued.

I snagged it. "Yes."

"Don't know why you're annoyed with me," Brett said. "You stood me up."

Ugh. I forgot I had asked Brett to come to Season's Greetings to help me decorate Cassie's house. "I decided to attend church this morning. I didn't think you'd arrive this early."

"Well, I'm here. Hold up..."

There was a squeal of tires in the background.

"What the—"

Pop. Pop. Pop.

Brett said one curse word and was silent.

"Brett!"

The phone line went dead.

TWENTY-SIX

I felt cold. Then hot. Back to cold. Someone had hurt Brett. Because of me. Tears ran down my face. Had Brett paid a high price for my decision? The silence I heard wasn't golden. It was dark. Numbing. I grabbed onto the back of the driver's seat and tapped Jack on the arm. "Hurry."

"Sit back, buckle up, and I'll go faster." Jack said, inching up the speed.

Jack had followed me out of the church, grabbed the keys from my shaking hands and hoisted me into the back seat of my Traverse. The man had taken over, only asking me where to go.

I sat back and buckled in. I hit Brett's number on the speed dial. It rang and rang. "He won't answer. Please hurry. Turn left."

"I know how to get there, Merry."

Right. His uncle lived across the street from me. Cornelius! "I'm calling your uncle. He'll know what's going on."

"Do that."

"What's his number? I don't know it."

Jack shifted and pulled his phone from his jacket pocket, tossing it to me. "Use mine. Corn will block any number he doesn't know."

The phone was locked. This was taking too long. The screen wanted a fingerprint. "I need your finger."

Jack reached his right hand back. I grabbed it and placed his index finger on the correct space. His warm skin was a sharp contrast to my icy hands.

"It'll be okay, Merry. He'll be okay. I'm sure he knows how to handle whatever situation has happened."

"He was shot at!" I screeched. "He can't deal with that."

"I'm sure he can. You might not want to know he's trained for it, but he is."

"People don't shoot at him." Or did they? Lawyers made people mad, especially the kind of cases Brett took on. He went after those who abused their authority. "Oh God." I couldn't stop the wail from erupting from me.

"Merry—"

"Shut up, Jack, you're not helping."

Jack turned down my street, tires squealing and the back fishtailing. Two neighbors stood on their porches, eyes directed toward my house. I leaned forward, the seatbelt digging into my shoulder and stomach.

My carefully arranged front yard Christmas display was now a tangled heap of wires, beheaded reindeers, and turned over lighted-bumper cars. The world tipped. Amongst the carnage of my decorations was Brett. Lying still on the ground. One hand on top of Hammy.

The car started to slow down. I shoved open the door and jumped out, nearly falling flat on my face and under the tires.

"Merry!" Jack yelled.

I righted myself and ran for Brett's prone form. Shaky sobs escaped from me. This couldn't be happening. How would I tell our children their father was hurt? Killed. "Brett!" I hopped over the curb, hurtling myself toward Brett.

He started to rise and turn toward me. I was in flight and couldn't stop my momentum. I slammed into him, knocking Brett onto his side. We laid side-by-side, almost curled together.

I cradled his face in my hands. "Are you okay? Where are you hurt?"

His hair was mussed. Brown eyes filled with shock. My body shook, and he attempted to draw me closer. I had to get a good look at him. Every inch of him. I scrambled to my knees. He rose up on his elbows, an amused and smoldering look in his eyes.

He was fine. Totally fine. Not a scratch on him fine.

I swatted at him, emotions a jumble of relief and uncontrollable fury at the man. "Why didn't you answer me? Call me back?"

Brett snagged my flailing hands and stood, tugging me up. "Calm down, Merry. I dropped my phone when I dove for cover and then stepped on it. It's crushed. I also knocked the heads off your lighted deer."

"I thought you were hurt. Dead." Sobs shook me.

A soft smile crossed Brett's face. He pulled me into his arms. "Honey, I'm fine."

I relented, relaxing into him and wrapped my arms around his waist, letting out the last of my tears. Brett wasn't gone from my life. My children's lives. I held on tight, listening to the sound of his heart.

"I think your hamster is a goner. Some group of kids drove by and took out some of your lawn decorations." Brett's voice rumbled out, mixing with his heartbeat.

"I guess requesting your police department send a SWAT team, or whatever you have that's similar, was overkill," Jack said.

"Do you want me to flip the switch or not?" Cornelius's voice came from the area near my front door.

I left Brett's arms. My front door was opened. "Someone broke into my house."

"I borrowed our kids' key. I saw you hooked up my present and wanted to see how the hamster fit in with your other inflatable beings. I turned them on."

"You did what?" The screech in my voice didn't have an ounce of fear in it. I was angry. Livid. "You can't just go into my house."

"You invited me."

"You wait. You don't use Scotland or Raleigh's key to go inside."

Brett raised his hands and backed away from me. "I'm sorry. I didn't know that would be off-limits."

"We're divorced. Why wouldn't it be off-limits? You can't just go into my house whenever you want."

"You're getting an audience." Jack stepped between me and Brett. I hadn't realized I'd been stomping toward my ex-husband with fists clenched.

"Hold up." Fire sparked in Brett's gaze. "I have never entered your residence whenever. Even when our children lived at home. I respected your boundaries. Don't accuse me of doing otherwise."

"You haven't. Before," I corrected my prior statement. "I just don't want you thinking you can do so now."

Brett huffed out a breath and scrubbed his hand over his hair. "You invited me here today. I came to help you. Just like I always do. I'm getting the impression you don't want me here." He slid an unreadable gaze in Jack's direction, pivoted and stalked toward his car parked in my driveway.

Sirens grew closer. A lot of sirens. It sounded like the entire police force of Season's Greetings was heading our way. One by one, four squad cars whipped down the street. The last two turning sideways to block off the street.

"One of us should call Scotland," I said. There was no way my son wouldn't hear about this.

"I'll call if you loan me your phone," Brett said. "I'll tell him I was a little too concise with my report of kids and shooting. Left out Christmas decorations with a BB gun."

"From the tone of your voice, I thought it was your son in trouble." Jack handed me my car keys.

Now, Jack's comments made sense to me. Scotland was a police officer and trained in shooting situations, not that I really liked to think about it. I tried to avoid picturing my son in his full police uniform, made it easier to avoid the reality that my son carried a firearm to protect others—and himself. I preferred not to think about the fact that my son needed a gun for his job.

"Brett is my ex-husband. My children's father."

"I figured that out."

Officer Brianna Myers stepped out of the car, adjusted her utility belt, and headed over to us. "Seems everything is in order. Someone care to explain what is going on?"

Jack raised his hand. "I was overzealous. Thought an officer was in danger and turned out it was a hamster under fire not Merry's kid. And it wasn't Merry's kid who was at her place anyway."

Brianna frowned. "Merry, has anyone threatened your children? If so, I need to notify his department."

I shook my head. "No."

"Let's talk over by my cruiser," Brianna said.

I shuffled over.

"Do you need me, Merry?" Brett handed back my phone. Jack, and quite a few of neighbors, waited on my answer.

"Not sure," I said.

Having a defense attorney on standby was a good idea right now. I wasn't sure how Brianna would view my not calling the police about what I remembered last night and taking it upon myself to scope out the church and the pastor and his wife. Fearing for my reputation seemed like a silly thing to have worried about as it was going to take a huge hit now. Even worse was the fear I felt believing for those awful minutes that Brett had been harmed because of me.

Brianna faced me, arms crossed. "Since Jack Sullivan knows a lot about the incident, I'm taking it you were with him."

Did everyone besides me know that Jack was related to Cornelius? "You know Jack?"

"Of him. He's not really the topic of this conversation, why you showed up together is."

"He was with me when Brett called, and I heard shots in the background. Brett's line went dead. I thought—" I couldn't finish the sentence. Tears were clogging my throat.

"You thought someone shot your ex-husband. Is there a reason you'd think that? A case he's working on?" Brianna pulled out a notebook.

"Because of the naughty sign someone left on my doorstep," I whispered. "Jenna and Eric's names were on one and they're now dead."

"We're going to find out who put it there."

"Cornelius didn't see—"

Brianna sighed. "I understand that Cornelius usually knows everything that's going in your neighborhood, but the man does like his evening nap."

"Someone had stolen the first naughty sign I made for Rachel's store. Rachel thought it was Jenna because she wanted to copy it for her float sign."

"We'll check into it. We've pulled a lot of security footage from One More Page. I'll have the officer reviewing them keep an eye out for who might have taken the first sign."

"Or Rachel had lied to me and no one had stolen it," I muttered. "What if Rachel had put Jenna's name on the first sign and then changed her mind about including it? She didn't want to tell me the truth so said it was stolen."

"Why would she do that?"

"Because she was angry that Eric wouldn't leave her and wanted to embarrass Jenna."

"Jenna wasn't one to toy with." Brianna scribbled something onto her notepad.

"Exactly. Rachel came to her senses and asked for a new sign and threw that one away. Once Jenna was killed, Rachel put the old sign back up and hid the unaltered sign. The one with Jenna's name was placed there during the parade. It had to be a quick switch. Then she threw both of them away. Sarah took the one that didn't have Jenna and Eric's name on it." I tapped down my building excitement at having figured it out. "She added my name on to it to scare me, hoping I'd cover the shortfall in the town's budget."

"Sarah? Why in the world do you think she did it?"

"Because I found her scarf in the garbage bin along with the sign that had Eric and Jenna's names. I think Pastor Heath took the money from the town and she was trying to cover for him. You should check out the church's new sound system and van."

"We'll look into this, Merry. We need you to stay clear of the Heaths and anyone else who might be involved in this matter."

I wrapped my arms around myself. The chill in the air was getting to me. "What about Rachel? How much trouble is she in?"

"She committed a crime, Merry. There's no other way to look at it."

I was hoping there would be. "I think Eric threatened her."

"We got this. The truth will come out and if a judge thinks Rachel's circumstance deserves some mercy or leniency, it'll happen."

"But if not..."

"It's out of our hands, Merry," Brianna said.

"Everything okay?" Brett called out to us.

I nodded as Brianna headed to speak with Jack.

"I've given my statement," Brett said. "No reason for me to stick around."

"Wait, Brett." I jogged to him. "I'm sorry. I overreacted. I was so scared driving over here. I thought something happened to you."

"I'm fine, and that seemed to tick you off." Brett crossed his arm and leaned against his car. "I'm confused by you. You invite me over, forget, and get mad at me. We've been talking all the time, and I thought that you were giving signals regarding a possible us. I was wrong."

I let out a breath. "If I have been, I'm sorry. I trust you more than anyone, Brett. I guess I've been leaning on you more than I should."

"Don't say that." Brett reached out to tuck a lock of my hair behind my ear. I moved back.

"I appreciate everything you've done for me. Are doing for me."

Brett and I stared into each other's eyes. I had hurt him. Confused him. Heck, I was confused myself. I had been absolutely terrified thinking something happened to Brett. That he was gone. I didn't want him gone permanently from my life, but I wasn't sure I wanted him to be such an active part of it either. Which meant, I couldn't keep relying on him—reeling him in and then throwing him back. It wasn't fair to Brett. He was a great guy and deserved better.

"I should work with someone else," I said.

"That's probably for the best." Brett unlocked his car door and leaned inside, pulling out a stack of papers from a briefcase. "For some good news, one of the issues is over with. I pulled some strings and got this for you today rather than waiting until tomorrow. You were divorced from Samuel when he died."

I took the papers from Brett. I was divorced. "Positively?"

"Yes. I was able to compile enough evidence to show you had believed you were divorced from Samuel and that was still your intention and wishes. That any fraud was perpetrated on you, not by you. The judge took pity and says it's all good. Samuel's signature and the date will be accepted. You're divorced."

"But?" There was a tenseness in his smile. While this was good for my heart, this decision was liable to hurt something else—the disbursement of the lottery winnings.

"If Bonnie can prove that her marriage was valid, it will call into question the ownership of the lottery ticket. Helen allowed Samuel to verbally claim it and a lot of people in town thought it was Samuel's and then yours because..."

"It appeared I was still married to Samuel. So, Bonnie will have a legal claim to the money."

Brett nodded. "Helen will have to prove it was hers and say that her son took it from her."

The first part Helen could do, the second she never would. There was no way she'd tarnish her son's name, even though he had in a way bullied the ticket away from her. "Is there another option?"

"You ladies figuring out an equitable distribution. I'll talk to you later, Merry." Brett stepped toward me for a goodbye hug.

I opened my arms to receive it, the gesture second nature to us. Our gazes met. We stepped away from each other, nodding a farewell instead.

TWENTY-SEVEN

Today was a disaster. I walked into my house and dropped onto the couch. Ebenezer squealed from his habitat and thumbed against it, demanding my attention. I tipped my head back. "Can't you get out of there yourself?"

He wiggled his cute little nose and sent me a look pleading for a rescue.

"I'm coming." I pushed myself to my feet, exhaustion sweeping over me. What I needed was a long, hot bath and binge-watching Christmas movies. What I had to do was set Ebenezer free for a while and get some work done. I was behind. I hated to ask Bright to handle more of our orders. Lately, it seemed I was getting good at using my friends to pick up my slack or clean up messes I willingly generated for myself.

It wasn't like the situations were entirely my fault. Samuel created the two issues Brett helped with: the divorce—now resolved, and the lottery ticket—still seeking an answer. The others I was running myself ragged with—Christmas parade, orders, and looking into a murder—were all on me.

I plucked Ebenezer out of his zone of entrapment. "Let's get a snack and you can run free while I get some work done."

His eyes lit up. There were two words the guinea pig loved: free and snacks. I tucked him under my arm and headed for the kitchen.

My phone rang. I snagged the receiver. "Hello."

"Merry, this is Angela," her voice was teary. "I was just calling..."

Oh no. Angela and I were scheduled for a craft session today, and I had totally forgot. "I'm running behind schedule, I'll be over in about ten minutes."

"Are you sure? We can reschedule. It doesn't seem like today is a good day."

"No, it's perfect. This was the first time I've attended church in a while, and it threw off my schedule. It was a spur of the moment decision."

"I wish I'd known you were coming. You could have sat with us." Her voice grew softer. "I'm really sorry about not stepping forward to defend you. I wasn't feeling well. I was afraid you decided not to stop by because of that."

"I'm so sorry I made you think that. My life has been in such a tailspin lately, and I always seem to be behind. I promise I'll be there soon," I said, running a list in my mind of needed supplies. "I just need to grab a few items and I'll be out the door."

I ran up to my craft room, Ebenezer following behind me. Either he was hoping to sneak into the forbidden area or he thought the snacks were up here. I yanked open the door and flung open the closet: ornaments, vinyl, cutting machine. The list was growing longer and longer. This was going to take me forever. I'd actually get more orders completed by working on them in my studio than dragging everything over to Angela's house.

But I had promised. Bonnie had said Angela had been so happy crafting. It had given her some spark back and there weren't many activities Angela could participate in with her heart condition. I couldn't disappoint her. It wasn't fair. I'd just call her back and tell her it'll take longer.

Unless I took the RV. Scotland had stocked it. I'd give the crafting space a test run. Angela and I could both fit in there. While I designed and cut out the decals, Angela could weed the designs and place the vinyl onto the ornaments.

I unhooked my laptop, placing it in a bag with my Cricut, and grabbed a box of ornaments. I opened up the box and moved around some of the ornaments, making a pocket for Ebenezer. "We're going on a road trip."

He ran over to me, excited about the tone in my voice. Usually that inflection meant a trip outside of the house. I picked him up and placed him in the box. "This will work to get into the RV, I have to think of a better way to keep you safe while I'm driving."

Would an infant car seat work? I envisioned Ebenezer in one, his little legs sticking up from the belt straps. That wouldn't be a comfortable position for a guinea pig. Pulling out my phone, I emailed myself a reminder to call a local vet for advice on traveling with my buddy. I should have done it sooner, but it was better late than never. Uneasiness traveled through me as the word "never" filled my mind.

Time was ticking away. I shook off the sense of doom and deposited Ebenezer and the items into the passenger side of the RV before jogging to the driver side and climbing in. I hoped Angela wasn't fretting about my tardiness. I hated the fact I made her think that I had decided to deliberately avoid her because of Sarah's behavior.

I started the RV and pulled away from my house, threading the needle between cars curbside parking on both sides of the road. The task would be easier if the cars parked closer to the curb rather than a few feet away. Didn't they teach people how to park on the street anymore?

As I neared the spot where Eric had died, my breath tightened in my lungs and sweat coated my hands. Eric's death replayed itself in my mind. The van pulled off on the side of the road. Eric tumbling into the road. A thunk against my car. I clutched the steering wheel, taking in deep breaths to settle the growing panic. I hadn't expected this reaction.

"Get past this spot, and it'll all go way." I repeated the mantra over and over again. The memory of last night faded and another one took its place: finding Samuel. Worse got to worse, I could ditch crafting in the RV and work on the projects in Angela's house.

"I can do this."

Giving myself a few more words of pep talk, I envisioned all the places I could take my mobile crafting studio. The RV brought so much potential to my business. I could travel farther to shows. Bring more inventory with me. Create more inventory on the go.

The best way to overcome a fear was to challenge it. Face it. That was what I was going to keep telling myself until I got there. The drive back home wouldn't be too bad since I would know that I had done it already once today.

The RV handled well on the local roads, and I was doing a good job of staying between the lines though Angela and Norman lived on a narrow road. My favorite thing about the RV, besides being able to cart around an arsenal of craft supplies, was my ability to see over every car on the road. I liked my height advantage.

The turn-off for Norman and Angela's road was a few miles away from the bar. With all the trees, I hadn't realized they lived so close to it. The small housing area appeared to be separated from Season's Greetings, tucked in a wooded, private area when in reality it was just a couple of miles away. The trees and dirt road gave it the appearance of being in a more rural area than the rest of town. I turned down the road, which was a mix of asphalt and gravel. The tires bumped along a few rough spots. I slowed, not wanting to skid and end up with a tire or two in a ditch.

I spotted Norman and Angela's cute two-story house. Christmas lights were strung on the roof and there was a plastic Santa, sleigh, and eight not-so-tiny reindeer attached to his roof. The garage was still the garage, not the toy shop as in previous years. Angela's health took a toll on their decoration. I liked the simplicity of their decorations. It was just enough. Perfect. I'd make sure to tell Angela.

The road grew narrower the closer I got to the house. Branches thumped against the sides of the RV. I was going to have a fun time getting out of here. By the time we were done, it would be dark. The best thing to do was to turn this baby around while there was plenty of daylight. I had a few feet on either side and planned to use the old plan of backing up a foot, pull forward a few inches, and repeat that process until the front of the RV was facing out. It wasn't the most time saving method but my skills in this area weren't what they should be to zip backwards without a risk to Norman's car.

I put the RV in reverse, looking in the rearview mirror as I turned the wheel, praying I didn't go off the paved area of the driveway into the gravel area that looked like a small road. I stopped and put the RV back into drive. Again, I went in reverse, this time turning the steering wheel sharper, adding a few more feet to how far I could back up.

In the rearview mirror, I spotted Angela on her porch waving her arms frantically over her head. "Stop! Stop! The porch."

I slammed on the brakes and jammed the RV into park. There was a slight jar and crunching sound. Ebenezer squealed. My heart pounded. Oh no! I hadn't realized he was roaming. I spun the captain's chair. "Are you okay?"

Ebenezer scurried under the couch, his derriere pointed in my direction. I deserved that.

"Sorry, buddy." Slowly, I unbuckled my seat belt and opened the door. I hoped I didn't do too much damage to the porch.

"Did I hit it?" I was pretty sure the answer was yes.

"A tiny bit." Angela pointed at the railing. "Don't worry about it. Norman can fix that no problem."

I walked over. The main rail was split at the bottom. Fortunately, the steps weren't damaged. "I'm really sorry. I thought I had it. I guess I need to practice my parking skills. Maybe the fire or police department will let me perfect my skills in their lots."

"It's not that bad. It was just a little tap. The wood was chipping away and needed to be replaced. I'll have Norman take a look at it when he gets home. I'm sure this is something he can fix. The bottom stairs are fine."

"Norman isn't here?"

"No. Our car needs some repairs and my medical bills have been chipping away at all our funds. Fortunately, he's been able to borrow cars. We hope to have some money in a few weeks to fix it."

I knelt down to examine the damage to the porch stairs. The RV had bounced forward a bit, leaving a few inches of space between the bumper and the steps. There was a crack in the wood. It shouldn't cost too much to fix it. If I'd hit it any harder, I could've brought the whole small porch down. Might have even hurt Angela.

Rachel's confession pinged in my head. Eric had said his wife was slouched on the bottom step. He'd have to hit her pretty hard to kill her. The steps to their home hadn't been damaged. I had seen Jenna—found Jenna—in the bag. There hadn't been any injuries to her head. Since she had been sitting on the steps, Eric would've struck her head with the car. There would've been visible injuries.

"Merry, is everything all right?" Angela's question sounded like it was coming from far away.

I nodded, not wanting to talk and stop the bits of memories floating in my mind and piecing themselves together. Unless of course, Rachel lied to me. She had lied to me about so many things, and who knew what else she lied about. Like the stolen sign and Eric's confession.

Something in me was warning me not to take everything at face value. I wanted it to have been Eric who killed Jenna. Eric was a good suspect. He was a drunk. A cheater. What I was seeing was saying the scenario Rachel described was wrong.

I was there Saturday morning and the porch steps of the Wilcox home hadn't been damaged, or recently fixed. They were still a little wobbly when Eric forced me into his house, showing the same wear from Thursday. Eric hadn't hit the steps. In his drunken state, he confused hitting his brakes hard with slamming into the porch and killing his wife. Someone else had killed Jenna.

Other memories flooded into my head. Norman's confusion about the parade. "Has Norman been having any memory issues lately?"

Angela blinked a few times. "What?"

"Forgetting things?" I never wanted so badly to hear a yes about someone having a health issue. "Not remembering what's going on."

Slowly, Angela shook her head and gripped the railing. "No. Why are you asking me? Have you noticed something?"

"I thought I had." Misery clogged my voice. I replayed that night. The truth settled around me, dimming the world and swallowing up my Christmas spirit. Norman had said Jenna was dead before I had told him. I had found her body in the bag. Saw her first. Norman hadn't looked in the bag. He knew Jenna was dead because he killed her.

Norman had access to the city budget. Jenna must've found out that Norman was embezzling money. Jenna figured it out blackmailed him. The only way to keep his secret was for Jenna to be silenced and the money returned. At the mayor's office, Norman had brought up to me about paying the money back. It was the way out for him, and I hadn't taken the bait.

My heart broke. Money. Why was money always so important? I was starting to hate it. The best thing to do with the lottery ticket might be to tear it up.

"Can we go inside?" Angela's voice was weak. "I'm not feeling so good."

I jerked toward the direction of her voice. She was clinging to a rail, complexion pale.

The better choice was getting out of there, away from Norman. I'd go a safe distance then call the police. I had to get us away from the house before Norman returned. "How about we go inside the RV?"

I jumped up and took hold of her arm. She struggled a bit, not wanting to go downstairs.

"I just want to sit in my chair."

"I should take you the hospital," I said. "Norman isn't here, and you don't have another car."

"I don't need to go to the hospital."

"I think you do."

"Norman can take me when he gets home. He had borrowed the church's van last night and went to return it."

Harmony van. Norman had tossed Eric out of the van. I bet Norman had borrowed the vehicle I almost collided with when I escaped Eric's house. Which meant—Norman knew I had been there and might figure out the truth about Jenna's death. We had to go.

"We can't wait for him." I wrapped an arm around her shoulders, drawing her against me and helping her toward the RV. I wanted her at the hospital where she could receive medical help when the truth about the crime her husband committed broke her heart.

She shook her head but allowed me to direct her steps. I got her inside the RV.

She sunk onto one of the cushioned recliners, pressing her hand to her heart. Tears filled her eyes. "Please, Merry..."

Panic welled up in me. She was having a heart attack. "I'm going to call for help."

"I just need some water. My medicine. It's in my house. The table near my chair."

"Okay. I'll be right back." I yanked open the door.

Norman stood at the threshold, pointing a gun at me. "Let's go for a ride."

I turned and grabbed my phone. Angela lunged toward me, hitting the phone out of my hand.

"No." Her expression was fierce. She knew Norman killed Jenna.

"We can't let you do that, Merry." Norman stepped into the RV.

I backed up.

"Sit down." Norman waved the gun toward one of the recliners.

I eyed the door then from the corner of my eye spotted Ebenezer staring at me from under the couch. I couldn't leave him and there was no way I'd make it out of the RV without getting shot.

"Sit down. Where are the keys?"

That was a good question. Maybe I could stall him long enough and talk sense into him. "Might be in my pocket." I patted my front and back pockets. "You do know, since I figured it out, the police will too. This won't help you."

"I'm not expecting it to help. Just to end it. What do you know? The keys are in the ignition. Sit. Down." He pointed the gun at my head.

I sat. Ebenezer squealed and jumped toward me. Angela cried, placing her hand on her chest and stumbled backward into the recliner.

"Are you okay?" I scooted to the edge of the seat.

"Sit back, Merry." Norman handed Angela the gun. "Keep that on her while I find something to tie her up."

"You don't want to do this," I whispered to Angela.

"I can't let him go to jail because of me." Tears streamed down her face. "He was going to give it back. Jenna didn't care, even after taking some of the money Norman borrowed as a payment to forget about it for a while. She went and told the mayor money was missing. He brought in the accountant. Jenna told us that the whole town would know Norman was naughty."

"You don't need to explain anything to her." Norman shoved me back into the chair and tied my hands together. Ebenezer whistled and screeched at him.

Norman knocked him off the chair.

"Don't hurt him." I kicked Norman's knee.

He lost his balance and fell onto me. I jammed my knees into his gut and pushed him backwards.

"Stop it. Stop it or..." Angela screeched. "I'll kill your pet."

I grew still.

Norman knelt in front of me and tied my feet together. "You should've let it be. Eric killed Jenna. He was a man who needed to be in jail."

Technically, so did Norman. "You killed him and Jenna."

"He didn't give me a choice." Norman walked to the front and started the RV. "We're going for a little drive."

"If you shoot me, how are you going to explain that?"

"I'm not. You're going to have an accident driving this mammoth beast. You haven't had it for too long. No one will question it." He drove down his road, carefully maneuvering the RV. Branches thumped the sides.

I stared at Angela. She averted her gaze. "That might not be too wise of an idea."

"First, we'll drop Angela off at the hospital. You took her there and went to get me. On our way back to the hospital, there was a horrible accident."

"What?" Angela drew in a deep breath. Fear filled her face.

Norman planned on sparing Angela, but not me or himself. He pulled onto the main road, picking up speed.

"Norman don't do this." I struggled against the rope binding me. "Killing us is not the answer."

"It's the only one I have, Merry. I'm so sorry I have to do this." Grief shook his voice. "All Eric had to do was accept the cash I offered and leave. Once the town heard about Jenna's blackmailing business no one would care anymore about her death. He was free of his demanding and abusive wife. That woman never had a nice word to say to anyone. Not even him. Told me he could no longer accept that deal. We had to tell the truth and save her."

Save her. Rachel. He loved her. My heart ached. It was so sad. In his drunken state, Eric hadn't thought clearly and panicked, making a tragic situation even worse and dragged the woman he loved into it. Now, Eric was dead and Rachel was in jail. All for love.

Angela's complexion was paler. Her body trembled and sweat dripped down her face. She gripped her shirt over her heart. Angela was dying.

Did Norman love her more than he hated me?

"Angela is having a heart attack."

"That won't work, Merry."

"It's the truth, Norman. Look. At. Your. Wife."

Ebenezer wiggled himself behind me. The rope. He loved twine. Rope. Wires. I moved my hands, trying to entice him to have a few nibbles. Come on, buddy.

Norman turned his head. His eyes widened.

Angela was gasping for breath.

Ebenezer's tiny teeth sank into my wrist. I pressed my lips together, stopping myself from reacting to it. He chewed on the ropes, delighted not to be scolded for once.

Angela slumped forward, chin touching her chest. The seatbelt held her in place. Her head lolled to the side.

"No!" Norman screamed. The RV swerved to the side, nearly putting us in a ditch.

I tugged on my hands. The rope snapped. I had a choice, untie my legs and stop Norman or crawl to Angela and start CPR. There wasn't time for both. I slid to the floor and scooted over to Angela. I unbuckled Angela's seatbelt and tugged her to the floor. "Hurry, Norman."

The RV picked up speed. "Stay with me, Honey. Don't leave me."

I breathed for Angela, praying we'd get her to the hospital in time.

TWENTY-EIGHT

I sat alone in the waiting room. Three couches were in the room, a color that was not quite blue but not quite gray. Old, worn, and well-used. Many people had sat here, anxious for words about their loved ones. A wall clock ticked. The sound echoing in the room, counting down the minutes, the moments. How many did Angela have left? How many did anyone of us have? I picked up a magazine, trying to cover up the morbid thoughts filtering into my head and heart.

The police had Norman sequestered in another room, handcuffed and with two armed officers with him. Chief Hudson had arrived and granted Norman the grace of staying at the hospital until we received word about Angela. The door opened. I jumped to my feet.

Orville walked in, carrying two cups of coffee and sat down in the chair next to the one I had occupied.

I sat back down, not having the energy to remain standing. I was terrified to know the truth about Angela, Rachel, and Norman.

"How's Norman?" I asked, sipping at the coffee Orville handed me, soaking in the warmth traveling from the foam cup into my hands.

He shifted sideways, body now facing me. "Why are you asking about him? He tried to kill you."

"Technically, he just said he was going to but didn't actually try."

"And that makes a difference?"

"It has to. Makes it easier to process." I looked into the coffee, not wanting to meet Orville's eyes. I didn't want to know what he thought of my opinion. It was easier on my heart to believe that Norman, my friend, made an idle threat against me rather than he intended to kill us.

"I can understand that. You should be able to trust your friends," Orville said, a deep sadness in his voice. Norman had been his friend also. Was he thinking his friendship with Norman kept him from seeing the truth?

"Should," I whispered. But I was learning that might be one of my flaws. I trusted my friends too much.

"Don't write people off, Merry. This is the second time you've put yourself in danger because you didn't reach out first. You don't have to fix the wrongs in Season's Greetings yourself. You have to trust we'll come through."

I wanted to tell Orville I still trusted him, but my brain wouldn't let me say the words. Something inside me told me to think about what he said, but another part of me was saying trust had placed me in danger. Was trusting too much worse than not trusting at all? Was a little Scrooge entering into my heart? Was it bad to question things and people at times and not just live by a child-like faith?

"How long will Norman go to prison?" I asked.

"Hard to say what will happen to him. But Norman is in deep trouble. There isn't a way around it. He killed Jenna and Eric Wilcox, strangled them with Jenna's scarf, and misappropriated some of the town's money. Jenna wasn't a nice woman. Doesn't mean she deserved her fate. She was going to tell the town about his wrongdoings even after blackmailing him for some of the money. She turned her back on him, laughing, and he lost it. Grabbed her scarf and twisted it until she crumbled to the ground. Said he didn't mean to. He left her and thought Eric would be blamed for it since the couple had a volatile relationship. The police had been called there a few times. Jenna hadn't put Eric's name on any of the bank accounts. He had no access to any of money, and since blackmailing worked for Jenna, Eric tried his hand at it."

"And once Rachel was arrested, Eric was going to give up Norman to save her."

We sat there quiet for a few minutes, lost in our thoughts. Everything about this was so sad.

"How's Angela?" I asked.

"She'll pull through this time, but long term it's not looking good for her. Her daughters are on the way and she'll be going home with one of them when it's safe for her to travel. Neither wants to see their father."

"Those poor girls." Actually, women as they were a few years younger than me. What a lot of heartache for them to bear.

"I'm glad the chief offered to talk to them. I'm about done giving bad news to people." Orville arched his head back, resting it on the top of the square leather cushion.

The tone of his voice told me there was one more piece he had to give. I took a swallow of coffee, prolonging the inevitable for just a bit longer. "What kind of trouble is Rachel in?"

He stared up at the ceiling rather than looking at me. "Now that we're getting the full story, it's likely they'll go easy on her. But you never know. Sad thing is if she had just convinced Eric to let the police do their job the night he found Jenna dead, we would've known Eric hadn't killed her."

I felt tiny pinpricks of pain in my heart. Oh, Rachel, why? Tears flooded my eyes. "She wouldn't be in jail. Eric would still be alive."

Orville stood and stretched then placed his hands behind his back. "Yep. But she had been more concerned about everyone finding out about the affair than what they believed, which was Eric having accidentally killed his wife."

The court might go easy on Rachel, but how hard would she be on herself? How would the community treat her? Things wouldn't be the same for her in Season's Greetings. Or between us.

"We found out who shot up your lawn decorations. A couple of teenage girls. The ring leader's boyfriend stopped at your house the other day and picked up a girl."

Garrett. Poor Cassie. She liked the guy. "Cassie stayed with me, and her co-worker gave her a ride to work since her car was still at the bookstore."

"The parents have offered to replace any of your items that were ruined."

"Do you know if Garrett was still seeing this other girl?"

Orville raised his hands in mock surrender. "I stay out of teenage romance drama. You can take that up with the other moms."

"You might want to if these girls are stalking Garrett."

"That's not the story I'm seeing."

"Look what happened with the other story that we all thought we knew how it was written."

Orville heaved out a sigh. "You have a point there. I'll dig a little more."

"Thanks." Like Orville, I was leaning more toward Garrett was trying to two-time his girlfriend, but it could be more serious than that. Sometimes the obvious wasn't what was truly going on.

"Merry!" Cassie busted into the waiting room, tears glittering in her eyes.

"I'll let you deal with this." Orville patted my shoulder and headed out.

How did Cassie find out I was here? I stood up and drew the girl into my arms. Oh my God! Had something happened to Helen? Before I asked, Bonnie stepped into the room and mouthed the problem was Garrett.

Helen was okay. This was about a boy. I waited for Cassie to speak.

Cassie dropped down into a seat beside. "He has a girlfriend," she whispered, the words barely louder than the ticking coming from the clock.

"I'm sorry, honey. He could've broken up with her. Orville told me that she and some friends took out my inflatables because they spotted you two together."

"No, they're still dating. He admitted it to me. I thought he liked me." There was hurt and confusion in her voice. "Said I was just his type of girl and I should give him a chance. He started working there to get to know me better. He lied."

I didn't doubt he wanted to get to know her better. It was his motives I was unsure about. The timing of the boy's interest in Cassie bothered me. I'd been so wrapped up in Jenna's murder, I hadn't thought much of Cassie's romance. I might've saved her some heartache. It was possible the young man had started to fall for Cassie and wanted out of his other relationship and it had nothing to do with the rumor that Cassie was likely to come into some money.

"Maybe he does like you and that is why he wanted to work there," I said. "It could be he fell for you also and is conflicted. It does happen."

"I wanted that to be the truth. But it's not." Cassie buried her head in her hands. "I heard him talking to her. It's the money. My mom wanted me because of it. And now Garret. Why can't people just like me for me?"

I wrapped the grieving girl in my arms. People were horrible. "I do. I love you for you, you know that. Raleigh does. Scotland does."

She lifted her tear-stained face. "But will anyone else once they find out about the money?"

Bonnie remained silent. The shame on her face told me everything I needed to about the woman. Bonnie regretted not having reached out to her stepdaughter sooner. She couldn't also say she cared about her. Cassie wouldn't buy it, and Bonnie would become one more person claiming to like her because of money. Was there a way I could help bridge the gap between them? Help Bonnie break down the wall she built around herself?

"Someone will," I said. "I believe that with all my heart, Cassie, and you have to also. Someone will love you for you. You're lovable. Not everyone places more importance on money than people."

"It doesn't seem that's true of this town," Cassie said.

The bitterness in Cassie's voice left me breathless and a tightness grew in my chest. Because she was right. Season's Greetings was showing a side of itself I hadn't known existed. My believe-in-the-magic-of-Christmas town had a dark side. It was like the Grinches and Scrooges were coming to life. I hated seeing her lost and without hope.

"Every town has those people that have wrong priorities. It doesn't make it true of everyone," I said.

"You have to look for the good, Cassie," Bonnie said. "Don't be like me. It makes for a small world."

Cassie looked up, meeting Bonnie's gaze. "My dad loved you. Your patients do too."

Bonnie smiled sadly. I was a little shocked. This was the first time Cassie ever admitted that her dad loved Bonnie, said anything for that matter to make Bonnie feel included. I was proud of the teenager. Even in her grief, she was reaching out. She'd be okay.

"It's a lonely world when I'm not working," Bonnie said.

So was mine. I did have my children, but they had flown the coop as most children do. "I'm available to hang out with the exception around the Christmas holidays. Though, I could use some help catching up on orders."

Bonnie smiled. "I can do that."

"I'll help too." Cassie hopped up and wrapped an arm around me and Bonnie. "We can work on stuff tonight. Create some happy Christmas memories."

"I could go for that," I said. The best way to counterattack the bad was building some good. And the three of us could use some good. Brett's suggestion played in my mind. It was time to end the speculation in my head—and the town's.

Not to mention have the truth out there. The three of us, and Helen, deserved it. She'd be at peace knowing the money her son died for did some good.

"The divorce was final," I said.

Bonnie and Cassie stared at me. Cassie's lips trembled. She

had hoped it wasn't. She wanted me to be her mother—have a mother.

I hugged her. "You'll always be one of my kids. My girl. So, don't think that gets you off the hook from being scolded or receiving my advice. I'll be butting into your life forever."

Cassie hugged me back. "I can deal with that."

"Are you sure it's final?" Bonnie asked.

"Brett brought me the decree earlier today," I said. "It was approved. I'm divorced."

"Did he know if my marriage license is valid?"

"I didn't think to ask," I said. "It was kind of a tense situation at the time. Happened right after those girls took out my blow-up hamster and a few other pieces."

"What does that mean for..." Cassie trailed off, her cheeks reddening. She dipped her head.

"The lottery ticket? It depends on us." I tucked a strand of hair behind Cassie's ear. "I know what your grandmother wants me to do. But I want it to be our decision."

"Dad left it to Grandma?"

"It was your grandmother's ticket. She was going to give it to your father. After his death—"

"Grandma gave it to you." Cassie battled the hurt I watched rise into her eyes. She didn't want the fact her grandmother sent me the ticket to affect their relationship or ours.

"She was scared you'd be hurt because of it. She wanted me to protect you."

"I understand why Grandma didn't want me to have it. I don't even know if I want it. Daddy died because of it and it won't help Grandma." Cassie aged before my eyes. She knew her grandmother was dying. "Maybe we can move her to Season's Living. It'll be more comfortable for her. She won't be alone."

I squeezed her hand. "I think that's a good idea, sweetheart. I bet she'll agree if you ask her."

Bonnie studied me. "You think the lottery commission will fight the disbursement."

"Brett thinks that will happen unless it can be proven who owns it, or we come to an agreement. If all the parties who could claim ownership agree, there's no fight to worry about," I said.

"The ticket belonged to Helen. I believe you. It was hers to give and she gave it to you, Merry. I don't have a claim to it." Bonnie clasped Cassie's hands. "And you, Cassie, deserve to find someone to love who you won't second-guess. I won't fight it. You both have my word."

"Helen wanted you taken care of also, Bonnie," I said. "It's important to her that Samuel treated everyone right. She needs to see that he did right by us. That's what this is about, doing right. For Helen's sake."

"For Helen's sake." Bonnie stuck out her arm, palm down and smiled at me.

I placed my hand on hers and squeezed it.

Cassie cupped her hand over ours. "For Grandma's sake. We'll do it together."

"And for our own." I said. "From here on out, we're family. You're not alone, Bonnie. Neither are you Cassie. You both got me."

Tears glittered in Bonnie's eyes. "Brought together by Samuel."

"The best thing my dad ever did."

CHRISTINA FREEBURN

Christina Freeburn has always loved books. There was nothing better than picking up a story and being transported to another place. The love of reading evolved into the love of writing and she's been writing since her teenage years. Her first novel was a 2003 Library of Virginia Literary Award nominee. Her two mystery series, Faith Hunter Scrap This and Merry & Bright Handcrafted Mysteries, are a mix of crafty and crime and feature heroines whose crafting time is interrupted by crime solving. Christina served in the US Army and has also worked as a paralegal, librarian, and church secretary. She lives in West Virginia with her husband, dog, and a rarely seen cat except by those who are afraid of or allergic to felines.

Mysteries by Christina Freeburn

The Merry & Bright Handcrafted Mystery Series

NOT A CREATURE WAS STIRRING (#1)
BETTER WATCH OUT (#2)

The Faith Hunter Scrap This Series

CROPPED TO DEATH (#1)
DESIGNED TO DEATH (#2)
EMBELLISHED TO DEATH (#3)
FRAMED TO DEATH (#4)
MASKED TO DEATH (#5)
ALTERED TO DEATH (#6)

Henery Press Mystery Books

And finally, before you go...
Here are a few other mysteries
you might enjoy:

FATAL BRUSHSTROKE

Sybil Johnson

An Aurora Anderson Mystery (#1)

A dead body in her garden and a homicide detective on her doorstep...Computer programmer and tole-painting enthusiast Aurora (Rory) Anderson doesn't envision finding either when she steps outside to investigate the frenzied yipping coming from her own back yard. After all, she lives in a quiet California beach community where violent crime is rare and murder even rarer.

Suspicion falls on Rory when the body buried in her flowerbed turns out to be someone who knows her tole-painting teacher, Hester Bouquet. Just two weeks before, Rory attended one of Hester's weekend seminars, an unpleasant experience she vowed never to repeat. As evidence piles up against Rory, she embarks on a quest to identify the killer and clear her name. Can Rory unearth the truth before she encounters her own brush with death?

Available at booksellers nationwide and online

Visit www.henerypress.com for details

PILLOW STALK

Diane Vallere

A Madison Night Mystery (#1)

Interior Decorator Madison Night might look like a throwback to the sixties, but as business owner and landlord, she proves that independent women can have it all. But when a killer targets women dressed in her signature style—estate sale vintage to play up her resemblance to fave actress Doris Day—what makes her unique might make her dead.

The local detective connects the new crime to a twenty-year old cold case, and Madison's long-trusted contractor emerges as the leading suspect. As the body count piles up, Madison uncovers a Soviet spy, a campaign to destroy all Doris Day movies, and six minutes of film that will change her life forever.

Available at booksellers nationwide and online

Visit www.henerypress.com for details

STAGING IS MURDER

Grace Topping

A Laura Bishop Mystery (#1)

Laura Bishop just nabbed her first decorating commission—staging a 19th-century mansion that hasn't been updated for decades. But when a body falls from a laundry chute and lands at Laura's feet, replacing flowered wallpaper becomes the least of her duties.

To clear her assistant of the murder and save her fledgling business, Laura's determined to find the killer. Turns out it's not as easy as renovating a manor home, especially with two handsome men complicating her mission: the police detective on the case and the real estate agent trying to save the manse from foreclosure.

Worse still, the meddling of a horoscope-guided friend, a determined grandmother, and the local funeral director could get them all killed before Laura props the first pillow.

Available at booksellers nationwide and online

Visit www.henerypress.com for details

A MUDDIED MURDER

Wendy Tyson

A Greenhouse Mystery (#1)

When Megan Sawyer gives up her big-city law career to care for her grandmother and run the family's organic farm and café, she expects to find peace and tranquility in her scenic hometown of Winsome, Pennsylvania. Instead, her goat goes missing, rain muddies her fields, the town denies her business permits, and her family's Colonial-era farm sucks up the remains of her savings.

Just when she thinks she's reached the bottom of the rain barrel, Megan and the town's hunky veterinarian discover the local zoning commissioner's battered body in her barn. Now Megan's thrust into the middle of a murder investigation—and she's the chief suspect. Can Megan dig through small-town secrets, local politics, and old grievances in time to find a killer before that killer strikes again?

Available at booksellers nationwide and online

Visit www.henerypress.com for details

CPSIA information can be obtained
at www.ICGtesting.com
Printed in the USA
LVHW030845200221
679495LV00043B/891